Lady of Lohikärra

L. L. Nelson

Nelding & Michcomb Publishing

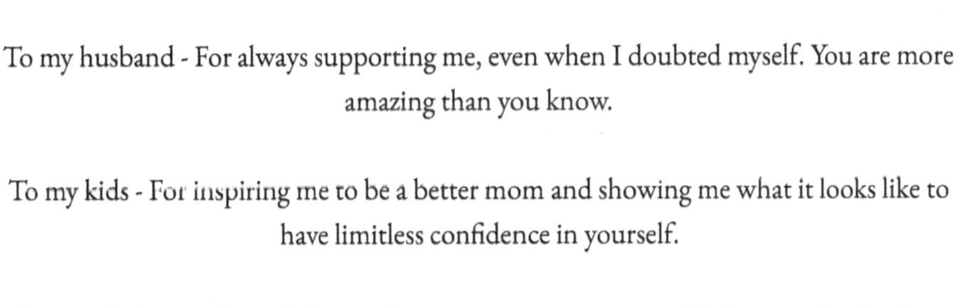

To my husband - For always supporting me, even when I doubted myself. You are more amazing than you know.

To my kids - For inspiring me to be a better mom and showing me what it looks like to have limitless confidence in yourself.

To my dad - For always believing I was an amazing writer and being my cheerleader.

To my sisters - For inspiring me and just being plain awesome.

Content Warning

This book contains references to content which may be triggering or upsetting to some readers. In particular, there are references to miscarriage and pregnancy within this book.

Your FREE book awaits!

A mysterious young woman, an elven invasion, and the tokens of the High King

Haldrek Rodreksson has known his entire life where his future lies and what is expected of him. But on the eve of battle, soothsayers show him three visions of a different future: a mysterious young woman, a new invasion, and theft of the High King's tokens. Visions which make him question his future and that of his homeland, Lohikärra.

When the capital of Lohikärra falls, Haldrek's world is thrown into disarray and he must scramble to keep the young woman from his visions safe.

Injured, weaponless, and with little support, will Haldrek be able to save the woman and change the visions he was given? Or will he, his homeland, and his loved ones fall to their enemies?

Get a free copy of the prequel
Visions of Lohikärra here:

https://www.llnelsonauthor.com/newsletter/

Contents

Chapter One

The bowstring cutting into my fingertips distracted me from my pain. I focused on the center of the target and relaxed my shoulders, loosing the arrow. It hit with a solid thud and I smiled for a brief moment. At least I could control *this* part of my life.

I pulled another arrow from the sheath and glanced out of the corner of my eye at the maidservant whose job it was to keep me company. A so-called perk of being the High Queen. I was never, ever, alone. Whether I wanted to be alone was another story. I didn't begrudge the girl—she was doing her job—but it didn't mean I enjoyed having an audience for nearly every moment of my life either.

The arrow flew as I released it and I took a deep breath. Grabbing another one, my hand brushed against someone else's right behind me. Spinning around, I pulled out my last arrow and handled it more like a dagger, pointing it at the person in defense.

Haldrek put his hands up and smiled as I relaxed, sheathing the arrow. That's why my maidservant had been silent. Haldrek had picked up a habit of sneaking up behind me and loving on me since we'd gotten married. I loved it—most days.

The servants knew better than to interrupt.

But today had turned out to be a lousy, horrible day and it was still early morning. The sun had only just risen over the mountains in the east. I sank my head into Haldrek's chest and let the tears I'd been holding back flow. His gambeson could take the wetness.

"I was looking for you," he whispered, his face burrowing into my hair. "If you're here..." He hesitated. "Did it come again?"

"Yes." I laughed bitterly. "My period started again this morning."

"I'm sorry. We'll keep trying. My men are still searching for Rorik. He will pay for what he's done. I promise."

I hated that I was crying right now. But my emotions kept crashing around inside of me like waves on the coast. My gift of shifting between the Realm of the Living and the Realm of Ghosts had turned into a curse. Nightmares plagued me nearly every night, leaving me exhausted. Now that my father was in Mirroth, there wasn't anyone within the Realm of Ghosts to aid me when Rorik would inevitably drag me there. Being a necromancer meant he had powers like mine. Only more sinister. His skills had been honed through practice, while mine were still instinctual. And he used his ability to shift between realms to torment me on a regular basis.

"I'm afraid, Haldrek. Part of me wants to get pregnant again. But if I do…" My throat squeezed tight at the thought. I didn't think I could handle what I'd gone through again. Even when Rorik wasn't tormenting me in the Realm of Ghosts, I still had nightmares about what had happened months ago. I felt guilty, wondering if my fears were preventing me from getting pregnant again. As illogical as it seemed, it could be possible. There were a lot of illogical things that were normal here.

"You're afraid that Rorik will take away any other children you may carry?" His voice was quiet enough that only he and I could hear his words.

I nodded. The memory of the dream where I had fought Rorik and lost, only to wake up to agonizing pain and more blood than I could imagine, still seared itself into my mind on a regular basis. I couldn't tell anyone, except Haldrek, about my fears and the emotions I was feeling. There was no one I truly trusted here in Drattüjert. Haldrek had mentioned talking to Mattie, but I was reluctant even with her. Not that she wouldn't be sympathetic, but she had her hands full with being the Thegn of Andrattür and her own newborn child. So I struggled, alone. As much as Haldrek tried to comfort me, there was little he could do to fight off the terror that Rorik sent my way.

"I'm also afraid." I hesitated. "What if I can't have any more kids? What if Rorik's magic did something to me—" There had been rumors spreading across the palace. Questions about whether or not Haldrek and I *could* have children. I let out a sob that shook me. Haldrek's hug grew tighter.

"I don't think he did. The healers and Rhaegos both said—"

"I know what they said. They said I would be fine. That my body would heal, but it would take time. But I also hear rumors. From the other women at court here." I pulled away and looked up at Haldrek. "They all think I'm barren and that Lohikärra is going to be plunged to chaos as soon as something happens to either of us. And of course Kamira is using that as a reason to say that I shouldn't be High Queen. That I am an infertile half-breed."

Haldrek sighed, irritation evident in his body language. This wasn't the first time I'd mentioned his cousin's antics. While it was normal for thegns to send family members to court on their behalf, neither Haldrek nor I knew why Raynord had sent his granddaughter to Drattüjert on his behalf. Not when there were other family members of his who could speak for him.

"I can talk to Kamira and Raynord once more. Reprimand her again and remind her of her place. Tell him she is being disruptive. But there isn't much more that I can do beyond that. Raynord chose her and even as the High King, I can't force him to choose another. For now, at the very least, ignore her. She's an immature girl who knows less about court manners than she thinks."

"I know. But it still hurts." My abdomen tightened again with more cramps and I leaned into Haldrek, trying to ignore the aches.

"I have some good news. While my men haven't found Rorik yet, they know roughly where he is. I received word yesterday he was seen holed up in the mountains of Etelaranikä. It's a remote part of Lohikärra, but that means he's cornered. Physically, at least."

"It's also in his backyard." I pulled myself closer to Haldrek, using the pressure of his body against mine to soothe me. The scent of honey and woodsmoke clung to him and calmed my mind as my body relaxed.

"It is. But my spies also tell me the people of Etelaranikä are suffering. I've sent *gifts* to aid them. Food, drink, cloth. All to help them while their thegn-heir has abandoned them. And I've made sure they know who those gifts are from."

I smiled. That had the potential for good. Maybe even make the Etelaranikäns rise up against Rorik. Not that I blamed them if they were still terrified of him. "Any other good news?" I asked, my cramps lessening for a moment.

"Bjorn's son Kotkel has said that his father is open to pledging his fealty to me. As has Drifa Kiimaami with her husband."

The idea of thegns who had sided with Gustav having people at Drattüjert still irritated and confused me. I didn't trust the four hersirs who spoke for those thegns, but Haldrek said it was wise. Something about keeping your friends close and enemies closer.

"Do you trust them? Or their words?"

"About as far as I can throw them." Haldrek laughed, his chest rumbling. It felt good in his embrace. "But I am open to the idea of them seeing the errors of their ways. All four hersirs know that they walk a fine line. Well, most of them do. But I don't think Sibila is a threat."

I nodded. Another strange choice for a hersir. I got the impression that Sibila was sent to Drattüjert less to advise and more for her safety, or to keep her out of the way. Her mother—Rorik's stepmother—sat in the thegn's chair in Etelaranikä and while her feelings toward Haldrek and I were unknown, she had disavowed Rorik as soon as Haldrek and I became High King and High Queen. She was an unknown factor, so I was leery of both her and her daughter.

Haldrek squeezed me once more, bringing my mind back to the present. "Don't worry. At least not for today. We will have children in the future, regardless of what any fools here say. Once Rorik is dead or has submitted to me, we'll be safe. I promise."

Despite my misery and my desire to hide from the world that day, I made my way to a common room on the third floor of the palace. It was a space that had once held living quarters centuries ago when the palace was much smaller, but now had turned into public spaces. They were still lavishly decorated, so they weren't exactly what I'd consider common, but they were set aside for mingling and socializing among those of abthanry and city folk. Either way, the meeting I hurried to was supposed to be informal and spontaneous, but as the High Queen, my attendance was required.

As soon as I entered the room, the half dozen or so women already there all stood up, bowing or curtsying to me. I did a weird little curtsy bow in return. It still felt strange to have people stop what they were doing and acknowledge me, even after all these months. Even after my time in Svangendom. The idea that I was someone of importance was still foreign and uncomfortable.

Surveying the room, I mentally noted the different thegn lands represented. On one side of the center table, Aallotar had sent Vilde's sister Ragnhild—and one of her top diplomats—to represent Heidrunefoss; Hrimfax had sent his mother, Lady Taimi, to represent Svarhestån; and her sister Lady Salla had come from Nerthusån on behalf of *her* son, Sigurd. On the other side of the table sat Sibila, representing Etelaranikä in name only; Lady Drifa from Itaranikä; and Kamira, last of all, from Drattrede. Only six thegn lands represented, not including myself, and plenty of gossip to go around.

I sat down at the head of the table, trying not to step on the long hem of my dress, and the women took their seats again. Taimi and Salla began whispering and giggling as they whipped stitches along the fabric in their hands. Much of Drattüjert had lost material goods or been reduced to rags in the past few years. After arriving back in the city, I had insisted we help the populace recover. The war had taken its toll on everyone, and I knew there were certain things that could help morale. There had been unanimous consensus on that part. But *how* to help the people of Drattüjert and the surrounding areas was still a subject of debate. Buildings were being rebuilt, but it was the little things—clothing, furniture, daily items—that we had bickered on.

In the end, it had been decided that we'd make clothing for those still suffering in Drattüjert. Nothing extravagant, but the shifts and smocks, in all sizes, that nearly everyone wore. Not a bad idea, but also something in which I had no prior experience. No one had ever taught me how to sew and so I fumbled with it. Every. Single. Day.

"That's not how you do it." Kamira sighed in exasperation, staring at the cloth I was working with. "It's not like this is hard." She grabbed at the cloth I was working with and I pulled away.

"Did I ask for your help?" I snapped. Irritation and humiliation bubbled up inside of me. Kamira, for all that she was supposed to be supporting Haldrek and me in her grandfather's stead, did nothing but complain and criticize my actions. It didn't help that she reminded me of a persistent childhood bully growing up. I had tried to ignore that thought, but her actions continued to reinforce the comparison.

"No, Lady *I-na*." She smirked as she mispronounced my name, emphasizing the 'I' sound. "But don't you want to give the people good quality clothing? So they know their queen cares about more than just herself?"

I bit the inside of my cheek, trying not to get sucked into her game. Before I could say anything, Ragnhild cleared her throat. "Queen Ina's sewing skills may be rudimentary, but your social skills are worse. She has already mentioned that this," Ragnhild gestured at the garments we were sewing, "is not something she was trained in during her youth. You, however, were taught how to speak to your superiors from a young age."

Kamira's cheeks reddened and I was grateful for Ragnhild in that moment. Ragnhild and I didn't often agree on things, but I respected her for the most part.

"When I have a chance to speak to my superiors, I'll be sure to address them correctly. *Lady I-na* is a thegn, so I am correct to address her by that title. Who knows how long she'll be queen if no aethlings come along soon."

The room went silent as I tried to stay composed. That hit like a punch to the stomach, and I blinked in vain as I did my best not to tear up. It wasn't my fault that... I pushed away the thoughts of everything that had happened. I'd insisted on waiting for an official announcement of my first pregnancy, but now that was biting me in the back.

"Ow!"

I looked up to see Lady Drifa staring daggers at Kamira. Kamira stared back as she rubbed her ribcage. Though Lady Drifa was no fan of mine, depending on the day, she seemed to resent Kamira even more.

"Your behavior is unbecoming of one raised at court. Before you seek to chasten others, you should look to your own failings."

Kamira gaped and a peal of laughter came from behind Lady Drifa.

"Tesroan is amused, isn't she? Though Naragos is probably not happy with her haldraga right now."

All eyes turned to Sibila. She was focused on her project, oblivious to the rest of the room. Given previous interactions, I assumed Tesroan was the dragon she was bound to. The thought occurred to me that she may have not been aware of what was going on when she became a haldraga. Or had her dragon taken that into account when binding with her? I shook my head as she continued.

"Yes, Naragos is probably not happy with Kamira right now. She hasn't been listening to her, has she?"

Kamira dropped her project and stood up, glaring at Sibila. "At least my family aren't full of traitors. Watch your tongue or you'll end up like your father."

Sibila turned to Kamira as if she'd just heard her, and my stomach clenched at the tension. Kamira was a hot-headed brat, and while Sibila was a fairly docile person, given her brother and father's traits, I wondered if there could be malice bubbling up within.

"Huh?" Sibila frowned and cocked her head. Her expression turned from confusion to fear as she leaned away from Kamira. My heart twinged and went out to her as compassion erased my suspicions in the moment, and I cleared my throat. For all I hated confrontation on my own behalf, I wasn't about to let Kamira bully Sibila.

"Maybe it's time for a break. Kamira, you seem tense right now," I said, mimicking some of the things I'd heard the older female abthanry say.

She turned to me with a sneer and I smiled, saying nothing.

As Kamira opened her mouth, Lady Salla stood up and said, "Oh, I think Queen Ina has the right idea. As much as I love sewing, I need to stretch these old bones. Kamira, would you be so kind as to walk with me?"

Kamira shut her mouth and grimaced. "Of course, Lady Salla." She slowly walked over to the door as Salla hobbled over. Unless something had happened recently, I knew Haldrek's aunt was exaggerating her limp. Though still older than either Haldrek's father or mine would have been, both Salla and Taimi were by no means ancient.

Once they left, I looked down at my work. It wasn't as fine as the others' work, and the critical voices in my head grew louder with every stitch. Still, I kept at it until the only people left in the room were myself and Hrimfax's mother, Lady Taimi.

"You know, I struggled with my sewing for many years. No one understood why I couldn't just do it when my sisters—Salla included—did it like they were born doing it."

I looked up at her, my heart still heavy, and smiled. I knew she was trying to help. Taimi and Salla were a few of the only people I truly felt safe around here, outside of Haldrek. Even if I didn't quite trust them with my innermost thoughts, they were still good women. "The sewing isn't the only thing bothering me."

"I figured out that much as well. You have a lot to deal with and...not much experience with it." My eyes widened as she waved her hand.

"I don't mean that as an insult or to make you think you aren't capable. You are capable. If Rhaegos bound herself with you, then you are probably the *most* capable of us all.

You're just having to learn more quickly than the rest of us have. But you are absolutely capable of that too."

My smile returned and I nodded. "I know. I just wish the learning curve wasn't so steep. Even Mattie seems to have adapted to being thegn quickly." Despite my own miseries, my chest felt lighter, thinking about Mattie. She and Llamryl, despite a small challenge from a former gesith, were now solidly ruling Andrattür from Mirratoft.

"Lady Mattie also had a thorough tutelage in Lohikärran customs through her father's stories. You have said as much."

"Yeah..." So had I. I hadn't delved as deeply into the lore and video game world of Lohikärra as Mattie, but I'd played the games and knew a lot of the lore that had been put into them.

She stood up and walked over next to me. "I also sense that you're still grieving, which is completely normal. Especially after the loss of a child." She squeezed my hand in comfort.

"How did you know?" My mind raced, trying to figure out how Taimi *would* have known. As far as I was concerned, only Haldrek and Mattie knew. Possibly Llamryl as well, but beyond that...

"I only bore two living children. Hrimfax and his older brother, Ulmer. But they were neither my first time with child, nor my last." Her eyes glistened as I turned to her. "And a quick illness took Ulmer when he was a child." Tears fell from her eyes as mine got blurry. "All this to say, I had a suspicion when you suddenly fell ill for a long period and then returned to public view looking more worn out than before." She hesitated. "Haldrek may have also sought me out to ask advice on how to comfort you, which confirmed my thoughts."

Her words brought tears to my eyes and I started bawling as she put her hand on my shoulder for comfort.

"It's never an easy experience, and it is normal to feel raw for many months afterwards. Especially when someone starts saying crude and awful things, like Kamira. She doesn't know a single thing about what's going on. She still has much to learn. Maturity to attain. Things you already know too well."

I nodded, wiping my eyes and nose with my sleeve. "And here I thought things were going to get easier."

Taimi laughed. "Things don't get easier as you grow older. You just get stronger. Not that it doesn't still hurt, but the weight isn't so heavy."

I nodded. "That's good to hear. It still hurts, but it'll get better. Right?"

She nodded as well and took a step back. "Something that may help in the meantime is some fresh air. I think that is a cure for everything. Unless you are needed elsewhere,

I would love your company while I—how did my sister phrase it?— stretch these old bones." She laughed and offered her arm to me.

"You're right, maybe fresh air will help. I don't have anything that I can think of, so I'd love to." I took her arm in mine and we headed out into the rest of the palace.

Chapter Two

Lady Taimi was right. Getting fresh air did wonders for my spirit. Even in the height of summer, a brisk cool breeze made its way through the outdoor parts of the palace, keeping our walk pleasant. Both my mind and body felt lighter in the refreshing summer sunshine. Making our way into the city, I made sure not to go any faster than Taimi was comfortable with, though she was still energetic enough that I questioned her excuse about old bones.

A few guards trailed us as we made our way through one of the rebuilt marketplaces. More of the perks of being the High Queen. I still hadn't gotten used to them, but I tried to ignore them as much as Haldrek or the other abthanry did. Heavenly scents helped distract me as we paused near a stall with a variety of fresh fruits and small pies the size of my palm.

"My queen! Care to try a sample? I have the best honey and cloudberry tarts you've ever tasted." The vendor scrambled to give me a small hand pie designed to look like some kind of flower or even the sun.

"I don't think I've ever tried that before." I turned to Taimi and she nodded.

"They are delicious. In both Svarhestån and Heidruncfoss, cloudberries are considered lucky. Or at least they are eaten at various celebrations to ensure good luck in the coming days. I've certainly made a glutton of myself in my younger days with those pies."

"Then I may have to try one." I took the pastry from the vendor and opened my mouth to take a bite as an anguished scream shattered the market's buzz. All the people around us turned to see what was going on. The pastry was pulled from my hand, and I saw one of the palace guards wrap it up and slip it away. I grimaced, remembering why for a brief moment before returning my attention to the situation at hand.

"Please, don't! I beg of you! It's not her fault!"

"Get off of me, you vile wench."

I moved through the crowd with Taimi as I heard a baby begin to scream. My heart froze and I pushed forward until I saw the open space in the middle of market. A man held a naked baby by its feet and struggled to untangle himself from the woman laying on the ground, her arms wrapped around one of his ankles.

"What is going on here?" I snapped.

The man turned his attention to me. "Nothing that concerns you, my queen."

The baby continued squalling, its cries becoming more frantic and in pain. Without thinking, I grabbed the child from him and wrapped it in the cloth hanging from my sleeves. Palace dresses were more decoration than anything, but at least the yards of fabric on this dress could serve a purpose.

"What are you doing? This does not concern you!" The man grabbed for the child as the woman began bawling again at his ankles and I ducked away from him. Two of the guards who had been following Lady Taimi and me stepped out of the crowd and toward the man. He put his hands up and stepped away from me.

"The well-being of my people is my concern," I snapped. "Why are you dangling a newborn baby in the middle of a market?" The child was now quiet except for a few muffled whimpers. "I can't think of a situation that calls for that kind of behavior."

The man's face reddened with anger. "I am ridding my family of a bane. This child is an abomination. A disgusting reminder of my wife's whorish nature, and I am getting rid of it like the trash it is."

"This child is a human being." My voice, despite being soft and low, was apparently ominous enough for the man to step back.

"That child is a half-breed. While I was out fighting with Thegn Heidrunefoss, my disgusting excuse of a wife was spreading her legs for every Blodnar soldier she could find."

"That's not true!" The woman wailed and looked up at me. "The Blodnar..." Her face twisted with anger and humiliation. "They took what they wanted, even if I refused. I never willingly laid with a Blodnar soldier."

"Yet you bred with one!" The man turned on his wife and shoved her away with the sole of his boot. "Everyone knows you can't be with child unless you enjoy the act. Did the Blodnar please you more than I ever did?" He took a menacing step toward her, and I nodded for the guards to restrain him.

"That's not true." I snapped. "*None* of that is true." I turned to the woman and glanced back at the child. It was still a newborn, but it had to be at least a few months old. My heart twisted with pity and I tried to keep my composure. "If you became... if this child has a Blodnar father, why did you keep it?"

The woman sank her head down. "I... I couldn't. The babe, she didn't cause me harm, and my husband and I have wanted children for so long. I thought—"

"You thought I'd raise some half-breed brat as my own?" He moved toward her, stopped only by the guards holding him. "How stupid are you?"

"Enough," I snapped, my patience gone. "This woman—your wife—has already dealt with enough misery. You shouldn't be adding to it." I focused on the woman. "Do you wish to raise this child?"

She kept her head low, not returning my gaze. "I—"

"Of course not. Why would she? If she has half a brain—"

"I asked *her*, not you. Shut your mouth, *ceorl*, or I will shut it for you." My fury surprised me and apparently him, as he stopped fighting the guards' grip on him.

I turned back to the woman as she shook her head. "If I am not with my husband, I have no way to care for my child."

Glancing down at the child, my heart twisted further. There was no way in Lyrroth, Hell, or Fargo I was going to abandon this baby or let it perish. But what exactly could I do? Lady Taimi placed her hand on the back of my arm as if to steady or comfort me.

I turned to her. "Is there no place in Drattüjert for abandoned children?"

She shook her head. "Not that I know of. You could create one. I'm sure there are many abandoned or orphaned children now who could be raised up."

"Maybe that's what I'll do," I said softly before turning to the woman. "If there is no way for you to take care of your child with *his* help," I scowled at the man still held by my guards, "I can ensure the child is taken care of."

The woman looked up at me with hesitation and wariness, but after a moment, she nodded.

"If, in the future, you need work to earn a few coins, there are always jobs in the palace to be done." I smiled at her, hoping she saw the opportunity. She nodded once more and rose to her feet. Glancing at the child for a moment, she bowed and slipped away.

As soon as she was gone, I gestured for the guards to release her husband. He rubbed his shoulders and sneered at me.

"The High King should put you in your place if he wants to be respected."

Before I could react, he darted off after his wife. An ominous weight dropped to the bottom of my gut and I turned to Lady Taimi. She smiled.

"Times are never boring with you, my queen. Shall we return to the palace?" She glanced at the child snuggled in my arms. "I have a feeling my nephew will want to hear about your latest endeavor."

By the time we returned to the palace, my anxiety had shifted from panic to determination. Why hadn't we created a place for orphaned and abandoned children? Solvange had

had one in Svartån, so it wasn't unheard of, but had they ever had something like that here in Drattüjert? If not, there absolutely should be one.

Lady Taimi and I arrived in the throne room just as a petitioner left. Haldrek had his head in one hand and I could tell he was tired. Next to him stood one of the many advisors who had returned to Drattüjert after we reclaimed it. For the most part, I ignored these men, as they ignored me. They cared more for Haldrek's ear than mine, and I'd learned to tolerate it for the time being. As Haldrek looked up at me, his demeanor brightened. At least for a moment. Then he cocked his head to the side as he stared at the baby in my arms.

"Ina...you're holding a baby. Whose baby is that?" He turned to Lady Taimi and asked, "Why do I have a feeling you have something to do with this, my dear aunt?"

She laughed and shook her head. "Your wife is something else. She has my approval."

He turned back to me and I tried to grin as brightly as I could. "I think we need to create an orphanage of some kind here in Drattüjert. Like what Solvange had in Svartån."

"All right...what does that have to do with the child, though? Is it an orphan?"

"It was abandoned. I got in the way of a man trying, at the very least, to injure the child, if not kill it."

"What of the mother?" The advisor, a man by the name of Gizur Englisson, butted into the conversation with his question and I grimaced.

"She didn't want to abandon the child, but her husband forced her to choose between him and the baby, and she admitted that she could not take care of her child alone."

"Why would a man want to abandon his own child?" Haldrek stood up and closed the distance between us, the advisor following a few steps behind him. As Haldrek reached me, he stared at the child as if it held some great secret.

"Haldrek... you know as well as I do the violence of war. The woman was raped by Blodnar soldiers. So her husband rejected the child."

"And he has that right, High Queen Ina," Gizur blurted out. I glared at him, annoyed that he was taking part in a conversation he wasn't supposed to be joining. "A man doesn't have to take care of a child that isn't his."

Irritation flashed through me. "But does he have the right to kill a child? I'm not saying he should be forced to take care of this child, but the child didn't exactly choose its parents either. It shouldn't be punished because of the actions of its parents."

Haldrek exhaled, shifting his attention between me and his advisor. He reached out, rubbing my arm in an attempt to comfort me. "You are right. A child shouldn't be held to blame for its parents' misdeeds." He hesitated, as if trying to find the right words. "I believe the Priests and Priestesses of Tenelth have some kind of orphanage here in the city.

Or they did before the Blodnar invaded. Not that I am against creating another place here, but—"

"Taimi said there wasn't any kind of orphanage that she knew of." I glanced at her and she nodded as I gently touched the child's forehead. "Would they treat the child like a human being, or would they act the same way as the Priests of Tenelth did with the Hethurin at Svangendom?"

"I don't know." Haldrek's voice was soft. "Are you afraid that will happen?"

I nodded, turning my attention back to him. "I've already heard people call children like this one 'half-breeds.' And I know how the Priests of Tenelth are with the Hethurin."

Gizur cleared his throat loudly. "With all due respect, Queen Ina, there is a valid concern about the 'half-breeds' as you call them. For all we know, they could grow up here and then side with their elven or Blodnar kin. That's not a weakness we need right now."

I turned my full focus to Haldrek's advisor. "Considering how the main person antagonizing us right now is a full-blooded Lohikärran thegn-heir, and considering how many Hethurin have loyally fought for me, I don't see that as a valid concern." I held the child out. "Does this child scare you?"

The man stepped back. "My queen... I know you didn't grow up here, but—"

Haldrek put his hands between us as I pulled the child back toward me. He faced Gizur. "I believe this is a conversation best left between my wife and I." He then glanced at his aunt and she nodded, walking over to the advisor and taking him by the shoulder. I heard her mutter something about 'her old bones' as she pulled him out of the room. A smile crept to my mouth.

"Ina." Haldrek's voice pricked at my heart and I focused on him.

"I know we have a lot on our plate in restoring Drattüjert, but I was thinking about it. If these children have a place where they can grow up, be safe, and I dunno, learn skills to help them in the future, they'll be less likely to turn away from their Lohikärran roots. It's like the Hethurin. What my dad did in Svartån *worked* and even when their neighbors hated them, the Hethurin knew that they were part of Svartån and there was someone there who would stand up for them, who wouldn't abandon them."

"You can't save everyone, Ina." His voice was soft as he leaned over me.

"I know that. I couldn't save everyone in Svartån, but I did what I could, and look how that turned out. Svartån survived. It's growing again. So saving some was better than nothing." I paused to collect my thoughts. "Plus, I'm not going to do this alone. I'll send for some of the Priests or Priestesses of Tenelth, talk to them, see how they can help. I can send for people from Svangendom to aid me if need be. But I know what it's like to be abandoned." Clenching my teeth, I whispered, "I know what it's like to be a so-called 'half-breed.'"

"Has anyone called you that here? Other than Kamira?"

"Not to my face. But I can still hear whispers." I shifted the child in my arms as I tried to brush my tears away. Haldrek wrapped his arms around me, squeezing me gently and taking care not to squeeze the child too tight.

"I see no harm in creating a place here within the palace. Much of it is still empty here and if this like your father's work with the Hethurin, perhaps it will work in Lohikärra's favor."

"Thank you." My spirits lifted and he let me go.

"Just...I don't know if part of this is because of our own trials of late, but if it is..." He squeezed my free hand. "I don't want you to worry. I believe that by this time next year, we will be rid of Rorik and have our own child to care for."

I smiled. That hadn't been on my mind as I'd rescued this child, but I could see why Haldrek thought it might have been. Still, his words comforted me.

He wrapped his arm around my shoulders and led me out of the throne room. "Come. If you're going to create an orphanage here, we need to find a good place for it."

Chapter Three

That night, I fell asleep easily with Haldrek's arms wrapped around my waist and under my neck. The mixture of mead, woodsmoke, and whatever soap he'd used tonight filled my nose, lulling me to sleep. Though I often worried that my nightmares might return, the nights when Haldrek was by my side were usually the most peaceful.

As I faded out of consciousness, I sensed my surroundings change. Opening my eyes, I found myself back in Fargo, but this time I was at my friend Henry's house. While I'd only been there a handful of times, those had always been pleasant memories. Even now, the scent of chocolate and cinnamon permeated the dream. I felt safe and happy.

Henry sat on the couch, deftly manipulating his controller as he played in a massive, epic battle with multiple characters fighting on his side, along with other computer-generated figures. I cocked my head in confusion. The game was from the Lohikärran series, but it wasn't any of the titles that Mattie or I had ever played. Instead, it looked more like one of the massive online role playing games. I remembered Mattie mentioning the gaming company that owned her father's games had been toying with the idea, but as far as I knew, they had just begun testing it when we'd been tossed into the real Lohikärra.

"Ina!" I jumped at the sound of my name and looked at Henry. He was younger than I last remembered. Like when we had started high school. I blinked and stared at him, wondering if this was an actual dream or something else.

Rhaegos?

She was silent. Usually, I could feel her presence when I shifted between realms, but all I could sense was me and Henry. Everything else felt suddenly...empty.

"Henry? What's going on?"

"I'm trying out the newest Lohikärra game. Wanna play?"

I turned back to the game and it looked different once again. The environment looked more like something from an Italian or Mediterranean role-playing game than anything I'd seen in Lohikärra.

"I'm fine just watching. What's the new game about? Is this still in Lohikärra?"

"Kinda." The voice grew deeper and I spun around to see Haldrek playing with the controller. What on earth? Even for a dream, that felt weird. I shifted away from the person, though they seemed oblivious to my discomfort. "It takes place in Etelaranikä and one of the..." he hesitated, "*Blodnar* provinces to the south of it. A place called Norycium. It's kinda cool. They've been creating games about Lohikärra for so long that it's nice to see something outside of that."

"Yeah." I kept an eye on Henry/Haldrek/whoever this was as I surveyed the rest of the dream. My body was on high alert. This wasn't a normal dream, but this wasn't a normal shift between realms, either. Which meant I had to be on my guard. For all I knew, this could be another one of Rorik's manipulations. But why would he pretend to be Henry or Haldrek? This didn't feel like his normal style of torment. How would he have known about Henry in the first place? Rorik had never used my memories against me before. He'd always used other forms of magic to torment me.

The person brushed their hand against my leg and I jumped again. Maybe asking them some questions would help me figure out what was going on now.

"What have you been doing recently?" I asked, trying to keep my voice as bland as possible. "It seems like it's been forever since we've had a chance to hang out outside of class."

"Class?"

"Yeah, class." I tried to keep my expression as neutral as possible. This wasn't a dream. This was someone or something pretending to be Henry. Playing off my memories. But whoever was doing it wasn't very skilled at magic. At least as far as I was aware.

"Oh, yeah...class. Eh, it's been, you know, *class*. I'm ready for it all to be over. Go somewhere new, you know?"

I nodded my head and looked at the screen. The character was scrambling over rocks and fighting off various types of wildlife now. "Where would you go?"

"Lohikärra."

"Lohikärra? Like the game?"

The game paused and I turned to see the person staring me. They were no longer Haldrek. Instead the person looked similar to Henry, just like the last time I had seen him. But there was something off. I knew it wasn't Henry—his presence was different.

"Lohikärra is more than just a game. As is Norycium. My mother told me as much."

That surprised me. Something churned in the back of my brain, however, like the idea wasn't actually that much of a surprise. I didn't expect Henry to say something like that, but at the same time it made sense. "Your mother? I know she liked the games, but I don't remember her saying there was more to them."

"She had her own secrets. Just like we all do." His voice grew warmer, less ominous. "But she spoke fondly of both Lohikärra and Norycium. Told me my father was from Lohikärra. So I'd like to go there one day."

I nodded, still trying to figure out why I'd been pulled into this dream or realm. Whoever this person was, it wasn't Henry, and I'd never interacted with them before. "It would certainly be a fun place to explore. I bet it's a lot like the games."

"Well, maybe when I get a chance to visit, you'll have to show me around?"

That statement made me wary. I hadn't mentioned anything about being in Lohikärra. "I don't know. You've played pretty much all the games. I'm sure you could find your way around Lohikärra better than I could." Now I needed to figure out how to get out of this dream. Whoever this person was, I was done dealing with them. I was ready to wake up.

"True. But it'd be fun to do it with a friend. What do you say?"

"I—" There was a loud thud and shudder. The dream disappeared and I flung my arms out wildly to catch myself. Something soft broke my fall and I opened my eyes to find myself back within the four-poster bed. It was pitch black, but I heard Haldrek grunt and groan beside me as he rolled over.

"Another bad dream?" His voice was sleepy as he wrapped his arms around me, pulling me into his chest. I relaxed and nodded, my face brushing against his shift. His breathing grew more regular and I soon found my heart in rhythm with his. As I dozed back to sleep, I sensed Rhaegos's presence return.

You were wise, little one. To be wary of the man in that dream. Tricksters come to play, and they will be as lethal as a necromancer.

In the morning, I was still wrapped up in Haldrek's arms. Light flowed through the edges of the bed's curtains and I wanted to hide from it, to stay in Haldrek's warm embrace a little bit longer. The dream had faded, but the feelings didn't, and I still felt unsettled from Rhaegos's message. As I tried to wrap my head around it, Haldrek began to stroke my hair, his breath tickling my scalp.

"Did you have another nightmare last night?"

I nodded my head, not saying anything. Haldrek would be curious and want to comfort me, but I didn't want to think about the dream or feel the emotions it gave me anymore.

"Was it Rorik again?"

I hesitated. It wasn't Rorik, but I had no idea how to explain Henry to Haldrek. Or the fact that the person had shifted between looking like Henry and Haldrek during the dream. I had no idea who the person haunting my dream was, only that the emotions were the same as whenever Rorik came to torment me.

"It wasn't. It was someone else. I don't know who, but it was just as terrifying as when Rorik taunts me." A cold, uncomfortable feeling stuck to the back of my neck, like someone was wrapping their hand around it and I shuddered.

"Did the person in your dream threaten you?" He pulled me closer with his free hand until our bodies were pressed against each other, his body heat wrapping itself around me. Despite the warmth of the summer air around us, I curled up into it. The feeling of his chest next to mine as our legs intertwined comforted me. The cold, uncomfortable feeling began to fade and I felt safe once again.

"No. Not openly. But the threat was there underneath everything. I knew the person wasn't to be trusted. Whoever they were. And then Rhaegos..." I stopped. Her warning didn't help me feel any better.

"Did Rhaegos protect you? I'd be surprised if she didn't."

"She warned me. Told me I was wise to be wary of the person in my dream. Something about tricksters being as lethal as necromancers." I didn't want to think about that. There was already so much on my—our—plates, that being on high alert for something or someone else would be exhausting.

Haldrek's chest rumbled as he began stroking my back. "Another thing to be worried about." He took a moment to rub the small of my back, the part of my body that always stayed sore the longest when I was on my period. It felt good as my muscles began to relax. "I had a thought last night. About what you said when you brought that babe in."

I stiffened up and he kissed the top of my head. "I'm not changing my mind on creating a small orphanage within the palace. Whether it's temporary or permanent within this place, the more I think about it, the more I think it is a good idea." His mouth moved down the side of my face as he continued to kiss me. I had a feeling I knew where this was leading, but we would see. If it did end up there, I wouldn't complain. Intimate moments like this with Haldrek were one of my favorite pleasures.

"I'm glad. This is important to me and... I know not a lot of my ideas are supported here. At least not at first."

Haldrek laughed softly and brushed his hand down to my legs. "You are the Reformer. People don't take to reform that easily. Not that it isn't important." He kissed me on the lips and I took in the taste of him, still enjoying our solitude. Even in the darkness of our covered bed, I could still sense him watching me.

"I'm just... I'm wondering if you're trying to replace your own childhood. Or at least make sure others don't experience the same things you did. Also, I know how badly... how Rorik's magic and our loss affected you. I don't know if taking care of other children is a way you're trying to cope with all that." He sighed. "I don't know if I'm making sense. I just want to make sure you're all right. If you're not, I want to help you."

Tears filled my eyes as he returned to kissing my collarbone tenderly. "Maybe? But is it a bad thing to want to help others? To keep others from dealing with what I dealt with? No one should go through that. And..." I hesitated. Haldrek's kisses stopped and I sensed him watching me again.

"And?"

"Part of me is afraid that I might end up like my mother when we have children. If we have this orphanage here, maybe I can watch the caretakers and see how they deal with the children. It's not like I had many good examples growing up. I... I wish I could have someone like Solvange here to emulate. Or," I paused.

"Or?"

My dream came back to mind. Henry's house had always been a safe and comfortable place for me. At least during the handful of times that I had been at his place. "Growing up, there was a lady I wished could be my mother. My friend Henry's mom. Anytime I visited, she was kind, welcoming, interested in what us kids were doing and, like, we weren't burdens to her. I remember wishing my mother would be more like her. Or, if I ever had kids, that I could be like her. But I'm afraid I don't know how to be like that."

Haldrek kissed me on the forehead and slipped his hand under my nightgown, stroking my belly and chest. "If how you treated your subjects in Svartån is any indicator of what kind of mother you will be, you will be an amazing one. There are plenty of women you can learn from and emulate if you wish. I know Taimi and Salla would be more than happy to act in that manner."

I smiled. "I think I'd like that. Taimi and Salla seem like nice women." For a moment, I wondered what it would have been like to be a daughter of theirs. Or have a mother with the same temperament as either of them.

"They are. They're good aunts, and I had many fond memories of them on the occasions where they'd return to Mirratoft."

"You think they'd help with the orphanage?"

Haldrek shrugged as he shifted on top of me. "I wouldn't be surprised if they would. And it may help others to come around to it." He pulled his nightgown off, tossing it against one of the bed curtains, and leaned over me, placing his arms on either side of my head. I stroked his arm muscles and smiled, pulling him down for a kiss. Given how I'd woken up after my nightmare, this morning was off to a pleasant start.

"And," He pulled back slightly to take a breath. "No matter what, you'll always have my support, *mine drawing*."

I smiled and pulled his head back toward mind for another kiss, grateful for him and savoring these last few minutes we had alone together before having to face the world again.

Chapter Four

I t was a good thing that Haldrek and I had started our day on a positive note. As soon as we were dressed and ready for the day, a palace messenger made his way to our fore quarters. Once one of the servants opened the door, he tumbled in, bowing on one knee to Haldrek.

"High King Haldrek, urgent news comes from your men in Lansiranikä."

Haldrek grimaced. "Speak."

"The warrior himself is in the war room. He has more details, but men loyal to Rorik have been found in Lansiranikä, and they are working with a gesith by the name of Hardbein."

"What?" I rushed forward from where I'd been standing near the bedroom door and the messenger flinched. Taking a step back, I said, "I'm not going to punish you. I'm just frustrated."

Haldrek turned to me and sighed. "I guess we should go down and see what other information the warrior has." He focused on the messenger and said, "Tell Kotkel Susi his attendance is required as well."

Without another word, the messenger left.

"Bastard." I curled my hands into fists. Turning to Haldrek, I said, "Hardbein is going after Svartån with Rorik's aid. He sees we're distracted here in Drattüjert, so he's going after my title. *Again.*"

Haldrek sighed. "We shouldn't assume until we speak to the warrior. Hardbein *shouldn't* have that authority. And yet..." He grimaced.

"And yet you wouldn't put it past him. He's been trying to take my title since before I arrived here. Bjorn hasn't been any better. You remember what he did after the battle for Aallotar's thegn hall. He was openly talking about what he would do once I was dead."

Haldrek nodded and gestured for me to walk ahead. "You're not wrong. I was just hoping Bjorn would be more reasonable. Either way, let's see what news awaits us."

When we arrived at the war room, Kotkel Susi—a tall but scrawny young man about Haldrek's age—was already talking to the messenger. Both seemed surprised to see me and Kotkel's attention darted to Haldrek as soon as he entered the room.

"My High King." Kotkel bowed to one knee. "I just learned news myself of the gesith's actions. I can promise you that my father will stop his unruly actions."

"Just like he stopped Hardbein from trying to take control of Svartån multiple times before?" I snapped. Worst case scenarios and guilt for being away from Svartån had been brewing in my head since we'd left our quarters, and I was in no mood for empty promises.

Kotkel glanced at me and then back at Haldrek as he stood up. "With all due respect, is it needful for the High Queen to be here?"

"Yes. Hardbein has tried to usurp her title as Thegn of Svartån multiple times. Unless the messenger tells me otherwise, I'm going to assume his connection with Rorik has more to do with taking the High Queen's ancestral lands than anything else."

Kotkel grimaced, nodding as he stood back. The messenger stepped forward and bowed to both Haldrek and me.

"My High King and High Queen. You are both correct in your assumptions. Hardbein is working with Rorik to foment discontent in Svartån. When I left, Hardbein was gathering warriors, intent on traveling to a city in southern Svartån."

"Sigreykir." I added, my irritation turning into full-blown agitation. "Hardbein's cousin is the gesith there. It wouldn't surprise me if he swore loyalty to him."

The messenger bowed to me. "That sounds in line with the information gathered thus far."

"My father wouldn't allow it. He would never betray a High King. His loyalty to Lohikärra and its rulers has always been steadfast." Kotkel blurted out. He focused on Haldrek, ignoring me completely. "I'll send word to my father. He'll curb Hardbein's actions. I promise."

"Will he?" I stepped forward, gaining Kotkel's attention. "Last I checked, he was pretty happy with the idea of Hardbein taking my place in Svartån." I didn't add the fact that neither Bjorn nor Kotkel had been at Haldrek's and my coronation as High King and Queen, nor had Bjorn officially sworn himself to us in the time since then. While Kotkel was in Drattüjert as a hersir—or representative—of Lansiranikä, sometimes I wondered how much loyalty he had toward either Haldrek or myself.

Kotkel's cheeks reddened. "I will send word to my father. That is my oath. No gesith should be trying to claim another thegn's lands from under them."

Haldrek nodded. "That I agree with. However, I wonder how ignorant your father is of the situation. He has certainly supported Hardbein in previous attempts to take my wife's lands." Turning to the messenger, Haldrek asked, "Any word on how independently

Hardbein is working on this? Does he have men from his fellow gesiths following him, or even warriors from the thegn hall itself?"

The messenger fidgeted with the rings on his fingers as he glanced at Kotkel. It was evident they had spoken about this prior to our arrival.

"Yes, my king. Among the warriors with him are others from various parts of Lansiranikä. And the thegn hall itself."

Kotkel sighed and I grimaced. "We're going to have to deal with this, Haldrek." I looked at him. "It sounds like I'll have to return to Svartån for a time."

Much to my surprise, he shook his head. "I should go in your stead. If Hardbein is working with Rorik," Haldrek glanced at Kotkel grimly, "and Bjorn is either ignoring or aiding this stunt, then this is about more than just Svartån. This is about pulling more of Lohikärra under the power of those who would not see either of us ruling from Drattüjert."

"My king—" Kotkel blurted out. He stepped back as Haldrek glared at him.

"How many times have you asked your father to send a token of his fealty, Kotkel?"

"Every time I speak with him, my king." He ducked his head, his ears turning the same shade of red as his hair.

"It's been nearly a year since the dragons accepted myself and Ina as the High King and Queen. What excuses your father from doing the same?"

Kotkel shook his head. "Nothing, my King."

"What excuses does he give for his behavior?"

Kotkel stood silent, refusing to look at Haldrek or me.

Haldrek bobbed his head and grimaced. "That's what I thought." He returned his focus to the messenger. "Return and tell those who sent you that I will be arriving in a fortnight with at least one sattar of men. If we can confront Rorik and his followers now, we may be able to bring peace to Lohikärra once and for all. You are dismissed."

The messenger nodded and hurried out of the room. Kotkel stayed for a moment, his hands balled up into fists.

"My father is not a traitor. He—we are Lohikärrans through and through. We have been for generations and we have laid down our lives for this kingdom. Which is more than can be said for others in this palace. The loyalty of Lansiranikä should not be in question." A sharp glance from Kotkel to me gave me all the needed subtext from his last line. Though he wouldn't say it out loud, he did not deem me to be Lohikärran.

Haldrek turned to him. "I never said your father was a traitor. But his actions thus far have made me wary. And his actions toward Ina and Svartån give me pause as well." Haldrek glanced out into the hallway before returning his focus to Kotkel. "You may go."

He bowed stiffly and I heard him mumble something as he exited, leaving Haldrek and I alone.

"That wasn't how I wanted to start off my morning." Haldrek sighed.

"I know. Me neither. But if you're going to Svartån to fight Hardbein, I should go too. I'm still technically the Thegn of Svartån, even if Skuti and the others are running Svangendom in my stead." It had been a few days since I'd spoken to anyone at the thegn hall. I made a mental note to do that the next time I had a free moment.

Haldrek grimaced. "Normally I would agree. However," he looked back at the door and took a step closer to me, "the two of us together are a much larger target now. Whether it be Hardbein, Bjorn or someone else, if both of us get killed, there's no one who can stop Rorik. And I need someone here in Drattüjert I can trust."

I laughed miserably, tears springing to my eyes as the weight of his words hit me. "So you don't trust your counselors?" Some of those from the various thegn lands I knew he didn't trust, but Haldrek had relied heavily on his uncle's counselors, the ones who had survived the Battle of Drattüjert at least.

"I trust them enough to get their jobs done. But if both of us were gone, I'm not sure they'd do anything for the city, unless it allowed them to be the only one in charge in our stead." He took my hands and leaned down so our foreheads were together. I soaked in the physical touch, knowing as soon as he left, it would be a long time until I felt his embrace again.

The next morning, Haldrek and I got up early. We made love once more before what we both knew would likely be two or more months of separation. Afterwards he got dressed in his new armor, fit for a High King, as well as to get a feel for the weapon that had come with his new title. I got up myself, wanting to spend every moment I could with him before he left. Sure, we'd have the pendants to talk, but the palace would feel so much more lonely without him by my side.

As he stretched his fingers and tested the joints in the armor, he looked up. "I'll be safe. I promise."

"I know. This is just me savoring every little bit of time with you." I walked over from where I'd been sitting and traced my hand along the edges of his armor before pulling him in for another kiss. His lips met mine hungrily for a few moments, and when he finally pulled back, I sighed. "Once you head out, I don't know how long it will take before you come back. Months? You'll likely be gone for our wedding anniversary and possibly the one-year anniversary of us being High King and Queen."

Haldrek bobbed his head side to side, thoughtfully. "It may take a few months. Depends on whether or not Bjorn is helping Hardbein or if it's just Rorik. If I'm lucky, I can take out both Rorik and Hardbein. Then, hopefully, this whole debacle can be put behind us." He stepped back to the table and sheathed his sword before stretching his arms out to the side. "How do I look?" There was a bit of nervousness in his voice. "I still think of this as my uncle's armor, not mine."

"You look like a bonafide High King." I walked up to him and pulled his head down for another kiss. Every kiss meant a few more moments together. Looking back up at him, I smiled with pride. "Proper and powerful."

He eagerly kissed me again and gently stroked my backside. As he pulled his head away, he whispered, "Good. Maybe I'll scare Hardbein into finally behaving."

I laughed. "Hardbein behaving? That'll be a miracle."

He kissed me once more on the neck, sending flutters up and down my body. Stupid Hardbein, taking my husband away from me. "I'll return as soon as I can. Until then, keep Drattüjert safe and let me know if anything changes."

A sudden feeling of foreboding hit me and I frowned, not wanting to let go of Haldrek. Rhaegos began churning inside my head. The overwhelming sensation that something would happen while Haldrek was away weighed me down and made me want to keep him close by. Pushing it aside, I tried to smile. "Of course. Hopefully nothing happens, but if it does, you'll be the first person I contact. Like always." I grabbed my pendant, being careful not to squeeze it. It was full and I needed to level up, but not right now.

Haldrek watched me for a moment and then asked, "Did Rhaegos just tell you something? Your expression shifted."

Shaking my head, I said, "I felt something, but it could just be nerves or anxiety. It's fine. I'll be fine."

"Are you sure?"

I nodded. "It's nothing. I think I'm just going to miss you a lot while you are gone, and I'm already feeling that." That was a lie. It was definitely more than that, but I didn't want Haldrek to start his journey with worry in his heart.

"I'm going to miss you too. I'll do everything I can to return home quickly." He squeezed me tight as we headed out of our private quarters.

The palace was quieter than normal as I walked with Haldrek outside. The large square in front of the palace was filled with more warriors than I could count, at least one or two sattars, and I knew there was another sattar of horsemen waiting outside the city walls. Haldrek's horse was saddled and ready to go just below the small landing where we stood.

Haldrek looked out over the warriors, as well as the throng of commoners who watched us from the edges of the square.

"Today, we go to show our might. Our brothers and neighbors have had their minds twisted by the necromancer Rorik's words and the greed of gesiths who aligned themselves with him. We will not stand for this behavior. The dragons will not stand for this behavior." He paused, looking over the men. "I know this will be trying for some of you. You've been away from your families for many months. You may not know what to expect back home, but know this: I will do everything in my power as High King to bring peace and prosperity back to Lohikärra."

The men began to cheer. Haldrek smiled and turned to me, his eyes wetter than before. He tugged at my belt, brushing his hand against my stomach. My chest tightened and tears bubbled up in my eyes as he leaned in.

"Once I've taken care of Rorik, we can resume trying for an aethling."

And that set off my tears. I ducked my head into his chest, unable to control myself. "You best come back safe. I don't know what I'd do if something happened to you."

"Don't worry. I've been fighting men like Hardbein my entire life, and Rorik...Andrattür is known for its dislike of the undead. I've fought plenty of undead creatures before. So Rorik and his minions will be gone soon."

I leaned back to wipe my tears. People were watching us, but I didn't care. "I believe you. Still, be safe."

Haldrek nodded, pulling out of my embrace. "I will. I love you, *mine drawing*."

Those words made me smile despite the tears and blotchiness that I knew was now covering my cheeks. I watched Haldrek as he descended the stairs and got on his horse. The warriors parted for him and, once he passed through, filled in behind him. I stayed on the landing until Haldrek and the sattars disappeared through the main gate at the end of the city.

As soon as I turned around to go back inside, the sense of foreboding came over me again, making my stomach churn. I placed my hand on my abdomen and groaned. It was heavier, more tangible this time. A part of me began to panic, wondering if Rorik was somehow invading my mind, despite being awake.

You are safe from Rorik for the time being, little one, though his power grows. What you sense is another person you must be wary of. Someone who also tries to wield my kin's magic without their permission.

"Is that person also Lohikärran?" I whispered as I hurried into the palace, hoping not to catch anyone's attention. For some reason, my dream came back to mind, and I got the sense that Rhaegos was bringing it back to my attention.

No, little one. This person is of Blodnar descent.

A chill went up my spine and I hurried back to my quarters as quickly as I could.

Chapter Five

The first few days after Haldrek left were relatively calm. Wanting to keep my mind busy, I doubled down on tasks Haldrek normally handled, including complaints from various groups and people within Drattüjert. While I never saw the actual people air their grievances, every morning started with a long list of issues from the day before. I quickly saw why this was Haldrek's least favorite task of the day.

"Queen *I-na*, are you listening?" One particular advisor, Thoreg Bjornsson, had picked up Kamira's bad habit of mispronouncing my name. As it was, I'd been trying to mull over a complaint that popped up every single day now: how to help the refugees who now flooded Drattüjert. Many of them were escaping the Blodnar's destruction as they had pulled back toward the border, but we needed to keep them from overwhelming a city still recovering from its own near destruction.

"Only when you say my name correctly." I turned to the man with a grimace. "Would you have called my father 'I-ngmar' or Ingmar?"

The man's mouth pinched together. "No, Queen Ina. But it's important you listen regardless." He began reading over the complaints again and I suppressed my irritation. Rhaegos had taught me more than a few things since we'd bonded. Not all of our conversations were vague warnings. One of the things Rhaegos had emphasized since we first bonded was boundaries. I had never learned them growing up, but now they were a needed skill as first a thegn and now as a High Queen.

"It's important for you to also say my name correctly," I snapped. Rhaegos had taught me boundaries, but now I struggled with keeping calm when people crossed them. "*And* I have been listening. Half of that list are complaints about refugees from the southern lands. Apparently, their 'ragged appearance' and smell make people uncomfortable here. Because no one in Drattüjert has ever been forced from their homes or been under the thumb of invaders."

Thoreg scowled and tossed the scroll he'd been holding on the table. Without a word, he marched out of the room. One of the other counselors, Gizur, lifted his head. "He was only trying to help, my queen."

"He needs to say my name correctly. You haven't had an issue with that, have you?"

Gizur shook his head. "All I'm saying is that perhaps you would do well to be more lady-like in your chastisements. Much like your predecessor, High King Kalle's wife."

I tried to ignore his verbal jab. "She had a name too. Did people mispronounce it as well?"

He glanced over at the two other men in the room. They said nothing. When he looked back at me, he said, "Perhaps we should focus on more important things than your name."

That snark made my anger grow further. Still, I wasn't about to pull back from my boundaries. "It's the simple things, counselor. No one likes it when others intentionally mispronounce their name. It's a sign of disrespect. Would you like it if someone continued to call you Gizzards or Geezer instead of Gizur? No, I don't think so." I took a deep breath and continued, ignoring him as he opened his mouth. "As for the other subjects we're dealing with... that's what the complainants must do. Deal with it. As High King and High Queen, Haldrek and I rule over *all* of Lohikärra, not just the city of Drattüjert. We're ending one war and trying to prevent another. This is a time of rebuilding, and I'm sure the refugees would love to rebuild their own homes instead of living in tents here."

"So what would you have these complainants do?" Gizur pursed his already thin lips until they disappeared.

"Have patience. If they must do something, help the refugees. Whether that is by rebuilding their homes or something else." I crossed my arms, daring the advisor to challenge me once again.

"You know it would be difficult for these people, those who come seeking your advice, to travel several days' time and do such things. Not to mention still dangerous. Would you have us send guards with them and limit Drattüjert's resources?"

I stared at Gizur. Long enough for him to straighten up. "Which is a more difficult task? Having patience or rebuilding the parts of Lohikärra where these refugees are coming from?"

The man looked away and the advisor on his right murmured, "Patience would be the best option, I suppose."

"Agreed. I can't keep other Lohikärrans from entering Drattüjert and I won't. They have just as much a right to be here as anyone else. Perhaps they might even help Drattüjert grow into an even more powerful city. Who knows? But now is a time of rebuilding and it will take exactly that. Time."

The advisors said nothing and refused to look me in the eye, instead focusing intently on the scrolls on the table.

"Are there any other complaints I should know about?" I gestured to the scrolls in front of me.

The men all shook their heads and mumbled various responses.

"Then we should take leave of this meeting. I'm sure we are all busy with various tasks in rebuilding both the city and Lohikärra itself."

They nodded and I left the room first, still irritated, but wondering if I'd handled the matter correctly.

You did fine, little one. I am proud of you for keeping your boundaries. There is power in one's name and they would be wise to remember that.

I exhaled, letting some of the worry and tension move from my body. There was still some clinging to me as I walked toward the nearest exterior door. Fresh air would help. It always did.

"High Queen Ina! Where are you off to now?"

I stopped and waited as Lady Taimi hurried to catch up. Her old bones didn't seem to be bothering her today.

"I was hoping for some fresh air. Possibly walk through the city as well and see how things are progressing." I put my arm out for her to grab. "It sounds like a lot of people are complaining about the refugees who are arriving and I want to see if there are any ways to ease the tension."

"A wise idea, I think. It's not good to be stuck inside the palace all day. Especially with lovely summer weather like this. May I join you?"

"Always." We linked arms and I watched movement following us out of the corner of my eye. While I knew who it was—the guards who were assigned to me personally—it was different than when Llamryl and his men guarded me. The near constant watch was something I was still adjusting to as High Queen. Returning my focus to the present, I listened to Taimi's pleasant chatter as we went down a set of stairs and followed the garden wall toward the front of the palace.

"I overheard that you've undertaken some of the tasks your husband usually deals with. How is that going?"

I sighed. "Politics have never been my strong suit. Even when I was younger, I avoided being in positions of authority." I omitted the main fact being that my mother had never liked me being in extracurricular activities, so even if I *had* been interested, I wouldn't have had the chance anyway.

"It is a skill that some people come by naturally and others develop over time. But I've found that one isn't necessarily better at those tasks than the other." She paused, then asked, "Have you kept Kalle's old advisors in line?"

"I'm trying. Though at least one is insistent on calling me I-na instead of Ina. It's getting on my nerves."

"A subtle jab, it seems. Did you correct him?"

"I did." We walked into the main square, active with city people. I noticed beggars on the far edge of the square and wondered how many were recent arrivals.

"Good. Keep them in line. Those men... I remember my sister, Tuliki, always fuming at their audacity. Especially after she and Kalle first got married. Many of them ignored her. It wasn't until after Kalleson, her eldest, was born that many of the advisors even acknowledged her existence."

"Did Kalle ever say anything to them?"

"They made sure not to insult or ignore Tuliki when he was around. Though it did take a few years for him to understand why what they were doing was bad."

"Did he not support his wife?"

Taimi firmly put her free hand on my arm. "Oh no, not at all! He loved and respected Tuliki very much. But sometimes it's hard to see things outside of your own experience and perceptions. Especially in one's youth."

I nodded, reflecting on Haldrek and myself. I was certainly learning a lot, but as always, Haldrek had a confidence and a presence I wish I had.

Taimi removed her hand and waved to someone wearing the robes of a Priest of Tenelth as we reached a far corner of the city that I had yet to visit. Much to my surprise, as the person came over, I realized it was a woman. For as long as I'd been in Lohikärra, I'd only ever met male Priests of Tenelth. Not only was she a woman, but I noticed that her skin tone was closer to Mattie's than mine. All in all, she stuck out as much as I did.

"Priestess Thwaya! I'm glad to see you!"

The woman's face lit up as she and Taimi embraced. As Thwaya turned to me, she bowed low to the ground. "Blessings of Tenelth and his kin be upon you, High Queen Ina."

I bowed as well. "Thank you." Hesitating, I added, "You too?"

Thwaya laughed and nodded. "One of the perks of being a priestess. The blessings of the dragons are never too far away. How are you this day, my queen?"

"As good as I can be, I suppose."

Taimi leaned in toward the priestess conspiratorially. "She's had to deal with the High King's counselors."

Before either Thwaya or I could say anything, a young boy, probably no more than two or three, came tumbling full speed into Thwaya's dress. Rather than being caught off guard by him, she grabbed him up and placed him on her hip. It was then that I noticed their similarity in appearance. I also noticed pointed tips of his ears poke out from underneath his curly hair.

"What have I told you about doing that, Alaion?" She sounded more amused than annoyed, "Where is Hallbera?"

The boy giggled and pointed behind us to a woman carrying a large basket of produce. "Priestess Thwaya! I've brought more vegetables for the Refuge."

Thwaya beamed. "Much appreciated, Hallbera." She continued to hold the boy as she turned back to us. "Hallbera is a dear cousin of mine. She and her husband own several large estates and farms in Heidrunefoss and Itaranikä. I could tell you the hows and whats of how they inherited those lands, but it would probably bore you as much as it always did me. Needless to say, before Drattüjert fell, Hallbera would bring foodstuffs here to feed the less fortunate. Now that you and the High King have reclaimed Drattüjert, she's been able to return to doing that. Which has been helpful…"

"Priestess Thwaya has taken it upon herself to manage the Refuge of Tenelth, and I thought you two should meet at some point, given your endeavors at the castle." Taimi hesitated. "I hope I didn't overstep my bounds."

I shook my head. "No, I appreciate it." Turning back to Thwaya, I said, "I want to create an orphanage or home of some kind for refugees, orphans, women and children who've been affected by the war. There's a lady, Solvange—"

"I know Solvange." Thwaya interrupted. "She's a dear friend, though I haven't seen her since I last travelled to Svartån. How is she?"

"As spirited as normal." I smiled. "I appreciate what she's done in Svartån, and I want to do the same here, but for more than just the Hethurin children." Now it was my turn to hesitate. "Though if the Refuge of Tenelth is already doing that, I don't want to encroach." I turned to Taimi, wondering why no one had mentioned the Refuge to me before.

"It's fine. The dragons see no encroachment when it comes to serving those in need. And," Thwaya looked past me, "there is always protection in having the High King and Queen's favor."

I turned back to see a few men staring at us. As soon as they caught sight of me, they disappeared into the crowd.

"There are those who dislike the Refuge of Tenelth, saying we harbor Blodnar spies, albeit unintentionally." Thwaya's voice turned firm. "I disagree. There has been nothing spoken among the refugees here except gratitude toward the dragons and those of us who serve them."

"Sounds similar to the situation I dealt with last year in Svartån," I murmured. Turning back to Thwaya, I continued, "If you have time, I'd love to see what you and the other Priests and Priestesses of Tenelth are doing here. Perhaps gain some inspiration or see how our efforts might be joined?"

Thwaya's expression brightened with a smile. "I would love that. Come, I would be honored if you and Lady Taimi would join me inside the Refuge."

Without another word, I nodded, and we followed Thwaya inside.

Chapter Six

My visit with Thwaya and the Refuge of Tenelth was a welcome reprieve from the palace politics that were quickly consuming my every waking hour. We agreed the 'High Queen's Home'—as Thwaya had nicknamed it—at the palace and the Refuge would work well together. Both then could provide more resources to those in need, with both refugees and those serving Tenelth traveling between the two places as needed.

Even though it was for refugees, I often visited those quarters. Officially, to oversee the work, and unofficially, as a refuge for myself. The facade I wore in front of the advisors and other abthanry often slipped as I visited with those in the High Queen's Home. I could relax among those who didn't necessarily have a home they could return too.

"High Queen Ina." One of the older priestesses bowed deeply, her long dress covering the stone floor around her. "It is an honor to see you again. What brings you here today?" We stood in the middle of a large room along the outer wall of the palace. At one point, I assumed, it had been a barracks or armory room, given the placement of the only windows was high above us. Most of the light in the area came from a few strategically placed hearths and plenty of candles. Almost two dozen refugees, mainly women and children, huddled in small groups around the room.

"Nothing special. I just wanted to see how everyone was doing." Children's laughter echoed through the room and my heart twisted. My thoughts went back to both my fears and desires. I'd never thought I was maternal—my mother certainly wasn't—but the desire to scoop up these children and keep them safe grew with every day.

"All is well, my queen. We've had a few new arrivals today. I'm sure they'd love to meet you," the priestess hesitated and ducked her head, "if you have the time."

It had never bothered me to meet with the refugees before, so I nodded. "Lead the way. And let me know if there is anything you all need. Food, blankets, clothing...I want those here to have some kind of stability." *Some kind of dignity.* Rhaegos's voice popped into my head. That... that I could agree with. I'd never been a refugee, at least in a traditional sense, but I knew what it felt like to desperately need something solid in my life. Something to hold onto in the middle of chaos.

The priestess nodded her head. "You have been very generous, my queen. Both here and with the Refuge. We are eternally grateful for your help." She took me into one of the smaller rooms where a handful of women sat. The youngest girl in the group peeked out of the window and giggled, watching whatever was outside.

"Maja!" An older woman, who had been sitting nearby, tugged the small girl back toward her. The woman looked tired, but a small smile crossed her mouth as she stood up.

"My queen, these women just recently arrived from Etelaranikä today. A family from Halsar." The priestess gestured to them. "Maja, the youngest, and her two sisters, Hallfrid and Gyda, as well as their mother, Bera, and their grandmother, Runa."

I smiled, trying to be as comforting as I could. While the youngest daughter, Maja, still seemed bright and cheerful, the mother and her two other daughters were very somber. The grandmother looked around the room, smiling, but seemed to be in another world entirely. "I'm glad you all could make it here. I hope we can help you in any manner you need."

Bera nodded. "You're the first person in Drattüjert, other than the priests and priestesses of Tenelth, to treat us with more than derision, Your Majesty. I know you have many duties, but thank you."

"I enjoy visiting with people here. How…" I hesitated to ask what was on my mind, and it didn't help that I was terrible at small talk. "How long did it take you from Halsar to here?"

"Over a week, almost two. But we weren't the fastest group leaving Halsar."

"What is it like there, right now?"

Bera grimaced. "Not good. It's too close to where Thegn-heir Rorik's men are camped and strange things have been rising in the forests around us." She focused on her feet. "Most people in Halsar are afraid. Rorik is a dangerous person and—"

"You shall be the one to slay him. In this life and the next." Runa faced me, and I noticed one of her eyes was white and the other one was closed.

"Mother…" Bera whispered, fear coloring her words as she glanced at me.

"It's fine." I was curious now why this woman had said what she did. Especially since I guessed they didn't know of my family's gift.

"You are the Lady of Lohikärra. Heir to Freya and many of her daughters. Those with that title are brought to Lohikärra in their greatest time of need. Just as Freya and Bjornulf slew Ryluth and his minions, so too will you."

"Ryluth has been dead for centuries, millennia now." The priestess sounded a bit taken aback by Runa's words.

"She is an old lady. Sometimes she speaks dreams and imaginings. I apologize..." Bera's eyes widened as she began to shake her head.

"I only speak what I see," Runa snapped. "My queen, you have many struggles ahead. There are those who would take your place as both Queen and as a Lady of Lohikärra. But they are weak and will take Lohikärra down a dark path. Your fate hangs like a thread which must be woven. Others will try to weave for you, but you must weave your own destiny or else."

"Or else what?" I hoped Rhaegos was listening. Or perhaps she or one of her kin were giving this woman her vision, if it was correct.

"Or else we are all doomed. You must weave your thread and balance it. When you do, you will be a true Lady of Lohikärra, like Freya of old." Her one eye closed and her head drooped down. As Bera touched her arm, Runa jerked awake.

After looking around at her entire family with a frown of confusion, she focused on me and bowed her head. "You *are* the High Queen. My apologies, Your Majesty. I thought I would be awake when you arrived. I hope I wasn't snoring." Her expression changed to worry and I shook my head.

"You weren't snoring. But you did say some interesting things about being a Lady of Lohikärra. I've only heard that term a handful of times since arriving in Drattüjert myself."

The old woman nodded and sighed. "Sometimes the voices in my head get a little antsy." She paused, looking me over for a moment, "I apologize if they offended you. But the title of Lady of Lohikärra is not given to every High Queen, I know that much. If they spoke about it, it was probably important."

I nodded and looked at the priestess, wondering how to end this conversation. While I wasn't offended, the 'voices' left me unnerved. The priestess smiled and placed her arm on my shoulder. "I'm sure you have much to attend to, my queen. Thank you again for visiting."

I smiled, taking the opportunity to leave without things getting awkward. Turning back to the family, I said, "I'm glad you are able to be here safe in Drattüjert. It was a pleasure to meet you."

With a wave, I departed and noticed that the priestess still looked uncomfortable. Once we were in a less crowded spot, away from the new family, she stopped.

"I apologize, my queen. I wasn't aware that the grandmother would speak as she did."

I shrugged. "It isn't the strangest thing that's happened to me in Lohikärra. Though now I may have to see if I can find more references to it. At least the Lady of Lohikärra part. Or ask Rhaegos. But for now," I sighed. "I should probably get back to the advisors and other abthanry. It won't be long before something happens that requires my attention."

She laughed quietly and nodded, still keeping her head bowed. "That is true, my queen. In that case, I hope the rest of your day goes by quickly."

"Thank you." I hurried out and let my mind ponder what exactly the old lady meant by her words, and by the term 'Lady of Lohikärra'.

Almost as if I had predicted it, just as I walked into the indoor garden room where Rorik had opened up a portal to toss me and Haldrek into, one year ago, someone grabbed my arm firmly, yanking me around to face them.

"High Queen I-na, we been looking all over the palace for you!"

I recoiled from the advisor, pulling my arm from his grip and scowling as anger and indignation flooded me. It was Thoreg Bjornsson, the same man I'd gotten into an argument with before visiting the Refuge of Tenelth. Even if I hadn't had that argument with him several days before, his entire demeanor told me that this would be an unpleasant interaction. His tone was patronizing, like I'd been scampering off to play instead of dealing with some of my other *more important* duties.

"I was speaking with a Priestess of Tenelth, if you must know. Don't ever touch me like that again. There are other ways of getting my attention."

"Not when you act like you are deaf! I've been screaming your name, chasing you these last few minutes." Thoreg looked at me wildly, shaking his head. For a moment I wondered how much of a danger he might be right now.

Either way, I had heard nothing to that effect. I knew that my hearing was fine. "I'm pretty sure that's a lie. If you were yelling for me, I would have heard you."

"One would assume, so why ignore me?" He crossed his arms and raised his eyebrows as if expecting some kind of lousy excuse.

I was getting irritated by this man, and his comments reminded me of my mother, always twisting my words and making me feel powerless.

Your intuition is correct. But you are not powerless.

Rhaegos's voice calmed me and strengthened my resolve. I wasn't going crazy. Thoreg was trying to mess with my head. If that was the case... "I wasn't ignoring you and you weren't shouting for me, at least anywhere in this vicinity. But that's not important. What's important is that I have a long list of things to do right now and you are stopping me. What do you want?"

"I..." he paused as I heard footsteps move toward us, "and a few of the other advisors, are concerned and wanted to speak to you about some of these *projects* of yours."

I saw a handful of Haldrek's advisors, as well as Kamira, Lady Drifa, and Kotkel walking toward us, both from the garden and behind the first counsellor. My muscles tightened as the feeling of being threatened grew. There were guards behind me, but now I questioned how loyal they were. Would they protect me if this group decided to fight? I brushed my hand against my dress, feeling the short blade at my hip. If nothing else, I could protect myself and escape to a safer location.

Rhaegos, help me.

They shall not harm you. Not today. Tell them that this is neither the time nor the place for this discussion. If they have issues, they know the proper way to bring them to your attention.

I straightened up, staring Thoreg in the eye and hoping it was intimidating enough. "This is neither the time nor the place for this. If you have issues with certain projects, there is a proper way to bring them to my attention."

"Not one in which you'll actually listen." Kamira stepped forward, and I bit the inside of my lip to keep from cussing her out here and now.

"I'm not going to listen here when you all are trying to ambush me. As I said before, if you have issues with certain projects, there is a proper way to bring them to my attention. *This* is not it."

Kamira sighed as if dealing with a petulant child. "You're spending too much time, effort, and money on your little projects and letting miscreants into the city."

I raised an eyebrow, crossing my arms. "Miscreants? Like whom?"

"Like all these refugees. The main Blodnar armies may be pulling back toward their lands, but you'd be stupid not to think they're not keeping spies here."

"So you've been spreading those rumors too, have you? I'm aware of what the Blodnar might be doing." In all honesty, Haldrek and I had been aware of potential spy activity since we became High King and High Queen. More so than most of the advisors, and definitely more than any of the thegns' hersirs.

"Yet you welcome them with open arms."

"The refugees? Yes. Because they are fellow Lohikärrans who have been displaced by the war. They are from nearly every thegn land bordering the Blodnar Empire." I focused on Lady Drifa. "Would you have me refuse refugees from Itaranikä because they might be Blodnar spies? There are people from Itaranikä in the High Queen's Home as we speak."

Lady Drifa pursed her lips and looked away, saying nothing.

"You don't think there are spies among those refugees?" Kamira brought her fist forward to knock on my head and I ducked, while pushing her arm out of the way.

"Don't you dare touch me like that." There was movement behind me and a few of my personal guards stepped forward out of shadows and from the central garden area. "Do you not think that there are people both Haldrek and I have put in place to protect

Drattüjert? Just because you don't know about something Kamira, doesn't mean it's nonexistent."

She continued to stare me down. "I trust the High King. It is *you* who I don't trust. We all know the stories. You appeared here out of nowhere and all of a sudden you're the Thegn of Svartån and have wormed your way into Haldrek's good graces. Then he makes you his High Queen in a matter of months. There is something strange about that. I—"

"Kamira," Lady Drifa interrupted her and Kamira looked back at her. "Your point has been made."

Kamira stepped away from me with a scowl. "I don't trust your loyalty to Lohikärra, *I-na*. Not with the miscreants you bring into the palace with your 'High Queen's Home.' I would bet most of the Blodnar spies in Drattüjert are among them. A real Lady of Lohikärra would disband the whole charade and send those *people* back to where they came from."

I was fuming. But before I had a chance to speak, a voice popped up from the garden.

"A true Lady of Lohikärra is merciful. A true Lady of Lohikärra is wise. And a true Lady of Lohikärra stands tall in the face of persecution." Sibila walked out of the garden, a small flower in her hand. She walked between Kamira and me, oblivious to everything around her except for the flower, stopping only when she was at the group. "Tesroan, you always speak of the Ladies of Lohikärra to me. They are lovely stories, but I never understand why you bring them up." Sibila stopped, smelled the flower, and laughed. "Yes, yes, I agree. The High Queen's Home has been a blessing to those cast out by my half-brother and his Blodnar allies. He would have no one in Etelaranikä except those loyal to him. His loss." She continued walking past everyone and out a nearby entrance. The space stayed unnaturally quiet for a few minutes after she left.

When I returned my focus to the group of advisors and hersirs, my expression hardened. In my head, I sensed Rhaegos prodding me to end the discussion. "Now that I know the truth of your feelings, I must return to my actual duties. If you have other complaints, you know the *proper* way to bring it up. Understood?"

Rhaegos's presence grew stronger inside of me and I sensed she was doing something, though I wasn't sure what. Much to my surprise, everyone bowed respectfully to me. Everyone except Kamira. Her hateful glare still bore into me. I ignored it.

Thoreg murmured, "We understand, High Queen Ina." He departed without another word and the rest of the group followed one by one, with Lady Drifa nearly dragging Kamira from my presence.

When I was alone, I whispered, "What was that, Rhaegos?"

I merely reminded my kin to keep their haldragas in check. We cannot force our haldragas to do what we wish, but we can guide them. It seems Kamira and her dragon are at odds right now. That may be something to keep an eye on in the future.

"You or me?" I remembered that my guards were still here, and though they didn't react as I spoke out loud, I still felt weird. Making my way back to my private quarters, I tried to focus on Rhaegos's presence. She roiled around inside my head, though it felt more of a busy sensation than anything else.

Both. Time will tell though. Kamira may question your loyalty to Lohikärra, but the dragons question her loyalty entirely.

A heavy weight dropped to the bottom of my stomach as I entered my quarters. If the dragons were questioning Kamira's loyalty and she had many allies here in the palace... things would get worse before they got better.

Chapter Seven

That afternoon, I called Mattie for the first time in a few weeks. I felt awful that our conversation had drawn farther and farther apart. While we had been close in Fargo, our different duties had slowly made our conversations less and less frequent. As much as I wished she was here at the palace, I knew she took her duties as Thegn of Andrattür seriously.

As soon as her face popped up inside the glassy stone of my pendant, I smiled.

"It's been a long time, Your Majesty." She smiled and I knew she was trying to hide a laugh. Still I felt like an awful, flaky friend.

"Mattie. I've been meaning to call. Things have been crazy here at the palace for the past few weeks. Still, that's no excuse."

"I know." There was the fussy cooing of a baby in the background and my heart twisted uncomfortably. Mattie and Llamryl's daughter was about six weeks old now. She would have been a month older than Haldrek's and my child, if I hadn't had the miscarriage. Mattie shifted and I heard a door close. "Sorry. I know that's probably not the sound you're wanting to hear right now."

"It's fine. How's she doing?"

"Good. Up a lot at night according to the nursemaids. I still don't know how I feel about having her with them most of the time. But I guess it's normal here for the abthanry? Llamryl and I try to spend time with her when we don't have other tasks. Or when I'm resting. My spell casting and magic use isn't back to what it was before Geirny was born, but I've been told it'll be back to normal by her first—" Mattie stopped. "Anyway, how is Drattüjert? I heard word from Jaonos that Haldrek left for Svartån and Lansiranikä?"

I nodded. Of course Jaonos would have kept Mattie up to date on what was going on. As her hersir, that was half of his job.

"Hardbein is making another attempt for Svartån, this time with followers of Rorik."

Mattie's eyes widened. "That's a bold move. Which attempt is this now? Fourth or fifth? In less than eighteen months?"

"Fourth attempt. I may hate him with every fiber of my being, but I can't say he isn't stubborn. I'm afraid Sigreykir will welcome Hardbein with open arms when he arrives, and I can't have Svartån fractured like that." Images of Svartåns fighting against one another entered my head and I shook them away, not wanting to entertain the thought. If Hardbein gained the loyalty of Sigreykir, he would certainly go after Svangendom next.

"Have you spoken to Skuti yet?"

"He was one of the first people Haldrek and I contacted. There is a sattar of men from the thegn hall going to 'check on Sigreykir' on my behalf. I made sure it was a mixed group of Hethurin and non-Hethurin. I know how the gesith is there." Yet another reason to keep Hardbein out of Svartån and his cousin under my thumb. Both would stir up conflict between the Hethurin and non-Hethurin again, destroying the current peace there.

"I remember you mentioning that last summer. If you and Haldrek would like, I can send a sattar of men as well. To show solidarity for their High King and aid their former thegn. Many still speak highly of Haldrek."

A smile crossed my face. Of course Mattie would know better how to play these political games. "I'm not opposed to it, and as Thegn of Svartån, they are welcome. But it may be wise to ask Haldrek if he needs more warriors. Or how they can help."

Mattie nodded. "How is everything else? I don't know if it's just me, but you sound worn down."

I sighed. "Palace politics are exhausting. Sometimes I wonder if I'm capable enough to be High Queen. Kamira is still being awful and," I hesitated, "I created a refuge of sorts within the castle. Like Solvange's in Svartån. People have been calling it the High Queen's Home. The Priestesses of Tenelth connected with the Refuge of Tenelth here in Drattüjert have been assisting me with it, but there has been pushback. Some of Haldrek's advisors tried to corner me today and demand I get rid of it."

"Why?" Mattie's eyes widened in surprise.

"There's a lot of hate here for the refugees. And fear that Blodnar spies may be among those refugees. I mean, Haldrek and I already knew about the possibility and have taken measures, but..." I faltered.

"But the advisors don't trust you."

I shook my head. "No. Kamira has been making it worse. She has all but accused me of being loyal to the Blodnar instead of Lohikärra." Tears filled my eyes. "I don't know what I can do. I'm not going to kick the refugees out. They're Lohikärran, for pity's sake. Not even Blodnar. But it seems like there's nothing I can do to convince the advisors I am loyal to Lohikärra. They were men loyal to Haldrek's uncle and they're loyal to him, but I'm still the outsider."

"I'm sorry. If you'd like, I can remind Jaonos to advocate for you more and call out those who are questioning you, but I know all of that is difficult. Not that you haven't dealt with difficult before. Bringing all of Svartån back together and killing Seirye was an accomplishment. If you can do that, you can handle some cantankerous old politicians." She glanced away from her pendant and nodded to someone. When she returned her focus to me, she said, "I have to go, but I believe in you. If there's anything I can do to help you, let me know. Andrattür is always loyal."

I smiled. "Thank you. I'm going to talk to Haldrek and I'll see what he says. Hopefully the advisors will come around without too much more issue." Not that I thought that was the case.

We each closed our pendants, and I glanced out the window that looked over the center city square. People bustled around, but even from here, I could see refugees sitting on the fringes. The sooner we dealt with Rorik and his allies, the sooner we could help people return to their homes.

Opening my pendant once again, I tapped my thumb on the glass stone and said, "Haldrek Rodreksson."

The half-filled number in my pendant disappeared as the black inky material began to ripple. After a moment, Haldrek's face appeared and a tired smile crossed it.

"*Mine drawing.* How are you?"

"Fine. Frustrated. I got ambushed today by Kamira, Lady Drifa, Kotkel, and some of your advisors in an attempt to talk about '*my projects.*' They want me to give up the High Queen's Home."

Haldrek frowned. "The High Queen's Home?"

I nodded. "It's the nickname Priestess Thwaya gave to my orphanage. The name has stuck for better or for worse. But they think that quarters for refugee women and children is a hotbed for Blodnar spies."

"Where are the refugees from?"

"Mostly Etelaranikä. Rorik's followers seem to going after those who refuse to follow him. There are also people from Bragidrattür and southern Heidrunefoss. Even Itaranikä, which I reminded Lady Drifa of. It's mostly villagers being attacked by remnants of the Blodnar army. I mean, theoretically, the Blodnar could have spies or sympathizers among the refugees, but too many of the stories I've heard sound legitimate. Usually, it's a small band of roughed up Blodnar soldiers going through outlying farms or grabbing travelers and doing terrible things. That doesn't sound too far-fetched."

Haldrek shook his head. "It doesn't. But it could also be a convenient story. Have you heard word from any of our information gatherers?"

"Yes and no. I meet with one or two every few days. Nothing abnormal has been going on. The strongest bits of information seem to be coming from warriors returning to the city from other parts of Lohikärra. But even that information is confirming the refugees' stories."

"Hmm." Haldrek pursed his lips thoughtfully. "Tell them to continue keeping an ear out for anything. I don't think the refugees are lying, but there are plenty of people who would like to see us fail."

"I agree." Part of me wanted to add that some of those people were probably already inside the palace. "What do you want me to do if Kamira and her crew come back with more complaints? I told them there are better ways to let their grievances be known than to try to corner me. I didn't appreciate Kamira taking a swing at me."

"She did what?" His expression turned serious as he focused on me.

I sighed. "It wasn't necessarily a swing as much as she tried to knock me on the head like it was a hollow log or something. I pushed her arm away and told her not to do that again."

"Did your guards do anything?"

"They became more alert and got closer to me, but before anything else could happen, Sibila started rambling about Ladies of Lohikärra, and her strange behavior defused the whole situation."

"Was she with the group?"

I shook my head. "She was in the garden area where Rorik tossed us into the vortex. I don't think anyone was aware she was there."

"If she wasn't so addled in the head, I'd think she would be more cunning than Rorik." Haldrek's comment surprised me.

"Why? And has there been any word as to why she is the way she is? I mean, given her family..." The few people who came with Sibila from Etelaranikä had said little about her past, or even why her mother had chosen her to be Etelaranikä's hersir at court.

"Gustav called her elf-touched, but I don't think that's it. The one time I spoke to her mother—Rorik's stepmother—she mentioned something about magic and a curse. Now knowing the kinds of things Gustav and Rorik were and are capable of, it wouldn't surprise me if one of them did something to her in her younger years."

The thought alone made me shudder. "Now that Rorik is trying to raise forces in Etelaranikä and elsewhere, Drattüjert is probably the safest place for her?"

Haldrek shrugged. "That wouldn't surprise me. Sibila's mother has pledged *her* loyalty to us, but I could see Sibila being used to manipulate her." He paused and closed his eyes for a moment. The way he was positioned in the pendant, I could tell he was laying down.

A flicker of desire popped up inside of me. I wished I could be by his side right now instead of dealing with palace drama.

"How was your day? You've heard about mine."

"We got into our first fight. And not with the people I was expecting."

"What? Who?" I straightened up and looked for any signs of injury from the small portion of his body that I could see.

"We're in Lansiranikä now. My intent was to speak with Bjorn. I tried through my pendant this morning before we marched, but he didn't answer. I thought it was because he didn't know about that aspect of the pendant. But when we reached the border of Lansiranikä, Bjorn's second eldest son, Kolfinn was waiting with a sattar of warriors to deny us passage. Bjorn spoke rudely to me through Kolfinn's pendant and told me that I was not welcome to harass his gesith, who was taking back what was rightfully his."

"That sonuva—"

"I told Bjorn that Hardbein was never the rightful ruler of Svartån and that if he was consorting with Rorik now, then he would be punished. Bjorn told me that he fully supported Hardbein's alliance with Rorik."

"What?" My head swam with the implications as I tried to keep my panic down.

"So my men and I fought against Kolfinn and his men. We won and I took Kolfinn as a prisoner, but that's one less ally we have. Kamira's actions and those of the others worry me. As much as I support the High Queen's Home and all you have done to aid Drattüjert and the rest of Lohikärra, tread carefully. We can't lose many more allies."

His words hit me like a chastisement and I fought to keep my tears at bay. I wanted to say something rude to him in the moment, but Rhaegos's presence wrapped tightly around me, calming me.

"I'm doing my best. Even when Kamira antagonizes me. But what do you want me to do with Kotkel? If his father is openly fighting against you, is it wise to let him have his freedom within the palace?"

Haldrek grimaced. "It isn't. But between him and Kolfinn, I think Kotkel is the more reasonable one. He is to be under supervision at all times, but afforded the privileges of a thegn-heir. If Bjorn has sided with Rorik and we win, which we will, if Bjorn is not dead, he will be stripped of his title as thegn and likely exiled from Lohikärra. If that happens, Kotkel will be the next Thegn of Lansiranikä. We need to keep him as our ally."

I nodded. "Then I'll do what I can here in Drattüjert. Hopefully he doesn't know what happened between you and his brother."

"I doubt it. Kolfinn's pendant has been confiscated, and my impression of the two of them has always been that of rivals. Kolfinn wants his father's power, but Kotkel is in line for it." Haldrek yawned. "I'm going to rest. Today was a long day and we have more marching—and fighting—ahead of us tomorrow." He smiled. "I love you, Ina. You are in my dreams every night."

I smiled, my heart still heavy and aching. "I love you too. Sleep well, Haldrek."

Chapter Eight

I slept fitfully that night, dreaming of darkness and someone hunting me. When I finally woke up, it was to pounding on the antechamber door. I quickly dressed myself and opened the bedroom door to see one of the royal spies—a man I only knew by the name of Egil—talking to a servant and gesturing quickly. This wasn't normal.

"Can I help you? Usually you're downstairs when we meet." I finished tying my belt around my overcoat. Despite the summer warmth, the palace was still drafty enough in the morning to need one.

The man bowed to me. "My queen. We've found a Blodnar spy within the city. He's demanding to speak to you."

"What? What are you—? He'd identified himself as a spy?"

Egil shook his head and laughed. "No, he claims he's here on behalf of the Blodnar Emperor and wishes to speak of peace."

"I'm surprised," My head was spinning again, this time as I tried to wake up. "Normally you and your people bring information, not act as messengers." Wariness flooded my senses. "Why should I entertain this spy's request to see me?" The man in front of me was one of the top information gatherers, the spymaster, so to speak. Haldrek trusted him implicitly, but this was the first time the man had come directly to the antechamber instead.

The spymaster pulled out a piece of paper. "He gave me this as a token, saying you would know what it is. It was interesting enough for me to think you should see it. Privately. I know how easily this could be used against you, my queen."

I frowned as I took the folded piece of paper. It didn't feel like a normal piece of paper, and it hadn't been folded like anything I'd seen before. Instead of being folded in half, it was folded into three equal rectangles. Opening it up, I flipped it around and gasped. I felt lightheaded for a moment and tried to steady myself on the nearby table without looking too obvious. The photograph in my hand was not something I ever thought I'd see again. The fact that I was holding a photograph in my hand had a multitude of implications attached to it, even if it wasn't a picture I knew.

"You recognized the token?" The man tried to peek at the picture I held and I pulled it back toward me, trying not to scowl. How on earth had this picture ended up in Lohikärra and in the hands of a Blodnar spy?

"I do. But the fact that a spy is holding on to it means something bad has happened. And I want answers." Different scenarios for why this photograph was here buzzed through my head, and I needed to sit down. "I... I need to get dressed, but as soon as I am ready, I wish to see the person who had this."

Egil nodded. "As you wish, my queen."

I hurried back to Haldrek's and my room. As I closed the door, Rhaegos's voice whispered in my head:

Be careful, little one.

A short time later, I found myself hurrying out of the palace with Egil and several of my personal guards. The token had been a photograph from years ago of Mattie, myself, Henry, and our mutual friend Alex. It was a silly, small thing. The picture had been taken during one of our first Lohikärra gaming sessions. But the memory was one of the few happy ones I had growing up and I knew for a fact Henry had a copy. Mattie had one as well, but I doubt she had had it on her either time we'd been transported to Lohikärra. So for there to be a copy here meant Henry, Alex, or someone connected to them had arrived in Lohikärra. Or in the Blodnar Empire.

"I demand to see the High Queen!" A man stood facing Thwaya and a few other priestesses at the Refuge, his back toward me. From that angle, he looked familiar, though his tone seemed *off* for either Henry or Alex. "I know she is connected to this place and I have an urgent message for her. If she isn't here, then I demand back my token."

Thwaya's face expressed a coldness I never would have imagined from her. Whatever he'd done must have pissed her off.

"I would not treat a priestess of Tenelth in such a way, whether you hold the dragons divine or not," I snapped as I stood behind him.

The man spun around and my eyes widened in surprise. It was Henry, but wearing a mishmash of Blodnar and Lohikärran clothing. Almost as if he'd scavenged discarded clothing while traveling here. I blinked in surprise, trying to see if my eyes were tricking me. He looked like Haldrek as well, if Haldrek was clean shaven and had a different nose. But the person staring at me was most definitely Henry.

"Ina?" His voice went quiet before he continued, "I *knew* you were here!" He leaned forward to hug me and I stepped back. Haldrek's spymaster and my guards stepped in between us, all brandishing a weapon of some kind. Henry's expression fell and my heart twinged with guilt. "It's me, Henry. Remember?"

"I know. What are you doing here, though?" I shook my head as soon as I realized how the words sounded. "I mean, what confuses me is why and how you're here? How did you know *I* was here? I haven't seen you in years."

He stepped back giving me some space. "People talk, Ina. I heard stories about the High Queen of Lohikärra just appearing one day and becoming the Thegn of Svartån. You were the actual Heir of Svartån, like the game!"

Haldrek's spymaster glanced at me, eyebrows raised, as I tried to stay calm and objective.

"So why are you here? In Drattüjert? In this world?" I hesitated, wondering how much information to give.

"That's the craziest thing. I was in a storm with my mom. We got hit by something and everything went black. I thought I was dead, but then I woke up in a grassy ditch and got captured by soldiers. They said I looked like the Emperor, which is crazy. But..." He paused and looked at the crowd amassed around us. "They brought me to the capital city. I found my mom. She's a freaking princess of some kind. And *my* dad is the Emperor. My real dad. Not the man who raised me."

My jaw dropped. His story seemed incredible. Too incredible. But then again, so was mine. I'd dropped into Lohikärra out of nowhere and was thrust into a position of power. So Henry's story could be true. But something still felt *off* in my gut.

"Why are you here then? In Drattüjert? You know as well as I do the animosity between the Blodnar empire and Lohikärra. The Blodnar have done many awful things to my people over the years." Anger colored my words, more than I expected. The intensity of my emotions surprised me.

Henry's eyebrows shot up in surprise. "Your people?"

"I am the High Queen now, and I am still the Thegn of Svartån. My father was the Thegn of Svartån before me, so yes, the people here are *my* people."

A small smile crossed Henry's face and I fought to keep my serious demeanor. "I'm here to parley for peace, High Queen Ina of Lohikärra. My father's empire is fracturing and many within the empire see this war as a lost cause, a petty feud among the rulers of each country. As you—and the High King—are new blood, there is a chance for peace now."

His words sounded diplomatic enough, and I'd been fighting for peace this entire time. But... Something was still off. I just couldn't tell exactly what. On the one hand, a ceasefire could allow Lohikärran forces to focus more on Rorik and his shenanigans. But I still needed to look tough. I knew that many already thought me weak for my actions thus far and, like Haldrek had said yesterday, we couldn't afford to lose allies.

"I am open to parley. However," I paused to gauge Henry's reaction. His expression remained unchanged. "This is a highly unusual situation. It is something that I must discuss with the High King himself. And our advisors."

"That sounds reasonable enough. Then should I find myself a room in a tavern and then come see you in a day or two once you have made your decision?"

I frowned at him in surprise. "Henry, you..." I shook my head and noticed Egil behind my left shoulder. How he'd slipped from his former position to there, I didn't know. While he said nothing, I got the sense he wanted to. I was sure a lot of people in this group wanted their opinions heard. I ignored the murmuring around me as I focused on Henry. "As you say you are the son of the Blodnar Emperor and we are still at war, you can't just be left to roam around Drattüjert."

"But—" Henry's expression faltered as I gestured to the guards to grab him. "You are not to be harmed while in the palace, but until further notice, you will be held under guard. Quarters will be made for you in one of the lower levels of the palace."

Henry jerked away as the guards tried to hold him, his expression darkening. "You're putting me in the dungeons? I thought we were friends. Think of everything I did for you when you were back at home. With your mother."

I grimaced, but thankfully, Egil stepped forward. "What is your title, *son of the Blodnar Emperor*?"

"Grand-Principis Henricus of Norycium." Henry's teeth clenched together as he spoke.

"Grand-Principis Henricus of Norycium, as an heir to the Blodnar Empire, I can assure you that there is no love for your kind here in Drattüjert. You may see staying in the palace dungeons as an insult, but as an enemy of Lohikärra, no matter your mission, that will be the safest place for you until the High King and Queen decide if they will parley with you."

The guards pulled Henry away as he stared at me, anger hardening his expression. "You've changed, Ina. You've changed *a lot*."

I ignored the ominous pit in my stomach. Once he was out of earshot, I whispered, "You've changed a lot too, Henry."

"Absolutely not."

Haldrek stared at me through my pendant, his expression hard and unflinching.

"Do you really want to fight two wars? Because that's what's going to happen." I had secluded myself in our quarters, sending the servants out to the antechambers so I could have some privacy. Haldrek had answered his pendant instantly, relief initially crossing his face before I told him what happened.

Now he was being stubborn.

"Ina, we are not negotiating *anything* with the Blodnar. You know what they are like. You've seen what monstrosities they have committed. They tried to kill you when you first arrived here. They've raped, murdered, and tortured innocents. There is nothing to negotiate. If their empire is crumbling because of this war, then their emperor can remove his soldiers from our lands and leave us be."

"What happens when the Blodnar gain strength again? Are we still going to be fighting a civil war?" I paced across the room, trying to stay far away from the door. "Even if we kill Rorik, are we going to go into places like Lansiranikä and fight more? People are exhausted, Haldrek and this could be a good way to ensure peace. Focus our attention on Rorik and the mess he's made."

Haldrek shook his head. "The Blodnar will never keep their promises. They started this war in the first place."

"Why?" The thought hit me hard, clearing out everything else. I knew he war had started sometime between when my dad had arrived in Fargo and when he returned to Lohikärra, but no one had told me of the exact event that caused everything. "Why did they start this war in the first place?"

Haldrek closed his mouth and stared at me in confusion. "You don't know, do you?"

"No, not really. This was all a fantasy world for me until a year and a half ago, remember? We've had a bunch of other stuff going on, so I never thought to ask."

"Hmm, fair enough." He grimaced. "My uncle Kalle had four living children: three sons and a daughter, Aina. Aina being Aallotar's mother. Of the sons, Kalleson was the eldest, the aethling, and heir. Akku, the youngest, was the Thegn of Heidrunefoss, and beloved uncle to Aallotar. But Kalle's middle son was Jaari. He was a warrior through and through, as well as being his father's best information gatherer. At least from what your father told me growing up." Haldrek looked away from the pendant for a moment to survey the area he was in. "Jaari was often working in the southern thegn lands like Etelaranikä and within the Blodnar Empire. This is all common knowledge. It is part of why the Blodnar emperor did what he did."

"Which was?"

"He accused Jaari of kidnapping his daughter, the grand-principia. The emperor demanded Kalle return her at once, but when Kalle sent messengers to tell him the grand-principia was not in Lohikärra, the emperor executed not only Jaari, but the messengers as well. He then sent troops into Lohikärra, claiming it as his own in exchange for his daughter. So we've been fighting them for almost twenty years."

"Huh." I twitched as Rhaegos tumbled in the back of my mind. The distinct impression that she had something to say came over me, but she remained silent.

"Huh, what?" Haldrek frowned into the pendant.

"Henry is my age, but he said the Blodnar emperor was his father. I'm trying to figure out how that's possible, because I've known Henry my entire life."

Haldrek's frown turned into a grimace. "The Blodnar lie through their teeth. It's a compulsion for them."

"It still doesn't make sense. Even if he is lying, why? Why lie to me? His connection to me is through Fargo, not the Blodnar Empire or Lohikärra. He wasn't a liar back home. He was one of the most honest people I knew."

"People change, Ina. Did he know his real father back in Fargo?"

I shook my head. "Henry lived with his mom and stepdad. The story I always heard was that Henry's bio-dad died before he was born. Which..." I groaned as I tried to make sense of everything. My head began to ache from everything I'd been dealing with over the past few days. It didn't help that Drattüjert had been warmer than normal either. I pulled the bed curtains apart and looked around for the watered-down wine drink that was sometimes placed in our room.

"Which means Henry lied to you, if his father is the Blodnar emperor."

"Haldrek!" I snapped, my irritation and the heat getting the best of me. As I grabbed a nearby pitcher, I sniffed it and poured it into one of the cups next to it. "Henry wasn't the one who told me that story. His mom did. So maybe his mom lied, because it wouldn't make sense for her to get laid by some otherwise imaginary emperor."

Haldrek snorted at that. "I wish the Blodnar Emperor was imaginary."

It was my turn to grimace. "Focus, Haldrek." I took a sip of the drink and let it cool me down before looking at the pendant again.

His scowl returned. "Where is this Henry right now?"

"In the dungeons. He's being held in one of the less crappy ones because of his status as a grand-principal."

"*Grand-principis*. It's a title all sons of a Blodnar emperor have." Haldrek's tone was heavy with annoyance.

"My bad." As much as I loved Haldrek, my irritation with him was making itself known. "For someone who hates the Blodnar so much, you sure know a lot about them." I regretted my snippiness as soon as I said it and I took another drink.

"Ina. I'm the High King. It's my job to know these things. I can't just brush them off for feel-good projects."

His words hit hard and I pursed my lips tightly, trying to keep myself from saying something I would regret. A heavy, awkward silence fell between us as I put the cup down and sat on our bed.

After a few moments, he sighed and said, "Ina, please help me."

I had no idea how to interpret that. Was he being genuine or patronizing? Did he think I wasn't helping him before?

"I have been. At least I've been trying." My voice was colder than I liked, but I was trying to be calm despite the torrent of indignation inside of me. "It's kind of hard when every choice I make seems to be the wrong one."

He grimaced as he looked into the pendant. "You're making good choices. I—I shouldn't have said what I did about your projects. You've been doing a lot of good things for Lohikärra and Drattüjert."

"But you don't trust me when it comes to dealing with Henry."

"I—It's not that I don't trust you. I don't trust him. You've already said something is off about him. I just…I don't want to make any longstanding agreements with the Blodnar Empire without getting back to the palace. I'm afraid that Henry will try to manipulate you because of your childhood friendship."

"You think I'm easy to manipulate?" I knew he didn't mean it that way, but his words poked at a fear I'd had for a long time: that I was a gullible, naïve fool. Another reason I wasn't good enough to be High Queen.

"I didn't say that. You aren't the one I'm questioning, Ina. I'm concerned about Henry. If we're going to talk peace, then I want to be there physically. I want to look him in the eye and see what he's up to. I don't think you're easy to manipulate, but I think he does and he's going to try something."

I tried to be understanding, but part of me wanted to refuse. To be stubborn and show everyone, including Haldrek, that I was competent enough to be High Queen.

"What should I do then? I can't hold him indefinitely. Look what the emperor did when he thought his daughter was imprisoned."

Haldrek sighed. "Either kick him out of Drattüjert and Lohikärra entirely, or keep him in the dungeons until I return to Drattüjert."

"Do you trust me to make the right choice?"

"Ina…" He grumbled. "I do. I wouldn't have made you my queen if I didn't think you were competent."

That eased the hurt I still felt, if just a little bit. "I'll think on it. And I'll let you know before I tell him. Either way, I'm going to do what's best for Drattüjert *and* Lohikärra."

Chapter Nine

By the next morning, I still hadn't made a decision. On the one hand, kicking Henry out of Lohikärra would go far to show my loyalty and help keep allies within the kingdom. On the other, this was Henry, one of my best friends growing up, and even if he'd changed since arriving in this world, who he was deep down was still the same. Right? Keeping him close would allow me to keep an eye on him.

But if he really was the son of the Blodnar Emperor, would that man then renew fighting at a time when Lohikärra couldn't afford it? My head spun as I let my maidservants dress me in my best clothing. If I was going to confront Henry on behalf of Haldrek and the rest of Lohikärra, I needed to look like a High Queen.

Be careful, little one. Haldrek is right to be wary of the new arrival, but casting the Blodnar out may not be the right decision.

"Then what is the right decision?" I glanced around, wondering how crazy I looked talking to no one in particular. Instead, the maidservants continued their tasks in silence.

I waited a few moments for Rhaegos's response, but she was silent too.

Arriving in the throne room, I stopped as the crowd of people who stood there quieted their chatter. This was new. Usually there were a handful of people milling around the throne room throughout the day, but there were easily a few dozen people standing around now. I hadn't expected a crowd to be watching as I spoke with Henry. My stomach twisted into knots as I tried to keep my breakfast down. A few people closest to me began to bow and as they did, the rest of the crowd followed.

"You may sit at your throne now, my queen." Haldrek's master spy spoke into my left ear and I tried not to jump in surprise. That man was skilled at his job. Whether I appreciated that, I had yet to decide.

Taking my seat, I said, "Bring the Blodnar man here."

The main doors to the throne room pulled open, revealing Henry in shackles and wearing the same clothes as yesterday. He stood tall and proud, or at least tall, as he walked toward me.

"Morning, Ina. Sleep well?" He winced as one of the guards nudged him in the shoulder with a spear tip. "Good morning, Your Majesty, Lady of Lohikärra. I hope you slept well."

"Thank you, Henry. I did." It was a lie, but I wasn't about to reveal my fitful sleep to anyone I didn't deeply trust. "I've spoken with the High King. He is hesitant to negotiate with a Blodnar grand-principis. However he and I are willing to listen to your reason for being here." I paused, trying to think of what to say next. "You have five minutes to convince me of your plan and whether or not you are more trustworthy than the Blodnar soldiers who have been ravaging Lohikärra, or those who tried to kill me when I arrived here."

Henry's eyes widened. "Ina, we're friends though. You should be able to—"

"We were friends in Fargo, Henry." I hated to be so cold and official to someone who had been one of my best friends growing up. "If we were in a different situation, I might trust you still. I would like to still trust you. But I am the High Queen and I have a kingdom to protect, alongside my husband."

"Fine. I'm technically here on behalf of my grandfather, the Emperor, to seek a truce, a peace agreement that would allow our soldiers to leave without harassment. My grandfather would honor the agreement during his lifetime."

I frowned. He had said his father was the Blodnar Emperor yesterday. Hadn't he? I tried to remember, but shook my head as the memories got fuzzy. "Why change now? Did your grandfather mention why he wants to stop fighting now?"

"There is much internal discontent in the Empire as we speak. People are leaving for other places, and it is causing difficulties for my family. Plus, my mother returned. I'm sure you are aware that her disappearance was the reason for this war. But since she has returned unharmed, and with a legitimate son in tow, my grandfather now sees no reason in continuing to fight with Lohikärra."

Warning bells went off in my head, and I felt like I was back home again, but not in a good way. This man, who looked and sounded like Henry, spoke words that reminded me of my mother on one of her better days. His vocabulary was different and how he emphasized his words felt wrong, creating a weight in my stomach and causing my chest and shoulders to stiffen. Rhaegos was right. I needed to be wary.

"It will take a lot more than conversation and apologies to make amends for the last twenty years. The Blodnar, your grandfather's soldiers, have done terrible things in his name. There are a lot of innocent people who are dead because of his actions."

"I understand. My grandfather understands. That's why he sent me here. To seek peace. That is my plea and parley." He bowed as best he could with the four guards around him.

This was bullshit. I wanted to cry. Whoever was standing in front of me was nothing like the Henry I remembered from Fargo. But I knew I'd changed as well. We had already grown distant by our senior year. More from schedules and life in general, but the person who stood in front of me was different in another way. Something I couldn't put my finger on. Part of me wanted to kick him out, to prove to Haldrek's advisors and the hersirs that I *was* loyal to Lohikärra. But another part of me wanted to figure out what was going on with Henry.

Keep this Henry close for now. He can do more damage unsupervised.

Rhaegos's words surprised me. I wanted more information, but I couldn't just blurt that out here. Not that her comment made no sense. It made plenty of sense. But she wouldn't have said anything if it wasn't important.

I focused on Henry. He watched me as well. "Your plea is an interesting one, but given the actions of the Blodnar over the past twenty years—our entire lives and then some—more than words are needed." My mind cleared for a moment as I continued, "I want to see if your grandfather, or *father* as you mentioned yesterday, actually wants peace. Just because someone is related to you doesn't mean they care about you." That was something Henry should have remembered about me. I knew that fact too well. "You may stay here in the palace, but you will be a prisoner until I or the High King can see physical proof of the Emperor's desire for peace. As long as you are here, you will be treated according to your title, but only time will tell if your father, or grandfather, is telling lies or not."

Henry's eyes widened more and he stepped forward. The front guards blocked him, putting their spear tips at his throat. "Ina, please—"

He sounded like his normal self for a split second there, and my insides twisted with guilt. But this wasn't about me. This was about more than just me. This was about Haldrek, Drattüjert, and Lohikärra. This was about keeping those I was responsible for safe. "Henry, go. I've made my decision. It is for the best, and I hope you are right about your emperor."

He stepped back, deflated, then turned around. After a few moments, he was gone. As soon as the spectacle was over, people began to disperse, their chatter and whispers following them out. I waited until I was nearly alone to sink into the chair.

This was going to be harder than I had thought.

I retreated to Haldrek's and my quarters after the evening meal, excusing myself with exhaustion. Despite feeling like garbage for most of the day, there was one silver lining. Most of the advisors and envoys seemed more congenial and less hostile after my interaction with Henry, so at least that was a win. I didn't know how long it would last, but after everything, I'd take it.

Curled up in the darkness of the covered bed, I closed my eyes, taking in a moment of quietness, only to feel the warmth of my pendant grow against my skin.

I pulled it out from under my shift and popped it open. Haldrek's face appeared on the other side with a somber smile. The tops of his shoulders were bare and, given the summer warmth, I imagined he was shirtless. It was a pleasant image in my mind and I wished I could see more of him.

"Good evening, *mine drawing*. How was your day?"

"Long. I feel like an awful person, even though I think I did the right thing."

"You dealt with the Blodnar spy?"

I sighed. "His name is Henry and he may not be a spy. Officially, he is an envoy for peace from the Blodnar Empire, though—"

"You wonder how much of that is the truth?"

I nodded, trying to stay positive despite my annoyance at getting interrupted. Haldrek wasn't meaning to be rude. He was just guessing my own thoughts. "The person I'm dealing with is different than the Henry I knew growing up. I mean, it's a been a few years since we really had a chance to hang out like we did when we were children, so it could just be that he's different now. Because everyone changes as they grow up. But something still feels off."

Haldrek was quiet for a moment before asking, "What did you decide to do?"

"Keep him in the dungeons. I want to see if he's actually here with peace in mind. If the Emperor was pissed off enough to demand his daughter's return when he thought she was kidnapped and Henry is truly here on his behalf, then we'll know. Whether it is envoys or an army, we'll know. If Henry isn't lying and the Blodnar Empire really is in rough shape, then I'm thinking it'll be the former." I took a deep breath and let my shoulders relax. Haldrek didn't look too unhappy with my decision.

"If it helps, I think you did the right thing. He can stay locked up, and when I return from dealing with Hardbein and Rorik, we can figure out what to do with this Henry then."

This Henry. The phrase passed through my mind as I remembered what Rhaegos had said in the throne room. She had made it sound as if there were multiple Henrys, which sounded ridiculous, even in a world full of magic.

"I also wanted to call and apologize."

My attention focused back on Haldrek. "What?" I could count on one hand the number of times someone had apologized to me in my life. It was nice, but confusing at the same time.

"I was thinking about our conversation last night all day today and I felt guilty for being so harsh on you. I've been under a lot of stress with everything, worried about whether or not I'm living up to how my ancestors were as High Kings, and I'm sorry. Hearing the news that Bjorn Susi has decided to follow Rorik and is willing to fight against his fellow thegns and King was a blow, but I should have been kinder. I'm sorry."

I stared at him, blinking a few times, trying to think of a response. What did you say when someone apologized to you? *Thank you? I'm sorry too?*

Ask him if Teminth told him what to say.

I laughed and said, "Rhaegos is asking if Teminth told you what to say."

Haldrek opened his mouth to say something, then started laughing. "I guess you could say that. Yes. I was feeling bad about our argument, but I didn't know how to say how I was feeling without making things worse. So Teminth and I may have had a long chat while we were traveling through Lansiranikä."

"I thought as much." A grin covered my face as the atmosphere around us became more comfortable. "I forgive you. I wasn't exactly in the best mood last night either." I stared at him and let my mind wander, imagining what we'd be doing at this moment if he was here at the palace instead of in Lansiranikä. The images that popped into my head made me miss Haldrek even more.

"I also wanted to tell you that I do trust you, even if—" He winced as I frowned, pulled out of my daydream. "What I mean is, you have a soft heart and I love that about you. It's part of what makes you a good leader. And a wonderful wife. You're compassionate. But it also means that people will try to take advantage of you or will think you weak. I don't want that to happen. Because I believe in you." He exhaled and I got the sense that he was trying to organize his thoughts. "Court life is vastly different than being at a thegn hall. You don't have much experience with that, and I don't either, but I think what you're trying to do is good and... I trust you to do the right thing." He grumbled and sat up. I saw a flash of his bare chest and a thrill went through me. "When did I start tripping over my words like this? I never felt this clumsy with my words before. Even when you first arrived and I was worried I'd scare you if I told you everything I knew."

I laughed. "Are you tired?"

"Very tired. We didn't have any skirmishes today, but it's been exhausting, constantly being alert and riding through what is now enemy territory."

"Then you're probably tired and need sleep. I need you to sleep well, so you can fight well and come home. I miss you. And you being shirtless is making it hard for me to focus."

A grin lit up his face and he pulled off his pendant so I could see more of him. He was definitely shirtless, and my thoughts of being with him started to get away from me as I imagined cuddling up next to him, skin to skin.

"I miss you too. You have been in my dreams ever since I left. I can't wait to return to Drattüjert."

I shook my head, trying to disperse my daydreams. "Me either. How long do you think it will take to find Hardbein? And then fight him?"

Haldrek sighed and returned to laying on his camp bed. "Finding him won't be that hard. He's headed to Sigreykir, so that's my destination now. What I'm concerned about is what I'll find in Sigreykir. I'm expecting a sattar from Svangendom to be ready to join my men and Mattie let me know that she's sent a sattar from Andrattür. It will be good to see those warriors again. But I don't know how many Hardbein commands, and I'm guessing the warriors of Sigreykir will fight alongside his cousin. If everything goes smoothly, it will be at least two weeks before I can return to Drattüjert. But I'm not expecting that. There will be bumps in the road. There are *always* bumps in the road."

"So at least another month?"

Haldrek nodded. "At least. I will be lucky if my men and I can return before winter begins to set in. But such is war. Long and exhausting." He closed his eyes and exhaled. The image of him wobbled as the pendant slipped out of his hand. He grabbed it and pulled it back up, his eyes now open.

"Then I should probably let you sleep then. I love you, Haldrek. Get some sleep and stay safe."

He smiled and kissed the pendant. "You too. I'll be back as soon as I can."

The pendant went dark as he closed it and my half-filled number returned. Turning over and snuggling under the blankets, I imagined him next to me as I fell asleep, praying to the dragons that it wouldn't be long before that was a reality again.

Chapter Ten

For the first time in many nights, I had sweet dreams. I was with Haldrek and several other people whom I couldn't see, but who loved me, and while I couldn't remember exactly what was going on, I was happy.

So when the curtains of our bed were pulled open the next morning, I wanted to hide from the real world and return to my dream.

"My queen, it's time to arise. The sun has already been up for many hours."

"It's summertime." I groaned. "We only get a handful of hours when the sun isn't up."

The maid smiled. "Still, your presence is required as High Queen."

I groaned, the last wisps of my dream fading away. "Where is my presence demanded currently?"

"You aren't late to anything, if that is what you are asking. There is time for breakfast. But then you are to meet with some of the thegns' hersirs." She paused as she looked through my wardrobe. "If you don't mind me saying, there has been much gossip about the interaction you had with the Blodnar man yesterday."

I straightened up, now alert. "What kind of gossip?" When I had interacted with the advisors and some of the hersirs yesterday, they had seemed satisfied with my response to Henry. Had I read them all wrong? Panic and flashbacks to misjudging my mother and Robert back in Fargo flooded my brain. The last thing I wanted was for Drattüjert to become my new Fargo.

"My queen?" The maid held out a dark red gown and I nodded, standing up to let her help me. "There are some who think you spoke too familiarly with him. And the fact that he called you friend—"

"Everyone has told me that the Blodnar are liars and to never trust a word from their mouths. And yet they believed him when he called me a friend?" I bit my tongue. Henry and I were friends. At least the Henry I had known growing up. The Henry I'd faced in the throne room yesterday, however...my gut told me that was a different story.

"You didn't correct him."

"I was busy sending him back to the dungeons until the High King returns. What more did they want? Interpretive dance? A public execution?"

The maidservant hesitated. "I do not disagree with you, my queen. Only speaking what I have heard."

I grimaced at my outburst. "I'm not mad at you. But now I'm worried how this meeting with the hersirs will go. Kamira is more than happy to see me fail."

"It is true that Lady Kamira has not refrained from spreading this gossip."

I groaned as my stomach tightened, and I wanted to throw up. Part of me wanted to contact Haldrek, but what could he do? He was in Lansiranikä, and he had more important things to do than deal with gossip. This was something I'd have to deal with myself.

"I think I will pass on breakfast. The thought of dealing with Kamira and her gossip is already making me sick."

"As you wish, my queen." The maidservant finished helping me into my dress and outer garments before bowing and leaving.

"Rhaegos, what am I going to do?" Anxiety flooded my mind as I anticipated what Kamira might say once I got down there. Who had she been gossiping to? And who had listened?

You will persevere, little one. Don't be afraid of your thegns' hersirs. There is little they can do at this point.

"*At this point* being the key phrase," I muttered, "The way I keep messing up, who know what will happen in the future?"

Rhaegos churned in the back of my mind, but didn't respond. I felt like a petulant child as I walked down to the room where I was to meet with the hersirs. As I made my way down the halls, I heard whispers in passing, and as much as I knew I shouldn't take heed to them, they felt harsher now than before.

I'd done the right thing, hadn't I?

Entering the room, I could feel a somber attitude weigh everything down. Most of the women rose for me, but Kamira and Lady Drifa both sat, engrossed in their needlework. A few undiplomatic words crossed my mind, but I decided to ignore their disrespect for now. I sat down at the head chair and began reading the text placed in front of me. Either the servants had given up on repairing my botched sewing attempts, or this was a subtle way to direct what I was learning.

Not that I cared. The text was a story of Freya and one of her many adventures, even after becoming High Queen, and it was an excuse to ignore the present situation. Historical texts were just as much an escape from the real world as any fictional story.

"I'm glad you were able to join us, Queen *I-na*." Kamira's voice dripped with condescension. "I heard you were busy entertaining the Blodnar spy. In the High King's quarters."

I continued to focus on my text. One of the runes was still vaguely unfamiliar. "Last time I checked, the High King's quarters weren't in the dungeons. You must have heard wrong."

More silence. I brushed over the offending rune and attempted to make sense of the text without it.

"Perhaps Lady Kamira isn't so much wrong as misinformed," Lady Drifa spoke, breaking the frigid silence. "Our *dear* Queen wouldn't be so bold as to do such a thing. No, I believe she visited the Blodnar man in *his* quarters. I've heard some of the dungeons have been set up to be more comfortable than others. Not that I've ever been down there."

"I'm sure a tour could be arranged," I mumbled under my breath. Why was this particular rune aggravating me? At this point, I didn't even know if it was worth dealing with.

"Ina!" Taimi's voice made me look up. There was an element of either panic or chastisement in her tone and it surprised me. Was she starting to believe Kamira's slander? She grimaced and took a deep breath. "My queen, I believe some of these stories should be addressed. There is some concern—"

"Concern about what? Gossip? Slander? Do you all really believe something happened with Henry beyond me sending him back to the dungeons?"

"You do speak familiarly of him." Ragnhild put her fabric down on the table. "There is valid concern that you are close to him."

I looked around the room at the various women, trying to control my temper. Sibila was the only person not staring back at me, but instead focusing on her fabric and humming softly to herself.

"First of all, I 'speak familiarly' of him because we were friends growing up. As children. He was one of the few people I knew who shared an interest in Lohikärra. Second, there should be no 'valid concern' about my relation to him. If I was close to Hen—him, I wouldn't put him in the dungeons. He'd be in the same situation as Kotkel, whose father has openly sided with Rorik. So, no, there is no valid concern. All I'm hearing is petty gossip." I wanted to add 'from people I respected', but I didn't know if I respected anyone in this room anymore. Did they honestly think I had snuck down to the dungeons and done something inappropriate?

"It's a shame what people do and say when they are afraid, Tesroan." Sibila's humming stopped as she began talking out loud to her dragon. Before I could say anything, she continued, "They think she's attached to the Blodnar man. Even in ways that the High

King doesn't know. With our kingdom in shambles, of course fears of loyalty arise first." Sibila bobbed her head side to side. "Yes, I think it is interesting too. They all make good points. Including the High Queen."

I was tempted to ignore Sibila's comments, but I got the sense that some of them might be onto something. Looking around the table, I asked, "Is this true? Do you think that I haven't been telling Haldrek everything, that I'm more sympathetic to the Blodnar than to my fellow Lohikärrans?"

Kamira began tapping her needle on the fabric. "It's a bit of a reach for you to say 'fellow Lohikärrans' when you're not really one of us, but yes, it's awfully convenient for this *Henry* Blodnar person to arrive in Drattüjert not long after the High King leaves to protect *your* thegn lands." She touched the needle to her lip. "As Thegn of Svartån, shouldn't *you* be the one to rush to your people's defense? If you do consider them your people."

I scowled. "Of course they are my people. I intended to leave for Svartån, but Haldrek, the High King, wished for me to stay here." A thick knot of anger and embarrassment began to grow in my throat. "I have *nothing* but devotion to my people, both those in Svartån and all of Lohikärra."

Kamira grimaced and shrugged her shoulders. "Likely story. *My queen.*"

I surveyed the group of women. None of them, not even Taimi or Salla, looked as if they believed me. That hurt worse than Kamira's ridiculous accusations.

"I want peace for Lohikärra. If that means talking to the enemy, then so be it. The last thing I would do is betray Haldrek or Lohikärra." I stood up. "Just because I didn't immediately cast out or execute a Blodnar envoy doesn't mean my loyalty isn't with Lohikärra or that I don't hold anger toward the Blodnar. They've tried to kill me multiple times. I've seen what they've done to innocent people here." Focusing in on Kamira, I continued, "So don't tell me you think I am loyal to them. That's ridiculous." Grabbing the scroll in front of me, I moved away from the chair. "If there is nothing left to discuss here, I have other affairs to attend to."

I should have stayed in bed. Drattüjert was turning out to be more like Fargo than I wanted. Sitting down in one of the many palace drevkés, I desperately hoped none of the hersirs or advisors would barge in on me. These were supposed to be quiet, sacred rooms where people could pray or commune with the dragons. I just needed a place to hide and cry.

As much as I knew I should talk to Rhaegos, I was too emotionally exhausted to start a conversation. I was sure she had better things to do than listen to me blubber on about the hersirs. Important dragon things.

Instead, I stared at the shrine. It was a statue of a man, but carved to look like he was part dragon. Was it supposed to be Tenelth, who could shape shift? Or a more interpretive design of Bjornulf, who was half dragon and half human? Honestly, it could have been either. Still, the statue looked noble, powerful, and confident. Everything I wasn't right now. Without thinking, I reached out to wipe some of the soot from the statue, surprised that it hadn't been cleaned yet.

"I wouldn't do that if I were you. Unless you are planning to make a substantial offering."

I jumped back and stumbled over the bench I'd been sitting on. Hands wrapped around me and pulled me upright to face the person who had walked into the room.

Much to my surprise, it was Senja, one of the dragons who had stayed in or around Drattüjert even after the Blodnar invaded. She and Paavo—her spouse? partner? companion? however the dragons did their relationships—they had accepted Haldrek's and my offering right before our coronation. I hadn't seen her since then and I had expected that she and Paavo had gone somewhere else for whatever reason. But I couldn't think of a reason why she was here, unless I really had done something horrible. Had I really done something horrible? She smiled and I started bawling, trying to wipe my face with the swathes of fabric I was dressed in.

"Ina, are you...?" She wrapped her arms around me, pulling me in toward her, and while a pulse of magic radiated through me causing all of my nerves to tingle, it was the mere embrace that caused me the most confusion. It felt comforting but strange at the same time.

"You are well. Healthy, that is. But I can feel your soul's exhaustion. Come, sit with me and talk."

I sat down next to her on one of the benches and glanced back at the door. Either she had been super silent, or I'd been too wrapped up in my thoughts to notice.

"No one will bother us." She waved her hand and though the door didn't close, the air in the doorframe began to shimmer. "You seem to need both privacy and a shoulder to cry on."

I nodded. "I promise I'm not trying to destroy Drattüjert or betray Lohikärra."

Senja laughed and leaned me into her shoulder. "I believe you. You are doing what Rhaegos would have you do, even if the others here don't believe you."

"How am I going to deal with that? I tried doing what made me look strong and loyal to Lohikärra, and somehow that got twisted into me lying to Haldrek and being in league with the Blodnar." More tears flowed from my eyes as Senja stroked my hair. "Even Taimi and Salla looked disappointed in me." Anger, hurt, and fear all swirled together in my chest, growing my misery by the moment. "I just can't win here. It's like Fargo all over again." That part scared me the most. I didn't want Lohikärra and Drattüjert to turn into another Fargo. This world had been my refuge for too many years.

"Does Haldrek know what you're doing?"

I nodded. "He's still uncertain about why I'm doing what I'm doing, but he trusts me. There isn't anything I'm hiding from him."

"And," she hesitated, "what feelings do you have toward this old friend of yours?"

I pulled my head up from her shoulder. "What are you implying? That I'm cheating on Haldrek by not executing Henry or kicking him out?"

Senja grimaced a little and shook her head. "I know nothing of this Henry person who seems to be causing so much gossip in the palace. I've heard the rumors, but there were plenty of rumors about me when I was your age."

I frowned at her. "I thought dragons were more peaceful than humans."

Senja threw her head back and started laughing. When she stopped, she shook her head. "Dragons fight, and they hold grudges longer than humans are capable of living. They just seem peaceful because it takes them a long time to come to blows. But when they fight, that is a terror. Plus, I wasn't always a dragon. But that's a story for another time."

She squeezed my hand and I got the sense that she was comforting me.

"Henry was a childhood friend. Growing up, he was one of the few people who cared about me. I had a crush on him at one point, when I was like ten, but that was only because he was nice to me. Not because I wanted to do anything with him. As it is," I hesitated, not necessarily wanting to pull Henry out of the closet here, even though he had been semi-openly dating Alex back home. "Henry would probably enjoy Haldrek's company in bed as much as I do."

Senja started laughing again. "He has no 'natural affection for women,' then? I think is how it's phrased now?"

I nodded. "And I respect that. I mean, I only want Haldrek, in that way at least. So I don't have feelings for Henry like that. No matter what anyone else says."

She nodded quietly. After a few moments of silence, she asked, "What do you know about your thegn weapon?"

I frowned. That was a strange question to ask after talking about Henry's sexuality and my feelings. "Freya once used it to fight Ryluth. And it can show a person's true self. Why?"

She shook her head. "I was just curious. It took me a long time to realize how powerful my own weapon was, as an aethling of Lohikärra." I looked at her in surprise as she continued talking, "But it's good that you know that. When was the last time you used your blade?"

"Like with training or in battle?"

"Either."

"It's been a few months." I sighed. Even though I'd been practicing with various weapons, I hadn't practiced with Freya's Menace in a while. I needed to do that. "I haven't had a chance to use it too much since the coronation. Though maybe I need to practice again, but with Kamira as the target."

Senja laughed once more and squeezed my hand. "Kamira will have her own trials to fight in the future. No need to add to them."

I grumbled, given how many times Kamira had added to my trials, but refrained from questioning Senja. She was a dragon after all, even if her backstory was still a mystery to me. Instead I asked, "Is that a skill that gets rusty?"

"What skill?" She turned to me in confusion. "Seeing people's true selves in the blade?" I nodded.

"It isn't, but you still have to be in the right mind to see it. You need to desire the truth of the situation, which might not always be *how* you want to perceive it. But having that skill is more valuable than ever now. It'll be useful in figuring out who your true allies here in the palace are."

I looked at her in surprise as she squeezed my hand once more. She smiled. "Don't worry. Rhaegos, Paavo, and I have complete faith in you, as do many of the other dragons who are around, whether they are bound to humans or not." She stood up and helped me up as well. "How are you feeling now?"

"Better. I'm still really confused, but Kamira's words hurt less now. Even if she thinks I'm a horrible person, that doesn't mean anything, right?"

Senja nodded. "You are correct. Her words may make you miserable for a time, but in the long run, they are of little value." She waved her hand and the shimmering at the door disappeared. "Come. I sensed hunger in you earlier. Let's get you some food so you can feel whole again."

Chapter Eleven

Senja's words—and food—helped me feel better. I spent the rest of the day avoiding the thegns' hersirs and working on matters that I could do more privately and without constant criticism.

The next morning, I woke up still feeling heavy and mournful. The palace felt more like a prison now, with everyone watching me. Whispers continued as I walked through the halls, only to stop when I was within earshot. Even Lady Taimi and Lady Salla were distant when I greeted them, being polite, but complaining of their 'old bones' when I asked if they would like to walk with me.

With no one to talk to, and a short amount of time before I needed to visit with advisors again, I figured checking on a few of the rebuilding projects Haldrek and I had started might lift my spirits. Though, honestly, just getting outside of the palace would help in that regard. While the chances that the palace gossip hadn't spread through all of Drattüjert were nonexistent, I could still check on the city's progress. Hopefully, that would help me feel better.

Walking along the main southern road out of the city, my thoughts were interrupted by a loud group arguing around the corner of some buildings near the gate. As I reached it, my guards pulled in closer to me and I noticed most of the workers staring down at something going on just inside the wall, where much of the city's refuse was tossed.

"What do you mean we have to deal with it? Do you really trust these Blodnar prisoners to not do something to weaken the walls? They're Blodnar, for Tenelth's sake! They're the ones who destroyed the walls in the first place. If you want to make them useful, let us kill them and use their corpses for mortar."

A few other men laughed and cheered at the comment as I got closer, my guards still keeping a tight square around me. The crowd cleared a path for us as I came across the confrontation. Several men stared at a man with an open scroll and tied-up Blodnar soldiers behind him.

"I am just following orders! My instructions were to put them to work. As part of some kind of agreement between the High Queen and the Blodnar prince. Payment for their destruction of the city."

I frowned. There hadn't been any agreement between me and Henry. He was still in the dungeons. "What agreement?"

Suddenly all eyes were on me. The man with the scroll straightened up and then bowed. "My queen. I was given instructions to use these men to rebuild the walls. As I said, there was some kind of agreement between you and the Blodnar man, prince, person, whoever."

Wariness hit me like a sinking weight. "Who gave you those instructions?"

"One of the High King's advisors. Thoreg was his name, I think. He said it was official and everything. My men and I took these Blodnar from the dungeons and we're going to use them for the most menial labor tasks. Not actually touching the walls, mind you, but chopping wood and mixing mortar. Is that what you were wishing, my queen?"

I gestured for the scroll and he eagerly handed it to me. Much to my surprise, I could read most of the runes and the words they made. But what made me pause was the runic signatures on the scroll. One was indeed Thoreg's signature. Dozens of questions popped up inside my head as I stared at it, the least being *why* he would sign something like this. This was the last thing I'd expect. But there was one thing more concerning and confusing than his rune or anything else on this document—*my* runic signature.

Or rather, what it would have been if I'd had a runic signature. Despite my time here in Lohikärra, I had never created a rune to sign documents. I always signed with the loopy cursive letters I'd taught myself years ago as a child.

Someone had forged this document, pretending to be me. I looked back up at the man in charge of the construction. While I hadn't signed this document and needed to find out who did, technically using the Blodnar for manual labor would allow the rebuilding projects to be finished faster, which in turn would help Drattüjert. But even I knew their mere presence outside of the dungeons would cause more gossip.

Whoever had created this document had put me in a difficult place. This could easily end up biting me in the butt either way. But I had to make a decision.

"Keep doing as you were. Use them as you see fit." I glanced at the crowd of laborers. "Without killing them."

"All hail the wise Queen of Drattüjert!" One of the Blodnar shouted, making me jump back. "Friend of the Magnus Principis Henricus of Norycium!" The men behind him shouted in agreement and my confusion increased.

"Did you all know about this? Before you were brought out of the dungeons?"

The first Blodnar soldier nodded. "We've been stuck in those dungeons since your husband and those blasted dragons captured us. By the mercy of the gods and goddesses,

Magnus Principis Henricus was brought here and he has spoken to you on our behalf. You in your feminine goodness have allowed us to see sunlight again."

I stared at the Blodnar soldiers for a moment, trying to gauge how serious they were. They looked serious. Focusing on the construction leader, I gestured for him to come over to me. He hurried over and I handed the scroll back to him. "Keep an eye on these men. If they've been in the dungeons that long..." I knew stories of people going crazy from confinement before. If these soldiers were that way, I didn't want them working on anything in Drattüjert.

"As you wish, my queen. I agree that their brains may be addled now. Beyond what is normal for a Blodnar." He paused, glanced at the soldiers, then back at me. "What would you have me do if they get unruly?"

"If they aren't assisting with repair or otherwise *starting* trouble, discipline them." I hesitated myself, wondering how strict I should be. At this point, anything less than full-on execution would make people think I was a Blodnar sympathizer. But I wasn't about to murder people either. "But if they start trouble, or kill anyone, then..." I nodded at the man, hoping he'd get my message.

He grimaced and nodded himself. "I understand, my queen. I'll keep an eye on them and make sure they stay in line. Once they are done for the day?"

I looked around at the crowd watching us. "Return them to the dungeons. Though they aren't a threat right now, we don't have space or guards for them outside the palace."

He nodded and bowed before walking away. I watched as the groups dispersed and the Blodnar were led out of the nearby gate, still marching as if untied and in a normal formation. It was eerie, and something felt off about them. I'd seen the Blodnar, I'd fought them. They were organized on the battlefield, but this group was different. Why?

"My queen."

I jumped and turned around to see Haldrek's master spy standing next to me. He smiled. "This is an interesting turn of events. Did you...?"

Despite my reservations about the whole situation, for some reason, he seemed trustworthy enough to confide in. At least right now. "No. My signature was forged. I don't sign with a runic signature. Ever. The document ordering these men had both mine and one of the advisors' signatures."

"Very interesting. You should go meet with them, then?"

I grumbled. "Unfortunately. I don't know what tasks Haldrek gave you before leaving, but would you... could you look into this and keep me up to date on this situation as well?"

He nodded, but said nothing. After an awkward silence, I nodded to him and hurried back to the palace, not looking forward to what I would find there.

My meeting with the advisors was uneventful and Thoreg, the particular counsellor I was looking to speak with was, much to my surprise, not at the meeting. When I asked about his whereabouts, there were no direct answers, only mumbles, murmurs, and averted glances. Totally not suspicious at all.

Afterwards, I made my way down to the dungeons. Thoreg had forged my signature somehow, on a document concerning Henry and his soldiers, and was now missing. Which meant he'd probably interacted with Henry at some point. As much as I wanted to believe Henry wouldn't do something to get me in trouble, I needed to figure out what the hell was going on and nip it in the bud before things got worse. The last thing I needed was someone pretending to be me.

Turning the corner with my guards and one of the head jailers of the dungeons, I stopped. In front of me stood Kamira, holding open chains, and Henry rubbing his wrists. He looked up at me and a grin lit up his face.

"Ina! Thank you! I knew I could count on you."

I stared at him in confusion and shook my head, trying to clear my thoughts. "What's going on here?"

"Your waiting lady, Lady Kamira, just arrived to free me from these cells. She said you sent her."

I turned to Kamira and she curtsied. "My queen, I took your words of peace between the Blodnar and Lohikärra to heart yesterday. There has been much violence between our peoples, but on the eve of a potential war between brothers, you are wise to say we cannot fight two enemies at the same time. So I took the liberty of aiding the Blodnar prince in his mission of peacemaking."

What. The. Actual. F—

"You took the liberty? Of doing what exactly?" My brain was screaming that this was a trap, a ploy of some kind. This was Kamira, after all. She wouldn't help me, even if her life depended on it. But I couldn't exactly tell her *no*. Nor could I send him back into the dungeons. If he was legitimately here on a peace mission, that would screw things up. But her taking the liberty of releasing him pissed me off.

"I," she hesitated, "I just wanted to help, Queen Ina."

The meek and humble facade wasn't helping her, at least with me. But I knew I couldn't look like an asshole either.

Gritting my teeth, I smiled. "Thank you, Kamira. I will take it from here."

She curtsied again and hurried past me. Even Rhaegos make a sound of annoyance in my head as she passed. Kamira was up to something, and I needed to figure that out as soon as possible.

"Did Kamira's help come as a surprise?" Henry's question turned my attention to him. Despite wearing the same long waist-length Blodnar tunic and Lohikärran pants that he'd arrived in, his facial expressions and mannerisms were *Henry* and a part of me wanted to relax around him. Rhaegos pushed against those feelings and I sensed her irritation. I tried to steel myself against being too sympathetic. I needed to be objective. Cold. But it didn't help that he looked like a near doppelgänger of Haldrek, whom I was missing terribly right now.

"It did. She hasn't been the most supportive of my projects. She has said some awful things about the Blodnar. This is completely opposite of what I expected from her."

"Perhaps that goes to show how good your oratory skills are? I remember you being very persuasive growing up." He rubbed the back of his head and grinned sheepishly. "At least from what I can remember of Fargo. The trip from there to here was a little chaotic."

I squinted at him in confusion and nodded with hesitation. Words like 'oratory' and 'persuasive' weren't exactly the kind of language Henry would use, at least normally. Plus, I wouldn't have called myself persuasive back in Fargo by any stretch of the imagination. But that was beside the point. Something shady was going on and I still needed to figure out what that was. Why was Kamira helping Henry and who forged my signature?

After watching him for a moment and trying to think of my next step, I said, "Maybe. You'll have to tell me how you got from Fargo to here when you have a chance. In the meantime, I need to figure some things out." I bit the inside of my lip in frustration. Kamira's actions had put me in a difficult situation. I couldn't put Henry back in the dungeon cell without looking like a jerk, but I couldn't just let him wander wherever he wanted. "I don't want you to be in the dungeons, honestly. But there are many people in Drattüjert who would hurt you, regardless of your peace mission. I don't want that either."

"Of course. Is there another part of the palace where I could stay? Under your watchful eye? I don't want to get you in trouble either." His voice was soft and kind, like it often had been back in Fargo.

I thought for a moment. There were empty quarters near where Kotkel and the other hersirs stayed. I could put Henry there, and order a few guards to be at his side at all times. "Yes." I sighed. "Follow me."

He hurried over to my side and gave me a squeeze. I smiled but pulled away, feeling awkward. "I'm married now, Henry. So, thanks for the hug, but..." My voice faltered as the awkwardness continued.

"I understand. Don't want your husband getting jealous?" Henry laughed and I grimaced.

"Haldrek knows I only have eyes for him. But there are others here who think you and I have a, uh, connection. Because we were friends growing up."

"Do we not have a connection? I mean, we were pretty close as children."

I stopped, my guards holding their formation around me. "We were always just friends, Henry. You, me, Mattie, and Alex. That was it. People think we have a *different* connection here. Not just friends, but like something else." I didn't want to say romantic, that felt too weird. But that's exactly what kind of relationship people thought Henry and I had. As far from the truth as it was.

Henry nodded, his expression faltering. "Oh. I understand now. No, you're right. We're just friends. Wouldn't want to have anyone thinking otherwise."

I could have sworn there was a hint of sadness in his voice, but I brushed it off. It was just the awkwardness of this whole situation. Right?

Walking forward, I continued, "I spoke again with Haldrek last night. We've decided to meet and consider your peace offerings together. He is currently outside of the city, but when he returns, we can talk more of your mission here. In the meantime, while you are here in the palace, you can be in the public areas, and I'll grant you quarters where you can sleep and take care of yourself. However, you will need to have the guards, that I assign, stay with you all day, every day."

Henry frowned. "Do you not trust me?"

I hesitated as we reached the hall where the hersirs stayed. A few servants were hurrying about, but none of the hersirs were around, much to my relief. I glanced at the room where Kotkel was staying. Just as I had asked, there were guards stationed outside. Focusing back on Henry, I shrugged.

"I trust the Henry I knew in Fargo. The kid I grew up with and who helped me when my mother and Robert were too intense. But this isn't Fargo. This is Lohikärra, and unfortunately, you are at least part Blodnar. Things are different here. Plus it's been a few years since we've really hung out. You were busy with sports and Alex, and I was busy counting down the days until I left my mother's place. We've both changed. Which is fine, it's just... things are different here. I hope that our kingdoms and empires can be at peace for once. Maybe then we can be good friends like we were in Fargo."

I gestured to the open door and he nodded. Without another word, he entered and shut it behind him. My heart fell as I assigned a few of my personal guard, warriors I'd grown to trust, to stay with him at all times. I didn't have many friends here. At least that I could completely trust. Haldrek was off fighting on my behalf and Mattie was leading Andrattür. Everyone else? One day maybe.

But, for now, I was alone.

Chapter Twelve

I had a few more duties to attend to that day, but as soon as I got a chance, I hurried up to Haldrek's and my quarters. The entire day had been emotionally exhausting and I needed solitude. As I slipped into the bedroom, my servants seemed to understand that need. Even those who usually puttered around within the bedroom kept their distance. As I collapsed on the bed, my mind went back to everything else I'd done today. As I had been listening to petitioners after dealing with Henry, Rhaegos had nudged me to talk to Mattie. Rhaegos had a point. Mattie may have been at Mirratoft, but I could at least get her opinion on what was going on.

Curled up within the privacy of the four-poster bed, I pulled out my pendant and said, "Mattie Gunvald, Mirratoft."

The black inky background swirled and rippled for a few moments before Mattie's face appeared, her eyes widening in surprise.

"What's up?" The shelves of books and scrolls behind her told me that Mattie was in Mirratoft's library. I smiled, glad that some things never changed.

"I wanted to say hi. And to let you know that someone else from Fargo is here now."

Mattie's eyes widened. "Wait. Another person from Fargo? Who?"

"Henry."

"*Henry?*" She laughed. "He must be in heaven right now, considering how much he loved the games. How did he get here? Is he there in Drattüjert?"

I nodded, grimacing as I tried to figure out how to explain everything that had happened over the last few days. And how to explain that Henry probably wasn't too happy with being in Lohikärra right now.

She paused and cocked her head. "Something's up. I feel like you'd be excited to see him. Is Alex with him? Or... if he's here, that means he has a connection to the world of Sethys. Don't tell me his bio-dad was from Lohikärra too?"

I shook my head. "His connection to Sethys is through the Blodnar empire, but I don't know how exactly. That's part of what is making his appearance here difficult. He popped up at the Refuge of Tenelth demanding to see me and threatening the priestesses there."

"Henry? Threatening people?" Mattie's brow furrowed deeper with confusion. "That's not like him at all. Even more recently. Remember how I had a class with him senior year? He wasn't cocky or giving anyone attitude. That seems way out of character for him."

"I know. And I remember. I mean, maybe threatening is a strong word, but he was being intimidating. He marched into Drattüjert wearing a mishmash of Lohikärran and Blodnar garb."

"What? I'm surprised he made it past the gates."

"Same. There are a few things that are off. He looks like Henry, he sounds like Henry, but I don't know if the changes I've seen are just him, all of us getting older, or something else."

"Where is he now?"

I sighed. "He's with the hersirs from the rest of Lohikärra as of today. There's some crazy, weird stuff going on right now and," I choked up, "I wish you or Haldrek were here."

"Ina—"

"I had to put him in the dungeons, but the other hersirs still think I'm being soft on him and I've been accused of sympathizing with the Blodnar, and then someone forged my signature to allow the other Blodnar soldiers out of the dungeons so they can work on repairing Drattüjert. Then when I went to see Henry and figure out what was going on because he's supposed to be here on a peace mission from either his father or grandfather or whoever, who's apparently the Blodnar emperor, and I saw Kamira, who's been awful this entire time, letting him out of his dungeon cell and pretending she was just doing what I told her to do and—"

"Whoa, whoa, whoa." Mattie rubbed her eyes and bridge of her nose as she groaned. "Henry arrived in Drattüjert, demanding to see you, right?"

"Yes."

"He's on a peace mission for the Blodnar emperor who is somehow related to him?"

I nodded.

"And since he's arrived, weird stuff's been going on with the Blodnar prisoners and Kamira?"

"Yes. And some of Haldrek's advisors. The document that had my signature forged was also signed by this particular advisor, Thoreg, who has been rude to me in the past. I don't know what to think."

"Have you talked to Haldrek about this?"

I nodded. "I've been talking to him every night, keeping him updated. He was pissed at first, telling me that if Henry is a Blodnar whatever, that he needs to be imprisoned or executed. I told him we don't need to be fighting two wars right now. Lohikärra is already worn out from almost twenty years of fighting. He agreed that we should keep Henry here until he can return. I know he doesn't trust him, which is understandable, but it still sucks."

Mattie nodded, her attention on something below the pendant. "You know, I'm not saying that Henry has changed, but I mean both of us changed after being here for a while. How long has he been here?"

I shrugged. "That wasn't something I thought to ask him."

"You should ask him. There could be a lot of things going on. Something that I just thought of... remember how close Henry was to his stepdad?"

"Kinda. I mean, Mr. Pollard seemed to care when Henry was doing well at sports and stuff, but usually Henry's mom was more invested in his life."

"I remember them not having that great of a relationship. Like, not as bad as you and your mother, but Henry would sometimes talk about the amount of pressure his stepdad would put on him. It made him miserable. Maybe... maybe he found his bio-dad in the Blodnar lands and they connected."

"Is that a bad thing, though?"

"Only if Henry is being used as a pawn. I mean, if his dad or granddad is the freaking Blodnar Emperor, then I could easily see him manipulating Henry in exchange for being a father figure to him. You know? Henry might be ready and willing to do what he can for someone who will accept him as he is."

"What should I do? I think I hurt Henry when I said I didn't trust him like I did in Fargo. And given how alone I feel..." Tears began to well up in my eyes. "Sometimes I wonder if I belong here."

"Ina, I wish I could be there with you. Has Jaonos been doing his job?"

I nodded. "He's probably one of the few hersirs who don't outright hate me right now."

"Good. If that changes, let me know. As for Henry, you don't have to be awful, but stay on your guard. Things are different here than in Fargo. There's a lot of bad blood between Lohikärra and the Blodnars. But you already know that."

I nodded, trying to wipe my eyes on my dress. "I'm just trying to do what's best for Lohikärra. And not create more trouble."

"I know. Silver lining though: If you keep Henry close, you can figure out what's going on. With him, with Kamira, and maybe also the advisor. Unless *his* signature was forged too, one might think that he's up to something as well. All of that is concerning."

"Yeah. That I need to nip in the bud. I can't have someone pretending to be me. That could make things a million times worse."

The sound of a baby crying in the background made Mattie look up. She turned back to me and sighed. "I need to go. Talk to Haldrek and keep a close eye on Henry. If you need anything from me, let me know."

I smiled weakly and closed my pendant. Laying down on the pillows, I let myself sob until I was too tired to cry anymore.

That night, I dreamt. As soon as I closed my eyes, I was in a haze of fog. While I couldn't see anything, there was no sense of imminent danger either. Instead, I felt the same as when I'd dreamt of Rhaegos interacting with my father back in Svartån. As light filtered around me, I realized I was in a place I'd never seen before, a place that looked nothing like Lohikärra. Lush grassy areas rolled out around me with a few trees sticking out along the edge of the horizon. To my left, a city wall stretched out in the distance, but I got the impression that it wasn't Drattüjert or any other Lohikärran city. Turning around, I stepped back as I realized I was in front of a shrine of some kind. The architecture was definitely not Lohikärran. Instead, it almost looked Greek or Roman. Or if the place I was currently in was still part of Sethys, something that might be in Blodnar lands. It was small and there were no doors, only arches for the two entrances across from one another. The interior was dark, but I could make out the shape of something on a pedestal.

Behind me, the sound of footsteps crunching on gravel caught my attention. I stepped out of the way as a woman, slightly taller than myself, strode past me in a rich, purple robe. A veil shadowed her face and covered her from head to foot. She looked like a character from one of my history textbooks detailing the ancient Roman world.

Several younger women, in simpler, beige colored robes, followed. The first woman stopped at one of the arches to the shrine and put out her hand. The others stopped as she entered the building alone.

I blinked and was pulled into the shrine as well, tucked away in the corner and facing the woman in purple. The shrine seemed lighter now as the woman bowed, placing an offering in front of the shrine.

"Blessed Rhaegaia, goddess of queens, empresses, and all women, hear my plea. Speak with me, I..." The woman paused as if the words were difficult to say. "I beg."

Footsteps came from the entrance opposite the woman. I turned to see Rhaegos walk into the shrine, a smile on her face. She too wore the same Roman-like garb as the woman, but in shimmering earth tones, not unlike the colors of her scales, or the clothes I'd seen her wear when I became a haldraga.

"Stand, little one. I have heard you and I shall listen."

The woman made a crying sound and I turned back to her. Tears covered her cheeks as they fell. Still she stood up, holding herself with a dignity I wished I could emulate.

"Rhaegaia, please protect me, and my child. Jaari is imprisoned, and I know that neither I nor my child will be safe in Jaari's homeland or mine. We thought our relationship would bring peace, but now... I beg your protection."

"My protection you shall have. You and your child shall be integral to peace between the Blodnar and the Lohikärrans, though not in the manner you expect. Do you trust me?"

"I—" The woman hesitated. "I have trusted you in the past. And I know I should trust you now. But my fear—" Her voice faltered as she bowed her head and her shoulders sank down. "I care only the well-being of my loved ones and myself. If you are promising protection, then I shall trust in you."

Rhaegos stepped around the shrine, opposite from me, and knelt so she was eye to eye with the woman, reminding me how tall Rhaegos actually was in her human form. She wrapped her arms around the woman, allowing her to sob freely. I got the sense that this woman had dealt with much emotionally in the near past, maybe too much, and this was the first time she could express herself.

As I watched the scene, feeling empathy for the woman, the area around me darkened until everything had disappeared and gone silent. I closed my eyes, still feeling safe, but letting my other senses take over.

"What do you think of that memory, little one?"

I nearly jumped away from the voice, but an unseen hand held me steady.

"Rhaegos?" Of course it was Rhaegos who had spoken, but I hadn't seen her in a physical form since I'd returned to Lohikärra. The space around me lightened up, and I saw her standing to my left, in the corner of my eye.

She wore the same shimmery earth tones of purple, green, and brown as I'd seen her in before, but the style of her clothing was now distinctly Lohikärran. She smiled at me and nodded. "We are safe, little one. For the time being. I wanted to show you a memory of mine, and I'm curious what you thought of it."

I stared at her in surprise. "It was interesting. My heart went out to that woman. She obviously was trying to protect her child, and I felt her grief over the Jaari man she was talking about. And you were—what did she call you again?"

"Rhaegaia. It is the name the Blodnar call me. I've told you before that the dragons do not care where the people who worship them come from. Some of us are even loathe to be worshiped. But it is something that many of the sentient races of Sethys do. The Blodnar know me and my kin only by our human forms. They have created a pantheon of gods and goddesses connected to many of my kin."

"And you are the goddess of queens, empresses, and women of all kinds."

Rhaegos nodded. "I have seen the struggles of many women across Sethys and I am one of many dragons who protect them. But that is a story for another day. The reason for this dream is simple: I was curious about your thoughts because you have met that woman before."

I stepped back in surprise. "What? When? Where?"

"Fargo, little one. She is your friend Henry's mother. The child she cared for so deeply in that memory is your friend, Henry."

"So, is it really Henry in Drattüjert right now?"

Rhaegos raised a brow at me. "You tell me. I knew his mother well, but you knew him far better than I ever did."

I sighed. "There's something off about him. Different. But I don't know if that's just us growing up or something else."

"What does your heart tell you?"

"Rhaegos..." I grumbled and she raised both brows at me. Instantly I felt embarrassed. "My heart tells me something is not quite right. But I don't know what it is."

"Then listen to your heart."

I grimaced, but didn't say anything for a few moments. Part of me wanted to be snarky, but I knew I needed to be respectful of Rhaegos as well. "Is Henry in Lohikärra? The Henry I knew growing up?"

Rhaegos nodded.

"Is he safe?"

She nodded again and I started to grow frustrated. None of this was helping me right now.

"Will helping Henry, or his mother if she's here, hurt Lohikärra or Haldrek?" As much as I cared for my old friend, I still had a responsibility as High Queen, and the last thing I wanted to do was hurt Haldrek.

"If you aid the correct Henry, not only will Lohikärra be protected, but it will finally see peace. Within and without."

The correct Henry? I opened my mouth to ask another question, but before I could get a single word out, a loud ominous rumbling boomed around us. Rhaegos's expression turned fierce and angry as I looked around for the source of the sound. Suddenly, Rhaegos gripped the front of my attire, her hands shifting into dragon's claws. She jumped, pulling me up through the space.

"Fly, little one! To safety!"

With that, she shoved me and I went tumbling away. I began to fall down through the space again, but Rhaegos's presence was gone. I screamed and right as I expected to hit something, I jolted awake.

Opening my eyes, I gasped for air, trying to calm my racing heart. The dream was still vivid, etched into my own memory. I had more questions than answers now, but the foremost thing on my mind was one question:

What did Rhaegos mean by 'the correct Henry'?

Chapter Thirteen

I didn't sleep much for the rest of the night. In the morning, I did everything I could to not fall asleep. More gossip abounded, but I was too tired to care as the phrase 'the correct Henry' swirled around in my head. At the same time, the strange booming sound in my dream which had changed Rhaegos's demeanor completely, unsettled me. I guessed we'd been in the Realm of Dragons while I slept, which meant something had happened there? Taking a moment to breathe as I stepped outside, I tried searching for Rhaegos's presence. She was still there, barely, but I got a sense of exhaustion from her. I'd have to ask Haldrek or Mattie if their dragons were acting off at all.

Walking around the city, the nice weather and the humming of a city returning to life improved my mood. People seemed cheerful and I was glad for that. Life in the palace may have been a hot mess, but at least something was working, right?

Detouring to the eastern gate, I watched as both Blodnar soldiers and Lohikärran laborers worked side by side on the walls. This had been the gate most heavily damaged and the one Haldrek and I had walked through when we had chased after Rorik. It was also the largest of the three major entrances into the city.

"Why are we doing this?"

My attention focused in on a couple of Blodnar soldiers on the inside of the gate, carrying buckets across their backs before dumping them on the ground. Their demeanor was vastly different from the ones I'd seen before. These men didn't seem so happy with their current situation. They also didn't seem to be paying attention to their surroundings. Even so, I stepped into the shadows of a nearby building and busied myself with looking at some repair work on the building.

"Because the Grand Principis demanded we do this. Who am I to question the Emperor or his heirs?"

"But we are soldiers of Norycium. Not stupid barbarians. This is slave's work!"

I glanced to the side as the second man spun around. "And are we not slaves now? Until those in the palace stop playing, our lives belong to them and their whims." He gestured to the large vat in front of both of them. Another man stood above, stirring whatever was in it, and another stood nearby, filling buckets full of whatever was in the vat. "Put your water in. We can't stop until these barbarians say we can."

Both men reached high above their heads and dumped their buckets into the vat before walking away.

"That's interesting."

I jumped and grimaced as Egil the spymaster stood near me. He bowed briefly. "My apologies, my queen. I didn't mean to scare you. Though it might be wise to keep yourself apprised of situations around you."

"Or maybe you're very good at sneaking around. What's interesting now?"

"The discontent from the Blodnar soldiers. Yesterday's group seemed blindly loyal to your friend."

"He's not...," I paused, trying to find the right words. "Henry is my friend, but I'm not so sure about the Grand Principis or whoever is inside the palace currently."

Egil raised a brow. "You think they aren't one and the same?"

"I'm not one hundred percent certain, no. But I have no proof to back up those feelings."

He smiled. "I can aid you in that, my queen. That is part of my job after all. You would just need to keep entertaining him long enough."

I nodded, a small bit of relief filling me, but also worry that I was overthinking things. My sleep-deprived brain wasn't helping. "I need to figure out who signed that document in my name yesterday as well. The advisor's name who was also on it? He has since disappeared."

Another raised brow from the spy. "Interesting. I will have one of my men look into that."

"Everything is very interesting to you."

He laughed, the first time I'd seen him do that. "It is my job, my queen. If I didn't find the most mundane things interesting, I couldn't serve the High King or yourself as I should." He stopped and a more serious expression crossed his face. "On that note, something interesting is going on in the High Queen's Home. Nothing worth alarm, but you may find useful information there."

I grimaced and turned back toward the palace. He wandered away and I made haste, not wanting to waste a moment. The fact that he mentioned the High Queen's Home made my anxiety skyrocket. Even if he thought there was nothing worrisome going on there, I knew I needed to return. For all I knew, one of the advisors could be harassing the refugees.

As soon as I entered the quarters where the High Queen's Home was, I relaxed. Nothing looked amiss, at least at first sight. There was no one there who wasn't supposed to be there. The Priestesses of Tenelth hurried around and a few babies fussed, but there was nothing that seemed off. The main room was busier than normal, but I assumed that was to be expected.

"My queen!" One of the priestesses came up to me and curtsied. "Is there something you have come here for?"

"I…" My mind went blank for a moment before inspiration hit. "Do you all need any help? I have some free time and I want to help those who have come here recently."

The young woman's expression relaxed as she smiled. "If you have time, there have been many children who have been brought here. Orphans, I suppose, and some left with only blankets or a basket. If you would like to sit with them, I'm sure they would find comfort in that."

I nodded and she gestured to a makeshift sitting area around a large fireplace. There was a small, resting fire in it, giving off a little heat and keeping some pots warm above it.

As I sat down, a young girl ran toward me, plowing into my leg and flopping on top of it, as if she thought I was an anchor of some kind. She looked up at me through a mess of tangled hair, eyes wet.

"I want mama."

My heart broke in that moment. Scooping her up, I sat her on my lap. "I'm not your mama, but I can sit here with you. Do…do you want a hug?"

She nodded and I squeezed her tight. As I released her, she nestled her head in the nook of my shoulder, relaxing and growing heavy. I smiled and looked up as the priestess from before brought over a bundle of cloth and placed it in the crook of my right arm. A small, familiar face stared up at me intently, looking me over before blinking and rustling in the swaddling. I wasn't sure, but the baby looked like the one I'd rescued just before Haldrek's departure. Regardless of whether it was or not, the child fell asleep within moments.

"You truly are a Lady of Lohikärra," the priestess whispered.

"What do you mean?"

"I always grew up hearing stories about Ladies of Lohikärra, and they always sounded like very maternal women. You seem to have a soothing effect on these children." She nodded to the small girl curled up against my left arm. "This one has struggled since her arrival here. She came with a group of refugees, but they said they found her crying and alone outside a burnt farmhouse."

"That's—" I couldn't finish the sentence. "How long has she been here?"

"Only a couple of weeks. She's been staying at the Refuge, but she would wake up screaming in the middle of the night. Priestess Thwaya thought she might do better over here. This is the calmest that I've seen her."

I nodded, thinking of what activities I was required to deal with today. If I could stay here long enough to let her sleep peacefully, I would.

There was more crying in the far corner behind me and the priestess looked up. "I should go check on that. Thank you for your help, my queen."

She hurried away and I returned to holding the children, relaxing against the back of the solid chair I was in. My thoughts came back front and center as I absentmindedly rocked the children. Rhaegos's words echoed in my mind as I tried to piece together what she could have possibly meant, as well as Haldrek's spy.

"You look like you are at home here."

I twisted around to see Henry watching me. The baby started to fuss and I tried to soothe it quickly. As soon as the child fell back asleep, I turned to Henry, who looked embarrassed.

"I'm sorry. I didn't mean to startle you."

"It's fine. What are you doing here?" My nerves were on high alert now, and a protective part of me started to grow, even though Henry didn't seem to be any kind of threat right now.

"I got tired of staying in my quarters. You said I was free to be in the public areas of the palace. Is this not one of them?"

I nodded. "It is. But most people, outside of myself, the servants, and the priestesses of Tenelth, ignore these quarters. The High Queen's Home isn't one of my more popular projects."

Henry frowned. "Why not?"

"Because it was created to help those who've been orphaned or abandoned due to the war. I... there was an incident almost a month ago where a man wanted to kill the child his wife bore because the child's biological father was Blodnar. I intervened and, long story short, the High Queen's Home was created." I stopped, wondering if I'd said too much. If this wasn't the 'correct Henry' as Rhaegos had mentioned, this was a stranger, and I didn't want to give him more information than I needed to.

"For those rejected because of their heritage?"

"Not only them, but refugees of the war overall. Many people from the southern thegn lands have left their homes because of what the Blodnar have done to my people."

Henry nodded and sat down on a stool across from me. "Your people?" A small, somber smile flitted across his face and I wondered what he was thinking. "How long...? You disappeared a couple of winters ago. Have you been here since then?"

I tried to calculate what a couple of winters could have meant, but my brain was too tired. "For the most part. I became the Thegn of Svartån and then the High Queen in that time. It's always been my duty to take care of people. And we've had so many enemies try to hurt us in that time. Not just the Blodnar. I've fought to protect the people here. I feel a closer connection to them than I ever did people in Fargo."

"Huh. So most of these children are the offspring of Lohikärran women and soldiers from Norycium?" He shook his head as I frowned. "You call them Blodnar, but that is a Lohikärran name for the people of my grandfather's empire. They called themselves Norycians."

I grimaced at his comment. Both at the implications—anger growing inside of me at the thought of what had been done—and at how he so casually brushed those actions aside, more concerned about names. Still, I didn't want to snap at him or do anything rash. At least not yet. "I'm afraid so. These children are innocent, but I think most of their fathers are not."

Henry nodded. "I understand. These aren't like the games we played back home, are they? I won't call them 'my men,' but the Norycians who have come here have not been civilized in any manner of speaking. That's why this peace mission is so important. Not only will it help the Empire, but it will help Lohikärra heal too."

"I think it will be a long time before Lohikärra will be fully healed." The words popped out of my mouth with a sharpness I hadn't intended. Henry grimaced and nodded.

"You are right. But we should do what we can to start that process." He looked around at the room and the people in it. "I think you are doing good work, Ina. Even if no one else here sees that. As someone who is half-Norycian and half-Lohikärran, I appreciate stuff like this. I wish there had been something like this for me and my mother."

Irritation from Rhaegos flashed in the back of my head as I stared at Henry in surprise. Before I had a chance to say anything, he stood up. "I'll leave you to your caretaking. Thank you. For being a good friend, a good queen, and for being an example."

He walked away and my anxiety went into overdrive. His words had technically been kind and understanding, but they confused me, as did Rhaegos's reaction to him. But there was nothing I could do right now. My arms were literally full, and once again there was nothing ominous enough for me to do anything but keep him at arm's length.

Chapter Fourteen

Another night of nightmares and lack of sleep had left me worn out. I'd fallen asleep early and though I felt my pendant warm up with what I assumed was Haldrek's call, I was too exhausted to answer.

In the morning, I ate my breakfast, and after showing my face for a little bit in the throne room, I made my way to the same drevké where I'd last talked to Senja. It would be a private, quiet place where I could pretend to talk to the dragons while I rested.

Unfortunately, I arrived to find the room not empty. There were only a couple of people in the room, and even though my guards stood outside the doorway, that was two people too many. As I turned around to leave, one of the benches creaked and I heard my name:

"Ina! Come sit with us."

I turned back to see Senja gesturing to me. A tired smile crossed my face. As much as I adored my connection with Rhaegos and appreciated her presence, I also liked how personable Senja tended to be. She was much less removed from humans than the rest of the dragons.

I walked up to her and sat down. On her other side, much to my surprise, was Sibila. She leaned forward, staring straight at the statue. A relaxed and peaceful expression covered her face as she smiled.

"Sibila asked for my company as she spoke with her dragon. She said she didn't feel comfortable alone."

"Rorik has been plaguing my dreams of recent. So much anger." Sibila continued to stare at the statue, though her smile had disappeared. She began wringing her hands and playing with the jewelry on them. I was unsure if her words were a response to Senja, or if she was talking to the statue. Senja acted as if nothing was amiss and put her arm around me.

"How have you been doing, Ina?"

"Tired. I haven't been sleeping well. Nightmares and such. Anxiety over you-know-who."

"Rorik thinks he can rule over all of Lohikärra, and yet he struggles to keep Etelaranikä under his thumb." Sibila laughed. "Even with his new ally, he rants and raves, lashing out at the simplest frustration." Her face fell. "He takes his anger out on me every night. Physically, he cannot touch me, but his emotions..." She sighed, letting her head sink into her lap. Her behavior surprised me. I'd never seen this side of her. Senja, on the other hand, seemed unfazed as she placed her other hand on Sibila's back.

"Do you still have the token Tesroan gave you before the two of you bonded, Sibila?"

Sibila nodded and pulled her right sleeve back. A chain connected three jeweled bracelets and a ring on Sibila's middle finger. Each bracelet and the ring had a round silver colored coin on it, inscribed with some kind of rune.

"May I see it? I fear Rorik grows stronger with each passing day, and his power is taking its toll on you."

Sibila said nothing, but took it off and gave it to Senja. The dragon closed her eyes and put the piece of jewelry in one of her cupped hands, covering it with the other. A low, rumbling, melodic sound came from Senja's chest and rose through her throat. The skin on her hands began to shimmer and shift into scales as she continued to hum. Rhaegos roused inside my head and the weight of anticipation fell over me. Whatever Senja was doing, it was powerful, and possibly even sacred.

Senja stopped and the scales turned back into skin. She exhaled and gave the jewelry back to Sibila. "That should help Tesroan's magic for the time being."

"The sooner we get rid of Rorik, the better," I muttered.

Senja turned to me. "He was not always this wicked. Spoiled, yes, but wicked, no. There's a reason he became a haldraga. No dragon would have bound with him if he'd been practicing necromancy at that point."

"High Queen Ina is right though. The sooner my brother is dead and gone, the better. He has tormented too many people for too long." Sibila kept her eyes averted as she put the jewelry back on. As soon as she finished, she groaned and leaned into Senja, closing her eyes. "He's angry now. His new ally was supposed to give him something precious and important, but he hasn't."

I hesitated, not knowing how proper or safe it was to ask questions at this point, but if Sibila was sensing Rorik's emotions, perhaps there was more she knew.

She laughed softly, her eyes still shut tight. "He's swearing never to trust a Blodnar again."

"Do you know who his new ally is?" I blurted the words out before I could contain myself.

Her eyes snapped open and she turned to me in surprise, as if she hadn't been aware I was there. "I don't know his name, but he is a foreigner, not long in these lands. There is a sinister nature to him. Matching Rorik's almost."

Excitement coursed through me, as did trepidation. Sibila had never been this coherent around me before. Her information could be valuable, but it also meant that she'd been hiding who she truly was from most of the court.

She sat up straight and frowned, putting her hands in front of her and holding her head in them. "The Blodnar doesn't look like a Blodnar, to be honest. Most of the time. Sometimes he does, but mostly he hides. He's pretending to be someone he's not. Is that the best way to describe it, Tesroan?"

More silence and then she nodded. "I'm glad you agree, Tesroan. Sometimes even I think my mind is gone and I'm only speaking gibberish." She stood up and walked out of the drevké as if Senja and I weren't there.

I watched her leave, confusion returning.

"There's much more to Sibila than meets the eye. I hope one day she is able to show that side of her." Senja twisted back around to face the shrine. For a moment, she almost looked like she was going to cry. Then the expression was gone, replaced by a firmness.

"Is she trustworthy?" I hated to ask the question, given that Senja seemed to trust her, but at the same time, there were a lot of things I didn't know about Sibila. "I mean, with a father like Gustav and a brother like Rorik—"

"We are not always like our blood relatives. Are you like your mother?" Senja's tone wasn't accusing, but I felt a slight twinge of guilt and anxiety. The last thing I wanted was to be like my mother. Or for people to think I was like her. A minor mercy of being in Lohikärra—outside of a few people, no one truly knew who my mother was, so they couldn't use that against me.

"I hope not. But sometimes I'm afraid I'll turn into her. Especially once Haldrek and I have kids." I turned back around and started playing with the dragon ring Haldrek had given me in Svartån as a ward against the undead. Despite the fact that I had gained some weight since arriving in Lohikärra, it still hung loosely around all my fingers except my thumb. "Not that that will happen any time soon." My mind flashed back to my first pregnancy and tears welled up in my eyes. I'd never have a chance to be a mother as long as Rorik was around.

"Did Haldrek give you that ring?" Senja tapped it.

I nodded. "Back when we were fighting the Isillas and there was a vampire threatening me."

"I can sense some of Teminth's magic in it. He probably blessed it for Haldrek before they bound themselves together. That's why the magic has faded. Would you like me and Rhaegos to add some of our magic to it?"

"Is Rhaegos able to, even though we've already joined together?" I knew it was a stupid question before the words left my mouth. Rhaegos's laughter and a sense of warmth flowed through my mind.

"As long as you are holding it, both of us can share our magic. There just has to be a dragon in physical form to perform the magic."

I nodded once more and held out the ring. Senja grabbed my hand with both of hers and began to make the same low melodic rumbling sound as when she'd blessed Sibila's jewelry. I felt energy course through my body and into my thumb as well. It was a comforting energy that made me feel safe, almost as if surrounded with some kind of protection.

After a few moments, Senja released her grip and smiled. The ring felt warm still, more so than it should for just being touched.

"That should keep any dark or necromantic magic away from you so long as you wear the ring. Whether on your finger or as a pendant." She smiled. "I noticed how loosely it fits your fingers."

"Thank you." I hesitated, wondering if I was hoping for too much. "So if, by some miracle, Haldrek and I..." My voice faltered.

"If you once again are with child, so long as that child is within you, they will be protected as well. There is now the magic of three dragons in that ring. No human or elven manifestation of magic could get through that protection."

Tears welled up in my eyes once more. My chest felt lighter and I wondered how long I'd been carrying around that fear. "Thank you, Senja."

She squeezed my hand. "You're welcome. I need to go rest now. Casting that kind of magic is exhausting."

I watched as she stood up and left. Now truly alone, I looked at the ring. My gratitude stayed, but the ache of being away from Haldrek came back, and I wished desperately for his quick return to Drattüjert.

That night, I was curled up inside the blankets of Haldrek's and my bed, lightly dozing. While the day hadn't been too busy, my lack of good sleep over the last few days had taken its toll and my body was completely exhausted.

Right as a thought of Haldrek being by my side once more began to form, my pendant warmed up. The thought of missing another conversation with him woke me from my dozing. I rolled up onto my elbow and opened my pendant. Haldrek's face lit up the clear stone screen, but his expression was grim and I could see streaks of dirt or dried blood on his face. He looked worn out.

Still, he smiled as he saw me. "Ina, I'm glad I was able to get ahold of you. Especially after the past few nights."

"I'm sorry." A strong yawn forced its way out of my mouth as I sat up. "I haven't been sleeping well."

"More nightmares?"

I nodded. "It's not always Rorik. Other dreams have been plaguing me. But I'm hoping that will be remedied soon." I showed him the ring still on my finger.

He frowned with confusion. "The dragon ring from when we were fighting Seirye?"

I nodded. "Senja and Rhaegos added their magic and blessed the ring to keep me safe from any dark or necromantic magic. Senja also said that the combined magic would protect any child I carried, so long as I wore the ring. But for the time being, if my nightmares are being caused by Rorik or any other magic wielder—"

"The ring should keep your nightmares at bay." Haldrek smiled, relief flooding his expression. "That's good news. And hopefully, after today's events, I'll be able to return home to you."

A thrill filled my chest. "What happened?" I knew they were still in Lansiranikä, or at least I thought they were. Had they caught up to Hardbein and Rorik's forces?

"We're currently camped outside the walls of Sigreykir. Hardbein's cousin joined forces with him, as expected, but between my warriors, Mattie's warriors, and your warriors from Svangendom, we had double their forces. Especially after many of the warriors of Sigreykir refused to follow their gesith."

"What?" That was a welcome surprise. I would have bet money they'd follow their gesith no matter what.

Haldrek nodded. "We still had to fight them. But most of the fighters were Lansiranikäns loyal to Hardbein."

"What about those that Rorik was supposed to send?"

Haldrek shrugged. "There were about fifty ill-trained mages casting necromantic magic at fallen corpses, but that was an easy group to dispatch. Many of the Andrattüran warriors are trained in dealing with necromancers. I sent them to deal with that group."

I smiled. "You were able to win the day. I love you. Thank you for dealing with Hardbein and his cousin."

His mouth lifted into a tired smile. "I love you too. But we're not quite done with Hardbein or his cousin. I had my men capture them, but not execute them. As Thegn of Svartån, that is your right. You get to choose whether they live or die."

A heavy weight settled in my stomach as I considered the ramifications. This was the fourth time Hardbein had tried to take my title since I arrived in Lohikärra. That had been how long ago? A year and a half. It felt longer. But still. The last time he'd tried to proclaim himself thegn, I had told him he was exiled from Svartån and would be executed if he returned. That brought up another technicality. One that I didn't want popping up in the future.

"Sigreykir is on the border of Lansiranikä. Did you do battle with Hardbein and his forces in Svartån or in Lansiranikä?"

"We were solidly within Svartån. If we had been in Lansiranikä, he would already be dead." Haldrek's tone held the implications of that. Between Haldrek's long-standing ire toward Hardbein and Bjorn Susi's recent alliance with Rorik, even I knew Hardbein's fight with Haldrek would have fallen under treason.

"Then it's my duty to punish him." I said softly, realizing my choice had already been made. At least if I wanted people to respect me as a thegn. Haldrek nodded. "The last time he tried to take my title, I told him if he returned to Svartån, he'd be a dead man. So that's my decision. He knew what I would do."

"Even if he didn't believe you. Where would you have me send him? I'm assuming you don't want his ghost hanging around in Svartån or the Realm of Ghosts."

"Lyrroth." The word came without hesitation. I grimaced. "Every action I've seen him take has been dishonorable."

"Agreed. And what of your gesith? Mercy or discipline? I have a feeling that he won't be happy if you execute Hardbein. If he was belligerent before, he'll probably be belligerent in the future."

I laughed morosely. While one could argue that the gesith of Sigreykir was only following his cousin's lead, he'd never been a fan of me and the feeling was mutual. "He assisted a man who would usurp my title. Has there ever been a time in Lohikärran history where that hasn't ended badly for the gesith?"

"Only when the usurper wins. But the gesith of Sigreykir signed an oath to you, did he not? Swearing allegiance to you as his thegn?"

I nodded. "Would that make his actions as bad as Hardbein's?"

"Worse. He swore an oath, acknowledging you as thegn. What he did is akin to what Bjorn Susi did when I arrived in Lansiranikä. It is treason."

The heavy weight in my stomach grew larger. I'd be responsible for the executions of two men. While I had no love for either of them or their actions, they had made their choices and now faced the consequences.

"Both he and Hardbein knew what would happen if they failed, right?"

"Of course. I doubt they believed it would happen to them, but every warrior, every member of the abthanry, knows what happens to traitors in Lohikärra. With enemies on all sides, there is no room for those who are faithless or worse."

"Then execute the gesith." The words felt heavy in my mouth. "And send him to Lyrroth as well." I paused, thinking if there was anyone who could take on the role of gesith in Sigreykir *and* whom I could trust. "You said most of the Sigreykir warriors refused to fight you?"

Haldrek nodded.

"Can you or someone there find one of those warriors who can become the next gesith? Preferably someone who will train and fight alongside the Hethurin. But even someone who will tolerate them." I hated setting such a low bar, but I wasn't going to deal with another gesith like Hardbein's cousin. If I was getting rid of one gesith, might as well find one who would be less difficult to deal with.

"Of course, my love." He finished writing something down and I sighed.

"Now how do I get rid of this heavy weight in my stomach? I know Hardbein and his cousin deserve this, but I still hate the idea. If they weren't pulling resources from our fight with Rorik..." I faltered as my thoughts dissipated.

"Understand that you can be both merciful and merciless while being a good thegn. As much as I would have, you didn't just call for their execution. Hardbein has been a thorn in your side from the very beginning, but you still checked to see if he truly returned to Svartån. As for his cousin, you're making sure he truly deserves the punishment he will receive." Haldrek sighed. "Handing down a writ of execution isn't an easy thing. Even when it is the right thing."

"It's difficult, that's for sure." I closed my eyes for a moment, but as soon as they got heavy again, I opened them and sat up. "But I hope this will mean less conflict and a quicker path to Rorik. The sooner he's dead, the better." My thoughts briefly went back to Sibila.

"Well, as much as I would like to let Hardbein and his cousin wallow in misery for the next few days, if it makes it easier on you, I will make sure their punishments are served quickly. As soon as they are, I can return home."

I nodded, without saying a word, trying not to think too hard about it. Haldrek wiped his brow with the back of his hand and then looked at it with a slight grimace.

"I should go wash all this grime off of me." A soft smile crossed his face. "I love you, Ina, and I can't wait to come home."

"You too. I miss you. Be safe."

My pendant went dark and I leaned back on the pillows underneath me. My mind buzzed with activity and I anticipated another sleepless night.

Chapter Fifteen

The next morning I found myself in front of all of the thegns' hersirs and court advisors, a meeting which Haldrek normally presided over, to keep them up to date with his plans and intentions, as well as to hear their opinions and grievances. As High Queen, it fell to me while he was away, and I did not look forward to it.

As I entered the room, I expected an icy, disapproving silence. Instead, most everyone bowed or curtseyed, then watched me with anticipation. Something had changed and I grew wary.

"Good morning. I'm glad everyone was able to make it." I smiled in an attempt to relax and lighten the mood, but it did nothing. Sitting down, I exhaled.

"There is good news," I hesitated, not wanting to glance at Kotkel, "coming from the High King. He was able to quell the revolt and attacks along the borders of Lansiranikä and Svartån."

"Is that good news for everyone, or just you, my queen?" Kamira's voice was sly, and hinted at mockery in her tone.

"It is good news for everyone who doesn't support Rorik taking over Lohikärra," I snapped. "Many of the fighters under Hardbein are, or were, followers of Rorik. But they are dead now and the High King is returning home."

There was a murmur of approval, but I didn't know if it stemmed from agreement or relief.

"The city is returning to normal, with much of the damage from recent battles being repaired. Especially the city walls. Those are nearly done."

"I heard there were Blodnar working on the walls," Ragnhild spoke up. "That is incredibly unwise. Do you let them meddle with the walls because of the Blodnar man you let roam free?"

I grimaced and glanced around at the table, looking for the advisor who had approved that. Much to my surprise, he had finally reappeared. Now Thoreg sat toward the end of the table with a smug look on his face. Where had he disappeared to?

"Why do you think it's unwise? I've visited the places where they're repairing the wall and the Blodnar prisoners are not actually touching or repairing it. They are being used for the more menial tasks, such as chopping wood and hauling water."

"Sabotage, my queen." Ragnhild stared at me, unblinking, her fist on the table. "You should know that."

"How are they going to sabotage water and wood?" I stared at her in disbelief, while worry began to creep up from my gut. I tried to brush it aside as fury emanated from her.

"Too much water will make the mortar weak, and damaging the wood will make it more difficult for the repairs to proceed. Plus, the fact that they now know how the walls are being repaired, if they ever fight against us again, they will know the weak points in our defenses!" She slammed her fist on the table in emphasis.

"I haven't heard reports of any of those things yet. I doubt the building and repairing of walls differs much between here and the Blodnar Empire. Stone is stone and mortar is mortar."

"I've heard reports, my queen." Kamira's voice was smug. "It surprises me that you haven't."

I turned to face her. "If you've heard reports, then please tell me from whom. Because those kinds of things I should be hearing from the High King's and my advisors." I glanced up at Thoreg, and he refused to meet my stare.

"Nothing official. Just various conversations." She picked at her nails and looked away.

"So gossip. That's different than actual reports, Kamira." I turned back to Ragnhild. "If you must know, the edict allowing the Blodnar wasn't signed by me. I have no runic signature, but whoever signed that document didn't know that."

There were a few gasps at the table and some murmurs, but I ignored them, keeping my focus on Ragnhild.

"But you didn't stop the Blodnar from working on the walls? Why not? Have you investigated who would sign your name on a document like that? Anyone in their right mind would put a stop to that."

"Like I said, I saw no harm in Blodnar chopping wood and hauling water. It shortens the time until our defenses are fully repaired. Which is important, given we're on the brink of a civil war. As for the signature, I *have* been looking into that. But given that the forger is likely someone here in the palace, it's not something I wanted announced until I had an idea of *who* would forge my signature."

"So you have an idea, then?"

I didn't, but they didn't need to know that. "Yes. It is something that is being dealt with as we speak."

Ragnhild sat back, but still didn't look pleased.

"What of the Blodnar *envoy*?" Kotkel's voice rang out with anger and I turned my focus to him. "You let him wander the halls of the palace, despite being one of the enemy, and yet there are those of us loyal to Lohikärra who are locked up and guarded like criminals."

"He—the Blodnar envoy is here on a peace mission." I wanted to add something snarky, insulting Kotkel's father and brother, but decided against it. "And he is guarded as well. Has he caused any trouble recently?"

Muttering and shaking of heads from the others at the table answered me as Kotkel continued to stare. I turned back to the rest of the hersirs and advisors, ignoring him.

"When the High King returns, he and I will deal with the Blodnar envoy. In the meantime, if he causes trouble, I will deal with it."

"By punishing him in your bed?" Kamira laughed and I glared at her until she stopped.

"What in Lyrroth does that even mean?" I spat out the words with the fury growing inside of me.

"He is your *friend* and mysteriously arrives as soon as the High King leaves. You let him roam the palace freely while others would have him locked up. It's not hard to put two and two together. Does the High King not please you anymore? Or perhaps you know you're not capable of bearing his seed?"

I scowled as I tried to keep the rage and pain inside of me from coming out. "Considering how often I have seen you around the Blodnar envoy and the Blodnar soldiers, perhaps it's me who should be questioning your motives, Kamira. I am faithful and loyal to Haldrek. And I am absolutely capable of having a child with him. But that is *none* of your business."

Kamira laughed. "Then why aren't you large with child yet? Not that I have experience, but I've heard of far too many women getting with child on accident to think that it's *that* hard."

"Just because it's easy for some women doesn't mean it's easy for all women." I seethed, fighting back my tears. The more I tried to control myself, the more I wanted to smack Kamira's head into the table. Glancing over at Salla and Taimi, I hoped I'd find a sympathetic face. Instead, Salla looked away and Taimi grimaced like she was disappointed. My heart broke at that moment, and I fought to keep from directing my anger at them. Did these people really think I was barren? Or that Haldrek and I hadn't been trying? Or, even worse, that I'd been fooling around?

Someone cleared their throat and I turned to see Lady Drifa staring at me. I steeled myself for what barbs she had in store for me. Even though she wasn't as nasty as Kamira, she was still no fan of mine.

"High Queen Ina, *with all due respect* I would suggest you calm your demeanor. It is unseemly for a High Queen to act out as you have. You seem to think yourself untouchable, given the High King's adoration for you thus far." She began picking at the tips of her nails as well. "A foolish Queen will burn her bridges quickly, but a wise Queen will be polite to even those she deems below her. Especially when she can be replaced due to a deficit in her body."

I gritted my teeth, trying to stay calm. Trying to keep from cussing out both Drifa and Kamira. Trying to act as a High Queen would be expected to act.

But in the end I snapped as an icy calm I'd never felt before came over me. A thin smile crossed my lips. "Lady Drifa, I was always taught that with age comes wisdom. But you have proven that statement very, very wrong. If you knew anything about what the High King and I have gone through in the past year, you would keep your mouth shut." I stood up and stared around at the group. "There is nothing more to report, as you all seem to care more for gossip than for facts."

Then, without another word, I stormed out of the room.

I rushed through the hallways, avoiding anyone or anything that might keep me from my solitude. Without thinking, I ducked into a nearby drevké and shut the door. This was a smaller room, more akin to a closet, with the only lights coming from the candles on the shrine.

Once I was well and truly alone, I let myself break down. Sliding down the door, I sobbed into my dress until my knees were soaking wet. For the first time in my life, I wondered if I'd made a mistake coming to Lohikärra. Did I really belong here? What was once a refuge was now just like Fargo.

A sharp rapping on the door made me stop. In as loud a voice as I could muster, I said, "Go away! This drevké is occupied!" A moment too late, I realized that I made the shrine room sound like a bathroom.

"It's Senja. May I come in?"

I scrambled to my feet and stepped away from the door as Senja slowly opened it. She cocked her head at me in surprise and I started bawling again.

"I'm sorry." My voice sounded horribly undignified as Senja closed the door again. She took me gently by the arm and gestured for me to take a seat on a stool facing the shrine.

"I sensed your distress as I walked past this room." She sat down next to me, keeping a hand on my shoulder. "This has always been one of my more favorite drevkés since it was built. It was a storage room when I was the aethling. But I think it works better as a private drevké, without so many people watching."

I nodded, trying to imagine this place when it was smaller. How long had it been since Senja was an aethling? A human? If I didn't feel so shitty at the current moment, I'd be more curious.

"Talk to me, Ina. I know what it's like to struggle with expectations."

I wiped my eyes and they burned, making me wince. "Were you ever High Queen? And told you were only worth something if you had a kid? Or that you were basically defective if you weren't pregnant already?"

Senja grimaced. "I was once the High Queen. But it wasn't the usual course. I certainly was expected to marry and carry on my family's line. Which I did, but not in the time or manner that the High King's court expected, at least under my grandfather." She wrapped her arm around me and lowered her head. "I was also condemned and criticized regularly because I had no love for the dragons while I was an aethling."

I pulled away slightly, looking at her in surprise. Now I needed to know her story. "Why? How?" I had so many questions, and it was tempting to listen to whatever story she had instead of dealing with my present reality.

Instead, she shook her head. "This is less about me and more about you. I only tell you these things so you understand why I say what I do."

Nodding, I wiped my face once more. "Haldrek and I have been trying to get pregnant again ever since…" I hesitated, not wanting to remember. "But every month has come and gone and I'm not pregnant yet. Part of me wonders if I only had one shot at having a kid and I lost it because of Rorik. What if I am defective? At least now?"

"You are not defective. Not in the slightest. You are young, though. All of this is very, very new. You will have children. Though I cannot see the exact future, your family's legacy won't stop with you or Haldrek. That much I *do* know."

"Will he take on another wife or a mistress if I don't get pregnant soon?"

Senja threw her head back and started laughing, startling me. "Knowing what you do of him, what do you think?"

I shook my head. "Haldrek doesn't seem to be that way. But what if I… what if nothing happens and his advisors start to pester him?"

"His advisors are those who survived his uncle. While they may have been helpful to Kalle, I think Haldrek will see that some of them may not fit anymore. If you don't think Haldrek would lay with another woman while you are still his wife, then he won't. Plus, if he's away frequently and you are not with child, there is no one to blame but himself." Senja laughed softly and squeezed me in a side hug. I felt a little better, but there was something else weighing me down.

"What about Henry?" The words rushed from my mind and out of my mouth before I could stop myself. "What do I do about him? He hasn't done anything outwardly antagonistic toward Lohikärra, and while I don't know if I fully trust him like I did in Fargo, I still don't want to burn bridges in case this is an actual peace mission. I want peace." My voice cracked and went higher. "That's literally all I want!" I started sobbing again and curled into my lap so my dress would muffle my cries. Senja stroked my back as if to comfort me.

"The situations with Henry is an interesting one. He certainly isn't what he seems to be, but you are right. You have to balance between not alienating him and the possibility of peace, and not alienating your advisors."

"I seem to be doing both at the same time." My voice was muffled by my dress as I sank deeper into it.

"What?"

Wiping the tears and snot from my face, I sat up. "I seem to be alienating everyone." I took a deep breath to try and calm myself. "Not long before Henry arrived, I had a dream. It was about him. But it wasn't. Like, I was remembering my childhood, but the Henry in my dream wasn't the Henry I remembered. He seemed different."

"Do you think your dream was a warning?"

I shrugged. "Maybe. But sometimes my dreams are just that. Dreams. And other times it's me getting tossed into another realm or something." I sighed. "Do the dragons hate me?" It felt like a stupid question, but given that everyone else seemed to hate or distrust me, I figured I'd check all my bases.

I expected Senja to be solemn, but instead she laughed and squeezed me tight again. "Do you think Rhaegos would hide whether she was mad at you or not?" A little puff of laughter tickled the back of my mind and I smiled. Rhaegos didn't seem like the type of dragon to hide her feelings. Ever.

"I guess not. No."

"Exactly. The dragons aren't angry with you. You're trying your best and *we* want to help you. We want to help you and Haldrek, even if there are forces within the palace who want to see you fail."

I groaned and leaned into Senja's shoulder. She didn't stiffen up or anything, so I assumed it was fine. It seemed like the right thing to do. As she wrapped her arm around me, she asked, "Has Rhaegos given you her thoughts on Henry?"

"Not explicitly, but I'm pretty sure she doesn't trust him. She's told me that she knew Henry's mother better than Henry, so I don't know." Another puff of something tickled my mind, and I sensed it was approval or agreement from Rhaegos.

"If Rhaegos doesn't trust the Henry who is here in the palace, then may I give some advice? Be cautious around him. I can tell that he's not what he seems, but whenever I've been around him, I can't sense what is beneath the surface."

I nodded, still anxious about what to do. Senja gave me another squeeze and stood up.

"I need to go check on some things right now, but if you still need help, I'll be around. Just remember that the dragons are proud of what you are doing to heal and reform Lohikärra. Even if the people here can't see the wisdom in your actions yet."

She left the drevké and I stayed, not quite wanting to face anyone again. Knowing I hadn't pissed off the dragons made me feel better. But my chest was still heavy from the other insults that had been hurled at me. Kamira and her cronies knew exactly where to hit in order to hurt me. While I knew some of the jabs were just to get a reaction out of me, others pricked at my mind and conscience, like letting Henry roam around freely.

There wasn't anything he could do in the public spaces though, right?

Chapter Sixteen

That night, I had my evening meal alone. Usually there would be some servants or guards around, but I'd asked for solitude this time. They'd humored me, but I could still hear footsteps rustling around outside of the antechamber. While I wasn't completely alone, I'd take what I could get.

The meal was delicious. It always was. But my appetite was almost nonexistent. After a few bites of beef and vegetables, I pushed the plate away and walked over to the small nook where I could rest and watch a sliver of the world outside. It was already dark, but I could see light from various homes and buildings down below. The sound of voices and murmurs came to me softly, but I couldn't tell if they were from the city below or if I was hearing people in other parts of the palace.

My mind returned to a memory of sitting here almost a year ago. Last November. Watching the celebrations and looking forward to the future. Now as summer had faded into fall, I wondered where we'd all be next November. Would there be celebrations? Or more war? Would Haldrek and I be here together? Or somewhere else? A brisk, cold breeze flew through the window and I hid my face from it.

A knock on the door made me look up and I turned to see Henry poking his head inside. In a moment, my insides turned as cold as the wind outside.

"What are you doing up here?" I stood, not at all comfortable with this surprise. Henry hadn't expressly been forbidden from coming up here. Even so, the quarters I shared with Haldrek were far enough removed from the public areas of the palace that Henry couldn't have just wandered up here without someone stopping him. "Where are your guards?"

Henry's face fell. "Is that any way to treat a friend? I've been trying to find you and you've been ignoring me."

"I have been busy dealing with stuff as High Queen." I'd also been in the public areas of the palace for most of the day, even with hiding in the drevké. If he had been trying to find me, he could have earlier. "If you think I've been ignoring you, you're mistaken. But I asked you a question. What are you doing up here and where are your guards?"

"Technically, that's two questions. But I'm up here trying to find you. I wanted to talk about a possible peace agreement. And my guards are in the hallway. There are many who would love for the war between Lohikärra and the Norycian empire to continue, so I thought it wise that we have this conversation in private."

"No." I walked over to him, fury fueling each step and gestured to the door. "We talk in the hallway. There is plenty of privacy there. This isn't a public space and I already have enough gossip going on about me. I don't need more."

Henry's expression softened. "What kinds of things are they saying? Obviously they are untrue, but you're my friend and I'd hate to see you being hurt by baseless accusations."

"It's nothing that concerns you. Just stuff I have to deal with as High Queen." I blinked back some tears, whether they were from sadness or anger, I had no idea. Gesturing to the door, I waited for him.

"Ina." His expression grew sadder as he reached out for me, his fingers grazing my arm. "You know little of court politics, and there are many who would see you fail. I don't want that for you. I want you to succeed as High Queen."

I pulled my arm away from him. "I am doing my best. But you being here, in mine and Haldrek's private quarters, does nothing but stir up more gossip. I'm fully aware that people want me to fail. But I refuse to give them any more ammunition."

"Ammunition?" He genuinely looked confused, but I was too angry to care. I pointed toward the steps and back to the hall.

"Yes, ammunition. You know what ammunition is. I've been doing everything I can to rebuild Lohikärra and help the victims of this long and exhausting war. But it's not good enough. So I have to do more. I have to make sure I don't look like I'm doing anything inappropriate, because even if my actions are innocent, there will always be some one who will twist it to make me look bad."

"I'm just trying to help. Like I've said before, you are a kind, amazing, and intelligent High Queen. The High King is lucky to have you. Any man would. But maybe you need to do some things without him. Perhaps if you took charge of this, of our negotiations, and let him know what I have to offer before he returns, this peace treaty will come along quicker." He reached out to stroke my cheek and I pushed his hand away.

"Stop. Don't touch me. I know you want to help me, Henry. I really do. But this is not the way to do it." I was tired, physically, emotionally, and mentally, and I struggled as I tried to get him to leave as diplomatically as I could.

"Then how? How can I help you?" He relaxed his shoulders and stared at me, as if searching for something.

I held his gaze. "Listen to what I say and leave these quarters. When Haldrek returns, the three of us will discuss peace negotiations."

He stayed watching me for a moment before nodding his head. "As you wish, Ina." He leaned in and closed his eyes as I turned my head to the side and moved toward the door. In a moment, his lips were on my cheek. I spun around and shoved him back. He stumbled back a few steps before catching himself.

"What the hell was that?" My voice boomed louder than even I imagined I was capable of.

"I... I was trying to apologize and accept your demand. Is a kiss too much? Between friends?"

"Yes! First of all, I'm married. The only person I'm kissing is my husband. Haldrek. Second off, you have *never* been interested in kissing girls. I'm pretty sure Alex was the only person you've ever been interested in kissing."

"She was a wonderful person, but—"

"*She?* Unless something changed after I left Fargo, Alex was always *Alexander.* Not *Alexandra* or *Alexandria*. You've *never* been interested in girls like that."

He stood there, wide-eyed and slack jawed, not moving, so I grabbed his arm and pulled him into the staircase and down to the hallway. Outside, all three of the guards I'd assigned him were standing around or leaning against a wall. They jumped up as soon as they saw me.

"What is the meaning of this? I said explicitly that Henry was to only be allowed access to the public areas of the castle, and that he was to be under guard at all times."

Before they could say anything, Henry pulled his arm out of my grip.

"You are being ridiculous, Ina. I am trying to help you. I want to bring peace to Lohikärra just as much as you do. Is this how you treat all envoys for peace? Is that why Lohikärra is constantly at war?"

I spun around to face him. "Shut up. What you did in there had *nothing* to do with peace treaties or negotiations. That was pure manipulation and I will *not* be manipulated."

He stood there stunned, and as he opened his mouth, I turned back to the guards.

"Henry is to be returned to the dungeons at once. He is not to be let out until the High King returns and negotiations can begin. Do you understand?"

The guards nodded, looking sheepish and not saying a word. I stepped aside as they grabbed him by both wrists and pushed him forward.

Henry twisted in their grip as he passed me. "Is this how you treat old friends?"

I glared at him, unflinching. "I could ask you the same thing." Not wanting to deal with this any longer, I marched back into my private quarters as the guards pulled him away.

I returned to the antechamber to find one of the servants taking my meal away. She stopped, staring at me wide-eyed.

A hint of fear colored her tone. "I assumed you were done, my queen. Do you want me to keep this out?"

I shook my head and sighed. "No, I'm no longer hungry. I just want to get ready for bed."

She nodded and continued cleaning up as I made my way into the bedchamber. Instead of curling up in bed, however, I stood in front of the wash basin and splashed ice cold water on my face. It stung and I gasped as it hit me. Grabbing a nearby piece of cloth, I wiped my face, scrubbing my cheek extra hard where Henry had tried to kiss me. I still felt disgusting and imagined a mark on my face where his lips had landed.

How dare he? What in the world was he thinking? This wasn't the Henry I knew. Not by a long shot. Rhaegos's words about the 'correct Henry' stuck in my head. If this wasn't the correct Henry, then who the hell was in the palace pretending to be him?

Sitting down on a nearby chair, I pulled out my pendant and debated who to call. Haldrek should know, but he'd have questions about why Henry was out of the dungeons in the first place. While I could tell him about Kamira's interference, he'd ask why I hadn't put Henry back in the dungeons afterwards. Which was a legitimate question and one I didn't know if I had a valid answer to.

Mattie, on the other hand, might know more about the magic being used. If this person was pretending to be Henry, that had to be pretty strong magic, right? And Mattie knew the 'correct Henry.' I felt like I was going crazy, being gaslit again, and I hated it. I hated not being able to trust one of my childhood best friends.

Pushing those thoughts out of my mind, I opened my pendant and stared at the number in it. Twenty-seven. It was almost full, but I'd leveled up a lot since arriving in Lohikärra. Yet I still felt like a beginner who was going to get their butt kicked every time they rounded a corner.

"Mattie Gunvald, Mirratoft."

The inky blackness began to ripple and then disappeared. The light on the other side was dim and I heard the bed strings creak. Had I interrupted something? My throat tightened with embarrassment at the idea and I started hating myself for a split second.

"You there, Ina?" Mattie's face lit up as she moved to another spot with better lighting.

"Yeah. Did I interrupt you? If I did, I'm sorry."

Mattie shook her head. "I was just resting. Llamryl is checking on a few things before he comes to bed." She yawned. "Geirny was fussy today. I'm worn out, even with the nursemaids' help. What's going on?"

"I have no idea what's going on." I groaned. "Today has been full of a bunch of messed up drama and I have no idea how to deal with it." Tears welled up in my eyes as I choked back a sob. "I'm sorry. I know you're super busy with being a thegn and being a mom and here I am, not being able to deal with my own shit."

Mattie frowned. "What happened today? Both of us have gone through some pretty crazy changes in the last few months. It's okay to feel overwhelmed."

I stared at her, wondering how she was staying so calm. She was right, but she seemed to being dealing with her crazy changes much better than I was. Even though I knew she meant well, I still felt like a blubbering idiot. She shrugged as she shifted the pendant to bring more light into it. "I've been having some heart-to-hearts with a few of the dragons here. They're really good therapists, if you ask them nicely."

That made me laugh. Not that I didn't believe her, it was true: but the thought of having a dragon for a therapist was amusing. For all of their vagaries sometimes, Rhaegos and Senja had been more than happy to play therapist with me. "You think it's because they've been around for so long?"

Mattie nodded. "I'm sure human drama is minuscule compared to the stuff they deal with. But you're ignoring my question. What happened today? I want to know what's going on."

"First, I had a lousy meeting with the stupid advisors and hersirs. I tried to explain everything that was going on, including the good news about Haldrek, but they were more curious about Henry, and the Blodnar rebuilding the city, and they were spreading all sorts of gossip. Ragnhild was losing her shit over water and wood, Kamira insinuated I was cheating on Haldrek, and Lady Drifa all but told me Haldrek would eventually leave me for another woman because I'm unable to have children."

Mattie gaped, eyes wide, and then shook her head as she grumbled. "I told Haldrek that having people from the thegn lands who didn't support him would be trouble. They're just working to undermine the two of you. I'm sure those people are poisoning the minds of those who would otherwise support you two."

"Technically Ragnhild and Kamira are hersirs from thegns who have always supported Haldrek. But you're right." I sighed. "I ended up hiding in one of the smaller drevkés here. Senja talked to me, which helped, but I've still felt like garbage because of all the gossip and the fact that I still don't know who forged my signature on that one document. My guess is either Kamira or Thoreg—the advisor who hates me—but I can't go accusing them of that, especially not now."

"Have you tried investigating the forgery at all?"

I nodded. "Haldrek's spymaster, Egil said he would look into it, but I haven't heard anything in the last few weeks, which worries me. There haven't been any other documents. It was just that one, but still."

"Forging or trying to forge your signature is a serious issue." Mattie paused to pop a piece of bread in her mouth.

"Yeah. Then, icing on top, Henry decided to invite himself into Haldrek's and my antechamber and start acting super weird." I groaned. "My gut's telling me that he's not the correct Henry, but if he isn't... then who is he and how the hell did he figure out how to look like Henry and know some of the stuff from Fargo?"

Mattie continued chewing. "Illusion magic is a difficult magic to keep up, at least from what I was reading in the library here. If a magic wielder tries to look like another living person, they either have to be highly skilled and trained, or have some object deeply connected to that person. Like that Isillas spy back in Svartån. He wasn't trying to look like a specific person, just somewhat Hethurin. That wouldn't have been difficult to pull off. But someone making themselves look like Henry? That would be difficult. And you said he was acting super weird when he came into your antechamber?"

I nodded. "He didn't have permission. I always remember Henry being super respectful about that kind of stuff. When I kicked him out, he tried to kiss me. On the lips. I moved out of the way, but still, the Henry I remember would have never done that. He also referred to Alex as a *she*."

Mattie frowned, her eyes growing wide in surprise, as she stopped chewing. "Okay, that definitely sounds like illusion magic then. The only other common reason that I could think of is some kind of possession, but there would be other obvious signs of that. Have you told Haldrek yet?"

"About today? No. He distrusts Henry, rightfully so, and I know he'll ask why Henry was out of the dungeons in the first place."

"Why was he?"

"Because Kamira let him out. Supposedly on my behalf. And at that point I thought it really could have been Henry, so I didn't want to be a jerk and possibly ruin any peace negotiations. The last thing we need to have the Blodnar war renewed because I was being an asshole."

Mattie nodded. "You should probably tell Haldrek that."

Standing up, I went over to the bed where I could wrap myself up in blankets. "I'm afraid he'll probably flip out. He's been stressed lately with everything and I don't want to add to that. I mean, with the gossip and everything, it's going to be a hot mess when he returns anyway."

"But if you give him a heads up, he'll have more time to prepare. We were talking through the pendants yesterday and he mentioned some of the frustrations he's been feeling."

My heart squeezed tight with fear. "With me?"

Mattie shook her head and hesitated. "In general, for the most part. But I know he's worried about how you're holding up in Drattüjert."

That made me feel worse and I groaned, bowing my head in frustration.

"If I may add something, Ina?" A new voice joined the conversation and I looked back up as Llamryl's face came into view.

"I think I can shed some information on maybe how Haldrek is feeling? Just as someone who has dealt with many sisters and female cousins. Oof." He grimaced as Mattie stared at him and I guessed that she had nudged him pointedly in the dim light. "I think his interactions with women have been likely limited to a handful of relations or servants. Being married and having wife is new for him, so he knows how to fight and rule over a land, but women are a different realm of experience altogether."

A frown crossed my face. "He's more familiar with being a bachelor than balancing family and kingdom responsibilities."

Llamryl nodded and I sighed.

"Call him and let him know what's up." Mattie said. "I think he'll appreciate that. Even if he's stressed."

I nodded and let the image in the pendant slip into darkness. Mattie was right. Haldrek needed to know, but I didn't know if I could handle anyone else being disappointed or mad at me today.

With a sigh, I said, "Haldrek Rodreksson."

The pendant rippled once more, but after a moment returned to stillness. Likely because Haldrek was already asleep. Still, it felt intentional, even though I knew it wasn't.

Pulling the curtains of the bed closed, I curled up under the blankets, trying to ignore my heavy heart.

Chapter Seventeen

That night's dreams were a mishmash of emotions and blurriness with nothing sticking in my mind. After only a few minutes, my chest grew warm and I imagined it was Haldrek, laying next to me, his body warmth soothing me as I nestled into his chest hair. The warmth intensified until I realized it wasn't a dream, but my pendant. I rubbed my eyes as I flipped open my pendant.

Haldrek's face stared at me, and though my initial reaction was to smile, his somber expression and the bags under his eyes told me something was wrong. Very wrong. Something had happened.

"Are you all right? What's going on?" Adrenaline woke me further and I sat up, looking for some sign of what time it was. Dim morning light seemed to filter through the curtains of the bed, but I couldn't be sure.

"I'm fine. Tired and pissed off, but fine. Svartån is secure. Hardbein and his cousin are dead and sent to Lyrroth. I also made sure to dispose of their bodies as befits traitors. But, and this is what angers me, my men and I got attacked last night by Lansiranikän warriors in a surprise raid. We were able to fight them off but they were a distraction." He sighed. "Kolfinn escaped and, I'm assuming, is headed back to his father's hall."

"Aren't you all in Svarhestån?" I remembered him mentioning a plan to take a different route back to Drattüjert since Bjorn had announced his loyalty to Rorik.

Haldrek nodded. "We are well within Svarhestån and I've already sent a messenger to both my cousin and the closest gesith. Hrimfax needs to know what Bjorn is doing. If the raiders go through any of the nearby towns, I want them stopped." He took a deep breath and exhaled. "This was essentially a raiding party with the goal of taking back Kolfinn. I feel stupid. Like I should have known better. And angry. These thegns who now side with Rorik were all men I looked up to when I was younger and now—" He scowled.

"I'm sorry, Haldrek. Is there anything you want me to do here in Drattüjert?"

"Add guards to those already watching Kotkel and order them to keep him within his quarters until I return. He is not to be allowed out. With Bjorn's actions, Kotkel is no longer a hersir, but a prisoner of war." Haldrek sighed. "Though... I don't want him to become my enemy like his father. Once all this is settled, I expect he'll become the new Thegn of Lansiranikä."

"Even with everything going on?" Kotkel already seemed bitter about his freedom being restricted. When Haldrek would eventually remove his father from power, I doubted Kotkel would have good feelings toward us. Given his current feelings, I wondered if Kotkel would just continue his father's actions, but with more animosity toward both Haldrek and me.

Haldrek nodded. "He is still the thegn heir of Lansiranikä. Even as High King, the dragons wouldn't let me take that from him. He'd have to do something awful—like Rorik—before they remove their power from him."

I nodded. "I'll get that done as soon as I'm up, then." Taking a moment to get out of bed, I wondered what else was causing Haldrek's somber mood. The attack was obviously an irritant, but there was more. More that was causing him to call me early in the morning.

He rubbed his face and brushed the hair out of it before continuing. "I also received word that Bragidrattür may be under attack soon. Some of my information gatherers have told me that a group of Etelaranikäns and Blodnar who have sworn loyalty to Rorik are heading for the thegn hall there." He exhaled. "I don't know if it's better to head there straight away or if I need to return to Drattüjert." His voice softened as he focused on me. "I miss you. The nights feel longer when you're not by my side."

Tears welled up in my eyes. I missed Haldrek terribly. "Same. I think that's part of why I haven't been sleeping well. I want you by my side again. Everything feels colder now."

The side of his mouth quirked up for a moment. "That could just be the fact that winter is on its way. It was the equinox not long ago. And winter comes quickly here."

I nodded. "I know. Do you think we'll be together on the anniversary of our coronation?"

"I hope so. I didn't like being away on the anniversary of our wedding this year." His expression faded back into exhaustion. "Is Henry, the Blodnar envoy, spy, whoever, still in the dungeons?"

I nodded. "Yes. Last I checked, he was still down there." An uncomfortable weight rolled into my gut as I wondered whether or not to tell him about Henry being free prior to that. It had never come up before in our conversations and with all of the bad news he'd received, I didn't want to sour his mood any more or have him get angry at me.

"Good." He sighed, closing his eyes for a moment. "Now that I think about it, if we're still dealing with your friend or whoever he is, it's probably best if I return to Drattüjert before heading to Bragidrattür. That'll probably be another week or so." Opening his eyes again, he stared at me. "Just keep things calm in Drattüjert for now and when I return, we can come up with a plan, both for Bragidrattür and for *your friend*, Henry."

I nodded, cringing inside at how he said 'your friend.' If I didn't trust Haldrek like I did, I would have worried his tone meant more than just annoyance. "It'll be good to see you in person again. I've missed you and—"

The sound of tent flaps opening interrupted as we heard a loud voice just out of my view. "My king, I have news you need to hear."

Haldrek sighed and nodded. He smiled tiredly at me. "We can finish this conversation later. I should probably hear what's going on."

I nodded, crestfallen, and watched as the pendant went dark again. My number, twenty-seven, was bright and nearly full. I didn't know what was causing it to grow so quickly, but at this point it didn't matter. It didn't give me the excitement I'd felt months ago when I'd first gotten it. My heart constricted, remembering Haldrek's adventures with me in Svartån. It hadn't been that long ago. But now...

Why did everything have to be so hard?

I got up reluctantly, still trying to rub the sleep from my eyes and making a mental list of all the things I needed to do, including confining Kotkel to his quarters. As much as I agreed with Haldrek that we needed to be careful with any of Bjorn's family right now, somehow Kotkel felt like a lesser threat than...pretty much anything at thing point. But maybe I was just being sensitive. Kotkel had argued against his treatment, but only because Henry had been treated better in his eyes. Even if I didn't like it, I could understand his logic.

Yeah, I wasn't looking forward to that conversation.

As I finished my morning meal, footsteps clomping up the stairs broke the near silence. I looked up in confusion, as did my maidservants, who seemed equally surprised. Just as I grabbed my eating knife, the door burst open and Henry tumbled in, quickly jumping to his feet.

"Ina, I found you!"

I gripped the eating knife in my hand, anger coursing through me as soon as I realized what had happened. "What are you doing here? Why are you out of the dungeons? Who let you out?"

Henry's expression darkened for a split second before he took a deep breath and exhaled. "We need to talk about the peace negotiations. *Now*." He looked at the maidservants and with a wave of his hand, gestured for them to leave. Their eyes widened and before I could say a word, they marched out of the room. I gaped for a moment before turning my anger back to Henry.

"Why? Why should I talk to you about anything when you ignore my orders and come barging into my quarters without my permission? This is the last place you're supposed to be. You know that."

"Ina, Norycian forces have joined that necromancer you and the High King are fighting. If you allow me some freedom, I can see that they stop fighting. I know I made a mistake last night. Both of us made mistakes. This is a very stressful time and—"

"You aren't LISTENING!" I shouted as loud as I could, raising my fists above my head for emphasis.

Henry flinched and took a step back. "I don't want to fight. Look, the Norycians accept me as the Emperor's heir. I can stop them. I can send a message to those heading for Bragidrattür and demand their allegiance. I can make them turn around and fight the necromancer. Isn't that what you want?"

"I want to know who let you out of the dungeons." My voice dropped lower and colder than I expected. "Who is undermining *my* authority?"

Henry's expression hardened. "You're not the boss, Ina." He relaxed, then smiled as if thinking of a great idea. "You want to show people that you're worth listening to? That you deserve to be the High Queen? Show them that you can bring peace to Lohikärra. Show them that you are more capable than you currently look right now. I know you, Ina. You are capable of great things. But you keep tripping over yourself. Show Haldrek's advisors just who they're dealing with."

I stared at him, anger flooding my brain until I couldn't think. Lowering my hand holding the knife, I took a deep breath and turned around. Or rather my feet did. For a split second, I felt out of control of my body. Even as I tried to call out for my guards to take Henry away, my mouth felt too heavy to speak. Instead, from the corner of my eye, I saw Henry step up behind me.

"Ina. I know how much you love Haldrek. What would be a better gift for him than peace? Peace between my father's people and my grandfather's people?" Henry's voice grew softer. "It may seem like you're undercutting him by negotiating peace with me, but you aren't. You're helping him. If the Norycian soldiers headed for Bragidrattür suddenly aren't fighting anymore, how much easier will Haldrek's job be?"

He slowly stepped around me and toward the large round table in the center of the room. Pulling a scroll from a hidden pocket on his person, he placed it on the table.

"Be the High Queen Haldrek wants, that Lohikärra wants. I've heard whispers of people calling you the Lady of Lohikärra. I don't know everything about what that title means, but the way I hear them speak it, it is an honorable title. Something every High Queen aspires to and the kind of person stories are written about. Tell me, are you a Lady of Lohikärra? Do you want to be?"

I strode over to the table, knowing that every moment that he spent in here made him more dangerous to me. But the voices of caution struggled to carry on as my head was full of strange visions. Of people bowing to me, of crowds cheering as I faced them, of Kamira groveling at my feet and begging forgiveness. Of Haldrek and I rolling around in bed, happy, and bodies intertwined as a sense of pride emanated from him.

"See? You are capable of so much. You are a queen and a Lady of Lohikärra." Henry's voice was soft, warm and comforting, like it had been as kids. Memories of us playing video games came back to mind and I felt safe listening to his voice. For the first time in a long while, I felt like I could relax. "Sign this, Ina. Sign these peace negotiations and show Haldrek that you are his equal. Become the Lady of Lohikärra you were destined to be."

I looked at the document. It was in two languages. On the top was a script that reminded me of the Latin alphabet, but the words were gibberish. On the bottom was the runic alphabet of Lohikärra, but most to the words were more complex than I was used to. This would be so much easier if Haldrek was here.

Don't sign it.

The voice was soft and distant, but familiar. It made me pause. Where did I know it from?

"Ina, time is of the essence. Sign this peace document and both Lohikärra and Norycium will praise you for being the wise and benevolent High Queen you are. No one will question your place as a Lady of Lohikärra."

Ina, listen to my voice. Focus.

The voice grew louder and the images of people cheering for me faded. I saw war instead. More battles like the one in Heidrunefoss before Haldrek and I were married. More buildings burning. The sense that Haldrek was gone and I was alone. The grief was overwhelming. I gripped the edge of the table with my free hand, trying not to fall to the floor.

"I can't."

"You can't what?" Henry's voice carried a sharp edge to it now. "You need to sign this document if you want Lohikärra to have peace. *Now.*"

"No." The haze from my mind cleared and I looked at the table. My hand was on a feather quill. Where had that come from? Where was the eating knife I'd had before? Something was wrong. Staring at the paper, adrenaline coursed through my body as I recognized Haldrek's signature on the document. Where had *that* come from? Anger fueled the adrenaline and I turned to Henry, realizing there had been some shady magic afoot.

"What the hell is going on?" I slapped the quill off of the table and grabbed the document. "What kind of magic are you using, Henry?" I pointed to Haldrek's signature on the document and stepped toward Henry. "What the hell is *this*? Haldrek hasn't even been here to sign anything. Where did this thing come from in the first place?"

His expression grew pale as he stepped back. "Ina, you need to calm down. This is for the best of both Lohikärra and Norycium. The High King is obviously taking his sweet time returning here to Drattüjert. They always do stuff like this. Drag things out until it's too late and—"

"They who? Who are you talking about? You *forged* my husband's signature!" I took the document in both hands and ripped it over and over until it was in small pieces all over the ground. Black ink seeped from the ripped edges, but I didn't know if that was some kind of dark magic or just ink.

"Ina—"

"I will *NEVER* betray my husband. I will *never* betray Haldrek." My throat turned raw from the screaming, but I continued. "Get out, Henry. Get out of here, now!"

I turned to the see if there was a servant or someone who would grab guards or warriors to confine Henry, but the two of us were now alone in the room. I remembered the maidservants leaving robotically. More trickery on Henry's part.

"You are fool, Ina Svanunge." Henry's tone made me spin around. It was low and ominous. "You should have signed that document. Now you'll be to blame when Lohikärra is destroyed. There is nothing you can do to save this wretched place. You will lose *everything*, you worthless *meertrix*."

I had no idea what he'd just called me and I didn't have time to think as the door to the antechamber creaked open. Spinning around, I watched as Kamira poked her head in.

"My queen—oh, I didn't know you were busy. I can wait." She slipped back out into the staircase before I could say anything.

"Ina, I can't." Henry's voice was louder than ever before and I spun around in horror, knowing what was going to happen next. "Though we once had something, you are a married woman now, and it would be wrong to betray your husband like that."

My eyes widened as I stood there, frozen in place. For a moment, this all felt too surreal. Like I was watching the scene unfold in front of me instead of being in it. Henry walked around me with a smug smirk on his face.

"You son of a —"

He shook his head and continued to smile as he reached the door. Much softer now, he said, "You made your bed, now you will have to lay in it. Alone."

I lunged for him and he slipped out of the room, closing the door between us.

Chapter Eighteen

Throwing the door open, I hurried down the stairs, chasing him into the main hallway. This was not the Henry I knew. Even if it was, all bets were off now.

"STOP RIGHT THERE!" I shouted, pointing at Henry. Everyone in the hallway froze and he turned around, looking amused. My anger grew as I realized that this had likely been a plan between Henry and Kamira.

"You want more of what I gave you before?" He smirked and I fought the desire to punch him in the face. I was much stronger now than I'd ever been in Fargo, but I still doubted I could go toe to toe with Henry.

"Shut up. I want to know what you are planning. You are a two-faced Blodnar bastard. I gave you a chance because of the person I knew as a child, and you betrayed me." Stepping forward, I kept my finger pointed at him. "You never wanted peace between Lohikärra and the Blodnar Empire. You wanted chaos. War. More destruction. I refuse to give that to you."

He laughed. "You are a weak leader, unfit to rule over anyone or anything. Most rulers would do anything in order to get what they wanted. If you wanted peace, you would have done whatever it took to get it."

Kamira cleared her throat and my attention turned back to her as I dropped my hand to my side. A few choice words entered my thoughts as she smirked.

"Perhaps you should keep your lover's spats more private, my queen."

There were a few muffled giggles around me, and I imagined tossing Kamira from the tallest tower in this awful place.

"This isn't a lover's spat, Kamira, though I doubt you'd know what that looks like. You'd have to have someone love you for that to happen." The words were sharp, but I was too angry to be regretful right now. "The only person I love is Haldrek." I pointed at Henry once again. "*He* was a childhood friend," I turned to him, "I was never attracted to. But now he is less than a friend." Kamira's mouth opened in my periphery, and I focused my attention on her. "Don't you dare say word to me. You need to leave. Things always get worse when you're around, and every time Henry has left the dungeons, it's been because of you. In fact, I'm pretty sure you helped him escape this time." The idea of yelling at the dungeon guards flitted through my mind, but I wondered how well that would work.

Kamira's face darkened as redness flushed over it. She opened her mouth once again, only to be interrupted by Henry:

"You're the only one making things worse, Ina. I came here seeking peace between our two kingdoms and you rejected me from the beginning, ordering me be sent to the dungeons not once, but twice. For all of your High Queen's Home and other projects, you seem to care little for peace. Maybe it's you and your husband who are the bloodthirsty warmongers." He paused and smiled as if a thought came to his mind. "That's it. That is your plan after all. You two wish to destroy Lohikärra and build it up into something very different. Something where you two are worshipped instead of the dragons."

I clenched my fists, repulsed by the idea. "Lies! Haldrek would never destroy Lohikärra and neither would I. As for the dragons, we worship them ourselves. They are honestly the only ones I trust in this place, right now. Why would we want people to worship us instead? That's stupid."

He smirked. "I couldn't have said it better myself. You are stupid."

I gaped at how easily he twisted my words. He turned on his heel and began walking away.

"Guards!" My voice came back and I pointed at Henry, hoping my personal guards were still nearby, but willing to take any palace guard's help right now. "Seize him and take him to the dungeons. Put him somewhere where he can't be retrieved. He is not to be released until either I or the High King personally request it. Understood?"

A couple of guards rushed from behind me and grabbed Henry. They restrained him as he tried to shrug off their grip. Instead, they dragged him away and out of sight.

I turned back to Kamira and glared at her. "I don't know what shady shit you're up to, but I will figure out what in Lyrroth you are doing. Other than Henry, you are the last person I trust in this place."

She glared back at me. "That's fine. I can handle one *unimportant* person not trusting me. The rest of the palace, though? They trust me more than they'll ever trust you." She spun around and hurried off, leaving me with a handful of onlookers as I rushed out of the hallway myself.

Letting my anger push me forward, I left the palace and made my way to the outer walls of the city. If Henry, or whoever I'd just dealt with, was going to play dirty, then I had no issue making him into the villain he already was. Just as the Blodnar had been doing every day since Henry or his imposter had arrived, they were hauling water, chopping wood and dealing with various menial tasks. But now, instead of seeing begrudging helpers, I saw potential threats.

Part of me wanted to be sympathetic. But Henry had shown himself to be two-faced, so now I couldn't risk any of the Blodnar soldiers also being two-faced.

One of the project leaders—a Lohikärran—came up to me and bowed deeply. "My queen, what brings you here today?"

"I'm here to check on the workers." Taking a moment to regain my composure, I smiled. "Particularly the Blodnar prisoners. Have there been any issues?"

The man shook his head. "Not with the group I've been watching. Dunno about the rest."

"Well, the peace talks with the Blodnar envoy have failed." I took a deep breath as the man looked at me in surprise. "The Blodnar currently working on the wall are to be kicked out of the city and sent back to the Blodnar empire. I have no love for these soldiers and they are to pay for their crimes. Let the people of Lohikärra deal with them how they may." The last sentence felt harsh as it rolled off my tongue, but my anger rolled on with it. Henry had betrayed me and the Blodnar had done awful things to my people. I wanted peace, but not at any cost.

The man nodded, eyes still wide in surprise. He turned to some of the men below and barked out a few orders. "They have been hard workers, but if this is your command, I will do as you say."

I nodded and made my way to several other groups still working on the walls, and delivering the same message. The Blodnar were to be gone as soon as possible. The guilt from my words faded with every step. I needed to protect my people at all costs. The Blodnar weren't my people. As I finished speaking to the leader of the last group, there were hurried footsteps behind me.

"My queen! Your attention, I beg."

I turned around with the few guards who'd kept up with me to see Haldrek's spymaster, Egil hurrying toward our group. When he stopped, he bowed. "My queen, you are quick-footed. I sense a foul mood about you."

"I would be lying if I said I wasn't angry right now. Why do you want my attention?" An inkling of fear slipped into my mind and I pushed it away.

"I believe I know who forged your signature. My men have found proof of one of the High King's advisors, Thoreg Bjornsson, corresponding with a Blodnar man by the name of Gaius Cassius."

"I don't know that name." My anger began to fade and wariness took its place. "Who is Gaius Cassius?"

"He is a man, a young man, who has sworn allegiance to Rorik. But prior to that, we know he lived in the heart of the Blodnar Empire and worked for the emperor's family. In what capacity, we're not sure, but given what we do know, it was likely as some kind of magic wielder."

"Shit. Have your men found him yet?"

Egil shook his head. "We have Thoreg Bjornsson in our hands, and are currently seeing what he knows."

I thought for a moment, taking the time to read Egil's body language. It was different than his usual, aloof self. "Am I in danger?"

"As far as I know, no. But perhaps it would be in your best interest to return to the palace. For your safety."

"In case Gaius Cassius is out here?"

He nodded. "From my knowledge, he had great skill with both blades and magic. If he has not yet made an attempt on your life, I'm sure he will now."

"Because I'm casting out all of the Blodnar soldiers?" I glanced back at where I'd come. Even though I couldn't see anything, I could hear shouting and arguing from the edge of town.

"Word has spread quickly of your falling out with the Blodnar envoy and there are some who are surprised you didn't cast him out earlier. Your anger and determination now also surprises some. Though I think it's because they have underestimated you for so long."

I sighed as I began walking with the man. He kept a fast pace while still surveying our surroundings. "I thought he was still the person I knew as a child." A thought popped into my head. "This Gaius Cassius? You said he has great skill with both blades and magic. Would that include illusion magic?"

Egil shook his head. "Not as far as I am aware." He stopped, scanning the market we were in. "That said, it wouldn't surprise me if he was skilled in such things. In fact, I would be more surprised if he *wasn't* adept at that kind of magic. Perhaps that's what made him all the more elusive."

We started walking again and, instead of cheery city folk and merchants, I saw more anger in the crowds today. Nothing large, but I sensed agitation and I didn't know whether it was just me or if it was something I hadn't seen before.

Once I arrived back at the palace, Egil disappeared. I was glad his men had caught Thoreg, the advisor who'd *likely* been forging my signature. That news just cemented my dislike of him. Though I was sure he wasn't the only one in the palace who'd been communicating with this Gaius Cassius person.

As I walked into the throne room, one of Haldrek's advisors, Gizur Englisson, hurried over, stepping in my path with a smug grin on his face. I groaned to myself. He hadn't been as at odds with me as much as Thoreg, but I remembered his comments from before and wondered what could be causing this grin. He hadn't been very supportive of me or many of my ideas, so I braced for what words would pop out of his mouth.

"My queen! I heard the welcome news! And I might say it isn't a moment too soon."

I did my best to keep my face neutral as my gut clenched. I could only imagine what the 'welcome' news was. For a man who usually deferred to Haldrek to approach me so eagerly only meant one thing.

"Please tell me what welcome news you're talking about swiftly. Today has been a busy day."

He continued to flash a wide grin and I suppressed the desire to smack it off his face.

"Ah, you sent that Blodnar spy who you called friend for so long to the dungeons once and for all, and I've heard word that you've expelled the Blodnar soldiers from our city. While execution would be preferable, so as to keep us from further issues, expulsion is a wise decision as well."

I grimaced in a way that I hoped looked like a smile. "It's good to hear I can get at least one thing right." The sarcasm was a bit strong in my tone as I stepped to the right to move around him.

"My queen, if I may offer an improvement?"

Despite the fact that I didn't think I could care less about his 'improvement,' I forced a smile. If I said no, he'd still find a way to give the improvement, and I'd look like the bad guy.

"You have one minute. I have other business to attend to." With any luck, that would keep him from rambling on and I could escape this conversation.

"Of course, my queen. With your newfound insight into the character of Blodnar peoples, or lack thereof, I would suggest closing down that 'High Queen's Home' that you created. While I'm sure it was done with noble intentions, you now understand that those with even a drop of Blodnar blood cannot be trusted. They are a weakness we cannot afford." He flashed his grin again and it took everything I had not to slap him as his tone became softer, more pleading. "I think doing so would certainly prove your loyalty to Lohikärra and to the High King for good. Something that, I'm sure you know, has been questioned for a long time now."

I scowled, dropping any pretense of pleasantries. "Those who question my loyalty to Lohikärra and my *husband* are fools who don't know *anything* about me, and have likely chosen to know nothing about me. As for the High Queen's Home, most of the people residing within it are Lohikärrans who have been displaced either by roving Blodnar bands or those who have aligned themselves with Rorik. The necromancer. And a true traitor to Lohikärra. If you had visited, you would know that. And, last time I checked, protecting children regardless of their ancestry didn't conflict with having loyalty towards one's kingdom or family."

He stepped back, jaw slack with surprise. Before he could say anything, I continued, "Now, as I said, I have other business to attend to." I twisted around and hurried toward the door at the back of the throne room, hoping to have some relief from *people* at some point today.

Chapter Nineteen

The next few days were miserable. Most members of the court avoided speaking to me or being near me, with the exception of Jaonos, on Mattie's orders, and Sibila, though she was back in her own little world, so I doubted she even knew I was around. The behavior of those I had thought friends would have broken my heart if I didn't feel so angry inside. As much as I wanted to confide in Haldrek, I tried to keep a positive demeanor whenever we talked, knowing he was dealing with much more serious stress than stupid court politics.

The only bright spot was the fact that Henry hadn't escaped the dungeons again, but even that wasn't all that bright. I got the uncomfortable feeling that Kamira had been helping him escape, especially given her general location when he had left the dungeons each time before.

But of course, as always, I had no proof of her interference. Which pissed me off even more.

One cold, dreary day, I left Haldrek's and my quarters, headed for yet another uncomfortable meeting with his advisors, the beginning of another long day of hearing how I was screwing up Drattüjert and Lohikärra. As I stepped into the hallway, Kamira stood only a few feet from the door, arms crossed, with a scowl that could kill plastered across her face.

I wanted to ignore her, but her body language told me she'd make a scene if I did. "What do you want? I have to meet with some of the advisors and I don't have time to spare."

"I want to see how you deal with the fact that you're a faithless whore who doesn't even deserve to be thegn." She spat at my feet and I stepped back in surprise. Apparently she had chosen violence this morning. My guards stepped forward and I put my hand up to stop them. If Kamira chose violence, I wasn't in a mood to stand down.

"What?" Cold anger ran through my whole body as I fought the urge to retaliate with verbal or physical violence of my own. She remained silent, glaring at me instead of answering my question, so I took the initiative and walked past her like she was a spirit in the Realm of Ghosts.

"You are a faithless whore. Everyone knows you were spreading your legs for that Blodnar spy. Did he fill you up full of—"

"Shut your mouth." I spun around quickly, knocking into her and making her stumble. "The only person I've ever slept with is Haldrek, my husband."

Kamira laughed. "And what was that? Once or twice for show? Obviously you did it once, because I know you were with child for a time. At least until nature rejected whatever disgusting spawn you attempted to create."

My stomach clenched as I attempted to fight back tears. Anger and sorrow fought to be the dominant emotion. "You—I was pregnant, but few people knew. How on earth did you know? And why do you insist on calling me barren when you know that I'm not?"

Kamira waved her hands at the hallway around us and I saw a handful of maids and other servants slip out of my view. "You live in a palace full of servants. There's no such thing as privacy. Maybe if you'd grown up in this world, you'd know that." She laughed in derision and continued, "I say you're barren *now*, because there is no way the dragons would ever let you get with child again. Any monstrosity that came from between your legs would only be fit for the dungeons or a ditch somewhere. Otherwise, Lohikärra would have to deal with some half or quarter breed creature as sane as Sibila. Nothing fit to be an aethling."

As I balled up my fist, a voice in my head told me to ignore her. Surprisingly, it wasn't Rhaegos's voice. Kamira was a stupid, spoiled brat who was jealous. Turning back around, I attempted to be the bigger person. She was winning as long as she got a reaction out of me. I tried to imagine what Rhaegos would do if she were in my situation.

I'd tell her to hold her tongue unless she had something useful to say. Even her dragon finds her difficult at times to deal with.

I chuckled as the image of a worn-out dragon dealing with pint sized Kamira throwing a tantrum flooded my mind.

"What are you laughing at, whore? The fact that the abomination inside of you died is a blessing to all of Lohikärra. You would have been a horrible mother as well as queen. The only thing that would have been better is if you had died as well, bleeding out in agony. As it is, the people of Lohikärra would all be better off without your existence."

Rage coursed through me as I stopped moving. A flash of my mother's snarling, scowling face erased the previous image from my mind. Kamira's words were a sucker punch to my gut and a reminder of all the abuse I'd dealt with growing up. Of everything I was trying to escape and move on from.

Forgive me, Rhaegos. I spun around and backhanded Kamira across the face, turning my hand into a fist as it hit her right cheek.

She went flying into the edge of a nearby door and grunted as her head hit it.

"If I were you, I'd hold my tongue until I had something useful to say. But for now, you should probably just shut up and get out of my sight."

She stared at me in disbelief and touched her cheek where I'd hit her. It was already pink from the impact and I figured it would bruise, but I hadn't broken any skin.

"You faithless whore! You pathetic wench! I promise you'll regret doing that." She scrambled to her feet and I was tempted to order her into the dungeons as well, but it might piss off more people. Plus, if she and Henry were in the same spot, even in different cells, that could cause more trouble.

"I promise that if you don't stay away from me, you will get more of what I just gave you. And I won't hold back next time." I paused and then added, "Remember who is the High Queen. No matter how much you hate the idea."

She scowled once more but kept her distance from me as she hurried down the hall. "Just you wait. You think you're invincible, but you're not. I'll see you grovel when *I* become High Queen."

I stared at her in surprise as she hurried away, her hand still on her cheek. Taking a deep breath, I walked the opposite way from her and braced myself for the crap that would inevitably follow.

I didn't have a chance for peace and quiet until well after the evening meal that night. While I would have rather eaten in peace, several advisors asked to share bread with me and I agreed reluctantly. The meal ended up being an extended chastising about something or another that I'd done to mess things up. While I tuned out the exact grievances, the shitty mood stuck with me. Though as miserable as the meal was, I was surprised they weren't yelling at me for how I'd treated Kamira earlier. Not that I regretted any of my actions.

Once I returned to the bedroom, I immediately pulled the bed curtains shut and wrapped myself in a pile of blankets, using the soft furs to muffle my crying. I could hear some of the maids rustling outside the bed, cleaning things up and tending to the fireplace, but otherwise I was left alone. Whether that was good or bad, I didn't know.

As the sobs wracking my body eased, a warmth emanated from my chest. I pulled my pendant out from underneath my dress and popped it open. Haldrek's worn face stared at me in surprise.

"Ina?"

"I'm here." I snuffled. The bed was completely dark and while I should have moved to somewhere with more light, I wasn't in any mood to leave my nest of blankets.

"Are you all right? What's going on?"

"I'm just tired and stressed and done dealing with people. I slapped Kamira today, but she deserved it."

Haldrek raised an eyebrow. "I believe you, but what did she do to deserve that? It takes a lot for you to hit someone outside of training or off the battlefield."

"I feel stupid saying this, but she called me a whore. Accused me of cheating on you with Henry. Then she went on about how she knew I'd been pregnant and she was glad our child died and that I should have died too."

Haldrek grumbled with annoyance. "Hasn't she been saying you can't have any children?"

I nodded, tears coming back with a fury. "She's been spreading stories about how my miscarriage was a sign from the dragons that I shouldn't be allowed to have offspring and that they've made me barren to keep me from producing any more monstrosities."

He grimaced. "I'm sorry, Ina. You shouldn't be dealing with this. I'll deal with her personally when I return to Drattüjert. I'll call on my uncle to send someone to replace her as hersir. What of Henry? Is he still in the dungeons?"

I nodded. "He managed to get out a few days ago, but I sent him back. I think he got out with Kamira's help, because she wasn't too far behind when he tried to get me to sign a peace document behind your back. I'm pretty sure she's involved with the whole signature forging thing too, but I can't prove it. Not unless your spy master finds something."

"*What?*" Haldrek's stare hardened and I stiffened up. "Why didn't you tell me this earlier? When it happened?"

"The signature forging thing? Because your spy master is dealing with it and I can't exactly go pointing fingers at people. One of your advisors, Thoreg Bjornsson, is being held by him because *he's* been writing back and forth with a known Blodnar spy."

Haldrek shook his head and swore in Lohikärran. "That's concerning too. But why didn't you tell me Henry escaped from the dungeons? That he tried to force you to sign some kind of document?"

"Because I dealt with it. I tore up the document and told the guards not to let him out unless you or I personally requested it. You've been dealing with lots of crazy stuff, like Hardbein and Lansiranikä, Bragidrattür, and all that. I didn't think you needed more stuff to worry about. Especially stupid palace politics." I gasped in frustration. "I'm trying to do my best! By you, by your advisors, by the people of Drattüjert and Lohikärra, and it feels like it's not good enough. Like it's never good enough!"

"But Henry escaping and trying to get you to sign a peace treaty is more than just palace politics." Haldrek sighed, then groaned. "I'm sorry you've had to deal with all of this while I was away, but at least now you know Henry can't be trusted."

The comment stung, and I felt like a child being called stupid once again. Yes, Henry was a problem, but so were Kamira and some of the other advisors. There were *Lohikärrans* here who couldn't be trusted. Kotkel's father had actively supported attacks on both Haldrek and myself, and Kamira was doing everything she could to torment and undermine me. It wasn't just Henry. My tears stopped and anger bubbled up inside me.

"The Henry I knew growing up wasn't like this person at all. Rhaegos told me that there was more than one Henry running around. So don't act like I'm some idiot," I snapped, instantly regretting my tone.

Haldrek looked up at me through the pendant, his eyes wide with surprise. "Do you think the Henry you've been dealing with is the real one?"

I grimaced, though I knew Haldrek couldn't see me. "After everything that's happened, I don't know anymore. But when he first arrived, he had a picture with him. Of me, Mattie, another friend Alex, and the Henry we knew. A picture that I'm pretty sure only Mattie and Henry had a copy of. Mine got destroyed by Robert. So I thought it was Henry. The one I knew. It's not like he's the first person from Fargo to be tossed here. But between his actions, and Rhaegos's reactions to him, my gut keeps telling me something is off." I laughed bitterly. "Just... I don't have any solid proof, only gut feelings and a few vague comments Rhaegos has made."

Haldrek nodded. "I understand." His expression was grim, making me wonder if he really did believe me, or if he was just trying to keep the peace between us. Doubts began to creep into my mind. Had I really messed things up? Would he still love me after this debacle? Or would I be cast off like some mistake?

"I'm sorry, Haldrek. I'm really trying, I promise."

"It's fine. My men and I are a day's ride from Drattüjert. We can deal with all of this when I return." He paused and closed his eyes, looking exhausted with dark circles under them. "I love you, Ina. And I miss you. One more day, and we'll be able to figure this all out."

Guilt wracked my body as I wondered how much of those phrases were real anymore, or if he was just tolerating me now. The idea broke my heart. I still loved him with my everything, but I hadn't done anything to make his life easier.

"I love you too, Haldrek. I wish you were here."

A small smile crossed his lips, then disappeared. He opened his eyes wearily. "One more day. I need to go to sleep now." A soft laugh escaped his lips. "I'm dozing off as we speak."

I tried to keep my voice more upbeat. "Sleep well, my love."

"You too. Good night, Ina." And with that the pendant went dark.

I closed mine, and sensing I was alone in the room, at least for the moment, I cried myself to sleep once more.

Chapter Twenty

The next day, I was able to find some time to privately look over some of the documents and reports detailing how Drattüjert and the surrounding areas had been recovering. I wanted to have some good news for Haldrek when he returned. Proof that not all of my time had been consumed with petty palace drama and botched diplomacy. And that despite some setbacks, we were actually helping Lohikärra recover from the decades-long war. With Jaonos at my side helping me translate some of the documents, I made good headway through the information. Drattüjert, according to the documents, was nearly back to what it had been prior to the battle that had killed the last High King and his family. Heidrunefoss had also been recovering, with a better harvest this year than last.

As my stomach grumbled for lunch, I turned to Jaonos with a smile. "I think Haldrek will be happy to know at least some things are going well in Lohikärra."

Jaonos smiled as well. "Agreed, my queen. Word around the city has it that this year's markets were bustling more than they have in a long time. A good omen for sure." His stomach grumbled as well and I laughed.

"Go ahead and take a break. I'm going to tidy up some of these documents and grab some food myself."

Jaonos bowed and left the room. Despite my somber conversation with Haldrek last night, my heart had been light when I woke up, knowing he was close and on his way home. I let myself think about our reunion, even if it was for a brief time, before he headed out to Bragidrattür. While I missed Haldrek every day and night, I'd been craving his *physical* presence more for the past few days. The thought of his body next to mine brought a smile to my face.

A knock at the door broke my reverie and I looked up. Gizur, the advisor from before, stood at the door, face pale and stricken with worry. Immediately, my mind jumped to the worst case scenario. Had something happened to Haldrek and his men?

"What's going on? You look ill."

He waved away my concern. "Not ill, my queen, but ill-informed, I hope. I heard word that you assaulted Lady Kamira yesterday. She has been wrathful this morning, causing disruptions everywhere she has gone."

Was that what this was about? Kamira was throwing a tantrum and Gizur was acting like we were being attacked by our enemies.

"Considering how she assaulted me yesterday, I'd call it self-defense." I turned back to the documents, signaling that the discussion was closed, but knowing that Gizur would likely ignore it.

"My queen, I saw the grisly, bloody bruise on her face myself. You do not seem to be injured, so I wonder how badly she assaulted you?"

Was he seriously defending Kamira? I turned back to him. "Not all injuries are physical, Gizur. Nor am I naked right now," I gestured to the many layers that made up my winter wardrobe, "as you can well see. Just because I do not look injured doesn't mean I'm not."

"That is true. Have you seen a healer then?"

"I have. They treated my injuries and gave me a salve to help the healing," I lied. What did it matter if I'd seen a healer or not? I doubted Gizur actually cared. He was more likely trying to wear me down or get me to admit to something he could then condemn.

"That is good to hear. Either way I think it would be in the best interest of the court, if you apologized to Lady Kamira for striking her. In this time of tension, a true Lady of Lohikärra would advocate for peace." He hesitated. "Starting with herself."

A wave of sickness and irritation washed over me as my hands grew cold. Was he actually serious? I stared at him in disbelief. He stood there expectantly, as if I were going to agree with him.

"Absolutely *not*! I refused to apologize to her for defending myself. By that same logic, you would say Lohikärrans should apologize to the Blodnar for defending themselves. That is absolutely ridiculous. No. I am not apologizing to Kamira for *anything*. She is a grown up. She needs to stop having temper tantrums because someone refuses to cower to her bullying. *I* refuse to cower to her bullying and I refuse to let her treat me badly just because she isn't getting her way."

He sighed, as if dealing with a stubborn child, and I scowled, fury welling up inside of me. Couldn't I have one day without someone nagging or belittling me? I was so done with this bullshit. It infuriated me that everyone in the court seemed to be taking Kamira's side when she was the nasty one.

"Honestly, I didn't think I'd have to tell you this. You *should* already know your place by now."

"My place?" His comment stunned me for a moment before I pushed through the disbelief. "Last time I checked, I knew my place. It's next to Haldrek. And before you say *anything* about the dragons, they have accepted me as the High Queen to Haldrek's High King. Otherwise they wouldn't have done what they did at the coronation. Unless you somehow think they were wrong."

"I'm not talking about the dragons. They are infinitely wise and never wrong. While I don't doubt their wisdom, I know their actions aren't always straightforward, and perhaps your acceptance by them is more of a cautionary tale."

"*What?*" It took all my self-control not to backhand Gizur like I did Kamira. He certainly deserved it.

"With all due respect, my queen, you are a half-breed. Your father, as loyal as he was to Lohikärra, sowed his seed outside of Lohikärra, then accepted you as his heir. There is no telling what kind of people your mother came from, and certainly you are aware that some believe she was a sorceress who cast illusion magic upon him. Though you may look like him, there is some credible doubt that you are even his. Either way, Lady Kamira is your better because she can actually prove where her ancestors came from. They are well-known for their heroics and feats on behalf of Lohikärra."

I stood there, stunned and enraged, no words coming from my mouth even as every single cuss word flew through my mind directed at him.

"Have the dragons bound your tongue to keep you from casting more lies? Good. Perhaps that's why you and the Blodnar spy got along so well. You're both used to casting vile illusions on people. Regardless, you are the High Queen and must be tolerated as such for the time being. That being the case, I would highly encourage you to apologize to Lady Kamira. The sooner the better. Maybe then she'll be more forgiving."

Then tension in my jaw released and I snapped, "There's no way in Lyrroth I'm going to apologize to an inbred, spoiled brat like her. She's no one's better just because of whose legs she popped out from between or because her parents are likely cousins, if not brother and sister."

Gizur gaped, his face reddening. He moved his jaw, but before any words could come out, a warrior came rushing into the room and past him, bowing before me on one knee.

"My queen, urgent news from the eastern gate. There is a large army of Blodnar soldiers moving away from the city, but they are causing mayhem in their wake."

"What?" I gestured for him to get up and rushed from the room. Making my way out of the palace, I saw a commotion just outside the eastern gate. From where I stood, it looked like there were men fighting on either side of the gate, but that the battle was being pushed out and farther away.

Haldrek's spymaster Egil came running up to me and stopped with a slight bow.

"My queen. It seems that some of the Blodnar who had been working on the walls tried to attack, but they're both being pushed back by our warriors and their own."

"What?" I'd expected our people to fight back obviously, but the Blodnar were pushing back their own soldiers? My gut told me something was seriously wrong.

"See, it's always a bad idea to deal with half-breeds and outsiders," Gizur sneered. I hadn't realized he had followed me.

"Shut up." Egil and I spoke at the same time, our words both directed at Gizur. I wanted to add a comment about Gizur licking Kamira's butt, given how he already had a brown nose, but even I thought that was too crude for the moment.

Instead I turned my focus back to Haldrek's master spy. "How many men do you think are in the group? Why do you think some of their soldiers are pushing them back?"

"Obviously it's because we have the superior forces." Gizur huffed. I gestured behind me towards the doors without looking and he grunted as a couple guards dragged him back into the palace.

Egil glanced back and smirked. "Thank you. As to your questions, I believe there are one to two hundred men total. It is the entirety of the Blodnar who were in our dungeons and then working on the walls. Why are their own soldiers pushing them back? I don't know, but I doubt it's for any reason beneficial to us." He sighed. "The High King returns soon, doesn't he?"

I nodded. "Tomorrow morning at the earliest."

"Very well. I'll continued to have my men watch what is going on and I'll have a report for him by then." He glanced at my pendant. "If you have a chance to speak to the High King before tomorrow, please inform him of what I've told you."

I nodded and he hurried away without a second glance. I closed my eyes and took a deep breath, trying to close out the sights and sounds around me.

All I wanted was a day of peace.

I wasn't able to sleep much that night and woke early. Haldrek confirmed he would be returning to the city by midday, so I took my lack of sleep as time to prepare and hope that nothing would ruin today or our reunion.

Rhaegos, please help me. And please let today go smoothly. I hoped I didn't sound too demanding or like I was begging. I just didn't know if I could take any more stress.

You will survive today. I cannot change others' actions, but I can strengthen you in your moments of weakness.

I stopped as she spoke. Her words should have been comforting, but after everything thus far, they felt more ominous. Rhaegos laughed softly in my mind.

You aren't out of the woods yet, but you have travelled far more terrifying forests than the one you are currently in.

That made me grumble, though I felt a little relief. "I don't feel like I've dealt with more terrifying forests before." Glancing in the mirror as one of my maidservants helped braid and decorate my hair for the day, I wondered if they thought I was as crazy as the rest of the court.

Don't worry. Speaking to one's dragon kin is far more common here than anywhere else. Now go. I sense Haldrek and Teminth at the city gates.

I gasped. "He's early!" The maid stepped back as I rushed out of the room, giddiness replacing my previous worries.

By the time I made it to the front doors of the palace, Haldrek was already entering them. As soon as I saw him, I stopped, my eyes welling up with tears. He smiled and I rushed into his arms, squeezing him as tight as I could despite his armor, not realizing how much I'd missed him. How much I'd *wanted* him.

"You're happy." He laughed, kissing me on the cheek.

"You're home." I twisted my head to the side so that our mouths could meet. The taste of camp kavasir was still on his lips and it reminded me of better times.

After a few moments of kissing, he pulled away with a gasp. Softly, he asked, "Do we need to finish this in our quarters?"

I laughed. The thought of us together again, in bed, excited me. "Yes. As soon as possible."

One more hearty kiss and he turned me around, so we were side by side. "What about Henry?"

"A few more hours in the dungeons won't hurt him. We can deal with him later. Or your spymaster can." It felt weird saying that for a moment, until I forced myself to remember that the person I'd been dealing with likely *wasn't* my friend, but an imposter. I had no love for an imposter.

Haldrek nodded. "Our advisors will likely want to see me—us—and I'll have to leave for Bragidrattür tomorrow, but before I leave..." He grinned.

I nodded and opened my mouth to respond as footsteps rushed toward us, echoing in the hall. Kamira curtsied deeply in front of us. Her left cheek was heavily bandaged and some of them looked like they had dried blood on them. Her temple was puffy as well, with mottled bruising around her left eye adding to the redness in it. She looked like the losing side of a street brawl or something. I may have backhanded her, but I hadn't done *that*. And... I frowned. I'd hit her with my *left* hand. That didn't make any sense.

"What happened to you, Kamira?" Haldrek looked between her and me in surprise. A sudden weight dropped into my stomach.

She glanced up meekly at me and then at Haldrek. "I fear I may have incurred the High Queen's wrath."

That stupid, effing bitch.

Haldrek looked at me in surprise. "You said you slapped her, not pummeled her."

"I did slap her. On her *right* cheek. I wasn't wearing any jewelry or armor, either." Inside, my anger already threatened to boil over. Knowing Kamira, this could go badly for me very quickly.

"I distinctly remember you hitting me with your right hand and falling back into a wall. But that is not why I came to find you two. I know I spoke poorly to you and your wrath is understandable. But now there is another issue."

"What's going on?" Haldrek's tone was low and dangerous. He was angry, but whether at me or at Kamira I couldn't tell.

"I merely wanted to know if the Blodnar spy was still supposed to be in his cell or if he had been moved elsewhere? Perhaps at the High Queen's request? He is no longer in the cell he had been put in and I do remember her saying that he was not to be removed from his cell unless either of yourselves requested it."

"Wait, what? He's gone? What were you doing in the dungeons in the first place?" Panic and anger flooded my brain and I stepped forward. Kamira cowered away from me and I sighed with frustration. "I'm not going to touch you. You're not worth my time right now."

"Answer the High Queen. Why were you in the dungeons?" Haldrek snapped, making Kamira jump away from him.

"I... I was merely trying to help? I know peace is desired and I thought—"

I turned to Haldrek, ignoring Kamira. "He should still be in the palace if his escape was recent."

He nodded and gestured to the guards. "Lock all the palace doors and start searching for this Henry person." Turning to me, he asked, "What does Henry look like?"

I opened my mouth, but hesitated as soon as the realization hit me. They actually looked similar. I always saw Henry as Henry and Haldrek as Haldrek, but hair color, body type, most everything was similar.

"Ina?"

"He looks like he could be your cousin, Haldrek. You two have the same body type, hair, eyes, all that. He was clean shaven when he arrived, but I'm guessing he has facial hair now and his nose is different. It has a bump at the top." I gestured on my own face.

Haldrek sighed. "Fine. So we're searching for someone who looks like the Blodnar version of me?"

I nodded. "We should probably talk to the guards and see when he escaped."

"Wouldn't you remember when you let him out?" Kamira turned to me, her voice soft and questioning.

"*I* never let him out. As far as I'm concerned, he could have stayed in there until Haldrek and I dealt with him. The man in the dungeon was no friend of mine."

Kamira raised her eyes in surprise as Haldrek walked between us and grabbed me by the arm.

"Let's go down to the dungeons." His grip and the tone of his voice both hurt. I pulled my arm out of his hand and hurried in front of him.

As soon as we got down to the dungeons, the sound of voices arguing led us to where they had placed Henry. It was a smaller, dirtier cell then I expected. The only door was a hole in the floor, perhaps four or five feet wide.

"Was this where you put him, Ina?" Haldrek's voice made me step back.

"I told the guards to put him in a place where only you or I could release him."

The guards who had been standing around were now kneeling as they faced Haldrek.

"High King, there was a lady bearing the High Queen's runes and saying that we must let the prisoner out or else."

"What runes?" I snapped.

"It was on a piece of paper, my queen." One of the men scrounged around in his clothing for a pocket and pulled out a grimy piece of torn paper. It had runes on it, but it wasn't anything I'd signed. Haldrek stepped up behind me, his breath on my neck. In any other circumstances, I would have appreciated the closeness.

"Can you two read?" Haldrek looked up and the two men shook their heads.

"The lady just told us we shouldn't question the High Queen's orders."

"We've been tricked." I hissed bitterly. "Haldrek, whose runes are these? You know I don't sign anything with runes. Someone forged—or tried to forge—my name again."

"These runes aren't anyone's signature. It's..." He sighed. "It's a common rune for whore."

The information made me sick. I looked at the men. "A lady gave you this and told you it was my signature? What did she look like?"

One of the men looked up at me. "She was young, like you. Dressed like a commoner, but held herself tall, like she was important. Couldn't see her face though. Too dark for that and she had clothing for the prisoner too."

"Damn it." Haldrek growled and began walking away.

"Haldrek—"

He stopped and looked at me. Even in the dim light, I could sense his anger. "Not now, Ina. We're running out of time, I just returned home and now I need to clean up another mess."

I stood there stunned, the weight of guilt hitting me like a bag of rocks, as he turned around and started walking away.

Chapter Twenty-One

I rushed after him, anger and fear fueling me. Anger at the fact that he was blaming me and fear that I'd messed up more than I even knew. The overwhelming desire to find 'Henry' and fix things myself fought with the overwhelming desire to beg for Haldrek's forgiveness. I hated both options and everything that had led up to this, including Kamira. Where had she gone? As soon as Haldrek and I'd gone into the dungeons, she had disappeared. Likely to help the imposter.

As soon as we entered the throne room, Gizur came striding up to Haldrek, only pausing for a second to throw me a dirty look.

"High King, it is an honor to see you back safe—"

"Not now!" Haldrek boomed as he kept walking.

Gizur stepped back, eyes wide in surprise. I passed him myself with my own scowl.

Stepping into the inner garden room behind the throne room, I caught up to Haldrek and grabbed his arm. Much to my surprise, he didn't shrug it off. He kept walking, making me hurry to keep up with him.

"I promise I did not release the Henry from the dungeon. I didn't even know what cell he was in. But Kamira obviously did. I'd bet money she was the woman who gave the guards my supposed orders, knowing they couldn't read."

He kept walking until I stopped him. "I think I know where to find the Henry I've been dealing with."

"Oh really?" Haldrek's snark filled the air and I glared at him.

"Don't. I'm trying to help. The Blodnar left after I kicked them out of the city. Some of them were fighting our warriors, but the rest were moving away. It was strange, but I think I know why they did that. They're headed to Bragidrattür. With the person I thought was Henry as their leader."

"Then why leave while he's in the dungeons?" He turned away from me and I pulled him back.

"Because they knew the people of Drattüjert would be more than happy to fight them if they stayed outside the walls. And if they had someone relaying messages to them from the palace—"

"I highly doubt Kamira is that much of a mastermind."

"I never said it was Kamira. But honestly, it could be." I snapped. "Go talk to Egil, your spymaster. Remember? He found letters from your advisor, Thoreg, communicating with a Blodnar man by the name of Gaius Cassius. It wouldn't surprise me if there were others in this palace who were up to shady stuff."

Haldrek glanced toward the inner garden room where we had come from and down the corridor where we were headed. "This is not the news I needed today." He pulled away and I kept following him.

"It's not the news I've needed during these last few months, but it's what I've dealt with. Look, if the guy I think is pretending to be Henry is leading the Blodnar to Drattüjert to fight and join Rorik's forces, I want to fight him too. He's hurt me as much as he's hurt anyone else and I want my own vengeance."

"No." Haldrek didn't even look back to speak to me and his tone was firm. But I wasn't in a mood to be a doormat to anyone else.

"Why not? I know how to fight. I'm a haldraga. And I care about Lohikärra just as much as you do. I want to ensure its safety just as much as anyone here."

Haldrek stopped as one of the guards ran up to him and bowed. "High King, we're searching the entire palace as we speak and have secured every doorway out of here. If the prisoner is still within the palace, he will be found."

"Good. If you find him, bring him to me immediately." Haldrek glanced over his shoulder at me before turning his attention to the guard. "I want to see who has been causing so much trouble while I've been away."

"Yes, my king."

The guards disappeared and Haldrek turned back to me. The corridor was still too dim to make out the more subtle expressions on his face, but I braced myself for some kind of rebuke. Not because I expected it from Haldrek, but because that had been my experience in the past.

"There are several reasons I don't want you out fighting when I confront this Blodnar bastard. First off, he has a vendetta against you now, since you didn't just go along with his plan. If you two met in battle, I'm afraid he would hurt you—"

"I can protect myself, Haldrek."

He put a finger up and continued. "I would be distracted if I knew he was going after you in battle. I don't need that distraction right now. Second, you are safer here in Drattüjert. No matter what anyone thinks or feels, if something happens to me while fighting, you are the only thing standing between Rorik and the title of High King."

"What about the dragons? You really think they'd allow him to take control of Lohikärra after all of the necromancer and dragon soul shit he's done?"

"I don't. But even if you, me, and Rorik all died and the title of High King went to the next in line, that would still be a lot of upheaval and chaos for Lohikärra. It's not worth it. I don't plan on dying, but if it happens, I want Lohikärra to be ruled by someone I think will rule it well and nobly."

"I think you are the only non-dragon who believes that." Even as I said that, I still wondered. "You do believe I'd rule Lohikärra well and nobly?"

He hesitated. "You'd do better than Rorik." Haldrek's lackluster vote of confidence hurt, and my anger welled up in defense.

I sighed in frustration, trying to will my tears back into my eyes. As difficult as it was for me to see all of Haldrek's expressions, I wasn't sure the darkness would hide my tears.

"Ina." His voice grew softer and for some reason that hurt more. "Let me deal with the Blodnar. I love you and you have many valuable skills, but," he hesitated once more, "this is a place I have more experience in right now, and the ice we are treading on is already very thin."

That's why it hurt more. Because, despite all my best efforts, I had still messed up. Haldrek's life was more difficult because of me. Kamira's accusations and those of the advisors bit at me like horseflies. In this moment, I couldn't think of a thing that I could do to make this situation better. My hurt bubbled up into more anger.

"So if I go fight this Blodnar bastard, you think I'm going to mess things up even further?"

"Ina, that's not what I said. I meant that we're in a difficult situation. The way you can help me best is by staying here. In the palace."

That didn't help me feel better in the slightest. But there was nothing else I could say to convince Haldrek—or anyone else.

"Fine. I'll stay in the palace. And continue to be your incompetent, worthless High Queen." I spun around and walked away as futile tears poured down my face.

The next morning, I found myself in front of the nondescript door that led to the dungeons. Haldrek hadn't been in our quarters when I went to bed and if he'd come in while I was sleeping, he had left before I'd woken up.

Guilt and fear twisted inside my gut, wondering if I'd pushed him away with my anger and attitude yesterday. I'd been angry. So angry at the thought that he wanted me to stay out of the way while he took care of my mess. Even if he tried to reword it to sound nicer, it still hurt. It still stung. So I figured I'd do my own work.

I was almost certain the Henry I had been interacting with was not the real Henry. Certain enough to bet money on it. And I was sure he was working with Kamira. But I need more information.

As I entered the dungeons, I saw a couple of the head guards rolling dice and cleared my throat. They looked up and dropped their dice on the table as I grimaced.

"Where are the guards who were supposed to be guarding the Blodnar spy?"

They stared at each other and then at me.

"I want to talk to them. They have information that's useful to me."

One of the men nodded and got up. "I'll take you to the cell they've been put in."

"They were imprisoned?" I tried not to sound surprised, but failed.

"Of course. You gave them a command and they didn't do it. So now a dangerous Blodnar spy has escaped. They'll be lucky if the High King doesn't execute them personally."

I focused on my feet to keep them moving forward as we went deeper into the dungeons. "How many times has the High King personally executed someone?"

The guard stopped and turned back, looking me over as if trying to calculate his answer. "Your husband, my queen? Only one, so far. A man he said hurt you as a child."

A cold wave of surprise washed over me. He'd killed Robert? Haldrek had never mentioned that to me, and while I knew he was capable of killing—he knew how to fight after all—I'd never thought he'd go as far as to personally kill someone who'd hurt me. The surprise turned to a flash of anxiety as we arrived at the cell of the two former guards. For a brief second, I saw myself in there—like I had been in the dungeon at Svangendom—but instead of Seirye on the other side of the bars, it was Haldrek and Kamira. I brushed the image away quickly, not wanting to ruminate on a future which might never come to pass.

Instead I focused on the two men inside the dungeon. Both were wrapped up in tattered blankets on opposite sides of the cell with maybe a foot between them. The cell itself wasn't much bigger than the one I'd been in when Seirye had captured me. The man on my right looked up and bobbed his head.

"High Queen."

"Good morning." I didn't want to sound like I was buddies with these two men, but I also didn't want to act like an interrogator. "I have a few questions."

The one man nodded while his companion on the left stayed still. Given how cold the dungeon was for me right now with my multiple layers of clothing, I could imagine how cold it was for them. Had the other man died in his sleep? I shook my head. He couldn't have. If he was dead, I would have seen his ghost.

"Were you two the guards for the Blodnar prisoner from the beginning?"

The man on the right stayed silent and averted his eyes. After a moment, his companion grunted. "Yes. This last time was the only time he escaped. That's why we're here."

"No, he escaped at least once more." I counted out the times the imposter had been put in the dungeon. "First when he arrived, second when he entered the High King's and my quarters without permission, and third when he tried to have me sign a forged document."

There was a grunt from the guard next to me and I looked at him. He turned away as I frowned. "The fact that he figured out how to escape a hole in the ground tells me that he's crafty."

The prisoner on the right cleared his throat. "With all due respect, High Queen, you didn't know that about him from your childhood? People don't just become crafty overnight."

"I have—the man you two had been guarding was not my friend. He was pretending, I'm almost certain."

Both men in the cell shuddered involuntarily and the one on the left grumbled, "I hate magic."

I watched them for a moment as a thought popped into my head. "You said he only escaped the last time, and with the help of a mysterious woman. I know Lady Kamira helped him get out the first time. But what about the one in the middle? After I sent him back to the dungeons for walking into the High King's quarters without an invitation?"

"It was the same lady as the first time." The man on the right blurted out. "She said you had had a change of heart or something. Wanting peace and all that. She had a note from you as well."

"Wait, so Lady Kamira released him all three times?"

Both men shook their heads. "Only the first two times. Last time it was a servant woman. Does Lady Kamira have a servant?" The one on the right turned to his companion, "I thought all of the abthanry had servants."

His companion shook his head. "Only the ones with enough coin."

"Enough." I snapped. As far as I was concerned, either Kamira or someone working for her had been releasing the imposter. Which meant she had been undermining me the entire time and had likely helped the man get me in to potentially compromising positions. I looked back at the prisoners. "Thank you for your help. I will speak to the High King on your behalf."

Both men mumbled their gratitude as I hurried out of the dungeon.

Once out of the dungeons, everything felt lighter as I tried to think of where Haldrek might be.

Go to the inner garden. He seeks peace and guidance there.

I followed Rhaegos's instructions and hurried through the corridors until I reached the inner garden. Despite the bright wintry light flowing into the room, there were too many memories of this place to make it very comfortable.

As it was, Kamira's voiced carried throughout the large space and I stopped to listen, hiding behind an evergreen shrub. I could see Haldrek's face as he sat on a small bench. Kamira stood in front of him with her back to me. Why was she here?

"My King, I only bring this information to you because I care. I care about my people, I care about the dragons, and I care about you. Lohikärra is not a place I want to see lose two High Kings in my lifetime."

Haldrek grumbled in annoyance. "If I wanted your opinions, I would ask you for them."

"Am I not one of your advisors? That's what I'm here for."

"You are a hersir. Here to speak on behalf of your grandfather. Not give me unsolicited opinions."

"Would you risk the well-being of your people because of some foreign half-breed? You don't know where her loyalty lies. If you'd been here when the Blodnar spy was running loose, you would have seen how she was throwing herself at him. It was disgusting. She said it was for the sake of peace, but it was obvious what she really wanted. Why do you think she was so amorous when you returned to the palace? She's trying to hide her manipulations."

"Kamira! Silence yourself!" Haldrek's voice boomed and I steeled myself against a flinch. Out of the corner of my eye, I saw a few servants hurry away from where they'd been watching the scene.

Glancing back, I noticed Haldrek now standing up, fury in his eyes as he stared at her, his fists clenched. If Kamira noticed his body language, she ignored it. Instead she put her hand on his upper arm and began stroking it, an action that pissed me off to no end.

"My king, please do not be angry with me." Her voice was softer, more submissive now. "I only wish to see you succeed. The dragons have willed it, and no one should stand in your way. Or make you look the fool."

A few choice swear words, both in English and Lohikärran, crossed my mind. I needed to end this meeting as soon as possible.

"My King, I know you love the Thegn of Svartån—"

"She is my High Queen, Kamira." He shook off her hand and stepped away.

"Apologies, my king." Kamira's voice tightened with a hint of annoyance as she shifted half a step to stay with him. "I know you love your High Queen. But certainly you must be asking yourself if she has made your time as High King easier or more difficult. You have many responsibilities, and it is better if your High Queen helps lift those burdens, not adds to them."

Haldrek sighed. "Ina and I both have much to learn about ruling Lohikärra. Neither of us expected our current situation when we were growing up."

"Yet you were raised to be a thegn. You know what is expected here in Lohikärra. Though her father may be the late Thegn of Svartån, what has she added since her arrival here?" Kamira placed her hand under his arm and tried to pull him toward her.

I'd had enough. Clearing my throat, I rounded the corner and into the clearing they were in. "Haldrek, I was looking for you. I have some information that I think you should hear." I glanced down at Kamira's hand and he shrugged her off.

She crossed her arms under her breasts, pushing them up while staring daggers at me.

"You can go, Kamira. I'd be surprised if you didn't already know what I'm about to tell the High King." I gestured for her to leave in the direction I had come.

"If it's something I already know, then you shouldn't have an issue with me staying." She smirked and pushed her boobs higher as she began tapping her foot. For a moment, she reminded me of my mother, and I resisted the urge to smack her again. As it was, the 'injury' on her left cheek had magically healed overnight and her bandages had shifted to the right cheek.

"Kamira, leave. If my queen desires a private conversation with me, then so be it."

She scowled and stopped tapping her foot. After a quick curtsy to Haldrek, she brushed past me and whispered, "Watch yourself. I'd be a better High Queen than you any day."

Chapter Twenty-Two

As soon as Kamira's footsteps faded out of the inner garden room, I looked back at Haldrek, not knowing where to start. I still felt bad from our argument yesterday, but the fact that Haldrek hadn't been more blunt or direct with Kamira also pissed me off. He hadn't exactly denied her accusations that I was an incompetent High Queen. Nor had he been quick to brush off her physical touch.

Rubbing the back of his neck, he asked, "What information do you have for me?"

"I spoke with the guards who had been in charge of watching Henry while he was in the dungeons. They—"

"So has Egil. He said they didn't admit to letting the Blodnar spy escape. Since they failed at the one job they had, he recommended they be put into the dungeons as prisoners themselves until further notice."

"That's where I found them." My words came out sharp and I tried to soften my voice. "But they didn't let him escape. At least as far as they knew. Each time, someone came, supposedly at my behest, to free him."

Haldrek huffed. "Did they say who? Or was it another mysterious serving woman?"

I glared at him for a moment, annoyed by his attitude. "It was Kamira the first two times. The second time, she had a note, supposedly from me, demanding he be released. As for the third time, they said they thought it was one of her servants. Which... I don't remember her bringing any personal servants."

Haldrek shook his head. "All of the advisors and hersirs are served by the same servants." He sighed and looked in the direction that Kamira had left. "Do you think she paid one of the servants to help the Blodnar man escape?"

"Or she did it herself with a disguise. Honestly, at this point, it wouldn't surprise me."

Haldrek sat back down and exhaled as he rested his head in his hands. His shoulders slouched forward and even without seeing his face, I knew he was stressed. Part of me wanted to comfort him and smooth things over, but I was still angry and hurt from his lack of faith in me.

"I'm sorry." He stood back up and faced me, straightening to his full height. Even though I doubted he'd hurt me, for a moment, our height difference felt larger than it was and I stepped back. "I'm sorry for getting angry at you earlier and for listening to Kamira just now. It's just..." He sighed.

"It's just what? Do you not trust me anymore?" The words were hard to speak and I wanted him to quickly tell me no, but instead he hesitated and looked away.

"I don't know. I *don't* know." He laughed sadly. "I trust you to be a competent thegn and to be a loyal wife. When Kamira said you were throwing yourself at the Blodnar spy, I knew those were lies. You wouldn't do that. That's not *you*. I know your loyalty to Lohikärra. You chose to come back here when given the chance. And your people, you were willing to sacrifice your life when Seirye threatened Svartån. You're like your father in that way. You're loyal to Lohikärra."

"So what don't you trust about me?" My tone was sharper than I wanted to be and immediately, I regretted it.

His expression hardened. "I don't trust your ability to *not* be manipulated." He exhaled. "That sounds awful, but the Blodnar spy was able to make you believe he was here for peace and negotiations and get you to let him out of the dungeons—"

"That was once, and that was because I was trying to play nice with Kamira and be diplomatic." I snapped, interrupting him. "I was trying to be a good High Queen and Lady of Lohikärra. Not burn potential bridges. I put guards around him to make sure he didn't do any shady shit, because I didn't know that he was manipulating me at that point. He hadn't done anything to make me think he was being shady."

"The fact of the matter is that you have a lot to learn to be a competent High Queen." He paused for a moment. "I believe the dragons when they say you will be a Lady of Lohikärra, but I don't see that happening soon."

Anger and humiliation flushed through my body. "What about you? You think you're the perfect High King? You don't think you have stuff to learn?"

"Of course I do!" Haldrek's body language became more animated as his cheeks and forehead reddened. "I have a lot to learn. To be anywhere close to the kind of king my uncle was or his predecessors. But I was raised to be a ruler. I had to learn how to rule from the time I was a child. I was ten when my half-uncle tried to kill me and take my title. You didn't."

"Oh, so it's my fault my father didn't bring me here when I was five? It's my fault that I didn't have the opportunities you had? We've both had to learn how to rule, Haldrek. I've just had to do it a much shorter time with a lot more people trying to kill me. At every corner, I'm fighting, not only with swords, but with words. Half the people here think

I'm worthless because they consider me a half-breed. I love Lohikärra, but it's inhabited by a bunch of fucking, baby-killing, racists."

Haldrek's expression darkened. "Lohikärra isn't perfect, but you're here now and you can't just shove your world's ideas on the people here all at once. You have to understand where they're coming from and what things are important to them. The Blodnar have been trying to erase our culture since I was a small child. They want to destroy the dragons and subjugate Lohikärra. I will be cursed to Lyrroth before I see that happen, especially because of some random friend of yours from Fargo."

I stood there stunned for a moment. This whole time I thought Haldrek had supported me and my endeavors for peace and restoration. His face softened, and he stared down at the floor.

"Ina—"

"No, don't try to apologize," I snapped. "You tolerate me because the dragons told you to. They told you to save me and save Svartån and that you'd be High King, but I'm not your perfect High Queen. I can't even give you an aethling because Rorik interferes and apparently my body is broken." I stared up at him, wanting him to feel the hurt I felt, the anger and frustration I was feeling right now. That I wasn't good enough. I would never be good enough. No matter how hard I tried, I would never succeed. "Tell me the truth. Do you regret marrying me? Do you regret not listening to your uncle and marrying his granddaughter? Because everyone seems to fucking love Kamira, even though she was the one getting Henry or whoever is pretending to be Henry released. But she's from noble blood and she knows her way around the palace and politics and Drattüjert."

"Ina, I don't tolerate you because the dragons told me to. If that was the case, I would have gone back to Mirratoft and done my own thing after you became thegn. If I only tolerated you, I wouldn't have asked you to be part of a romantic alliance with me. I love you. I always have."

I didn't feel very loved. "But do you think Kamira would be a better High Queen than me?"

Haldrek hesitated. "I think she would do better at court politics, yes. Likely because she grew up here and at her grandfather's thegn hall where people are always vying for power. That said, I never wanted her as a High Queen. I have no desire to change who my High Queen is."

"But you think she would be a better High Queen than me?" I wanted him to stop hedging and just tell me one way or another.

"I think there are things you could learn from her, yes, but—"

I spun around, frustration overflowing into tears. This was going nowhere. Why couldn't he just be honest? As I walked away, he grabbed my shoulder and stopped me.

"Ina, listen to me." His tone was more ominous than before, but for some reason I wasn't afraid. "Being High King and High Queen means having more responsibilities and to more people than when we were thegns. We're responsible to a lot more people and a lot more factions than before."

I shrugged out of his grip and spun around to face him. "If that's the case, then you should go take care of Bragidrattür, then go fuck your cousin, because apparently you think she'd be a better High Queen than me, but you're too much of a coward to tell me to my face."

Turning back around, I ran off, trying to find a place where I could cry and soothe my broken heart in peace.

I ran from the inner garden, my chest tight with anger, hurt, sadness, everything. I'd been looking forward to Haldrek's arrival for weeks, and now everything was in shambles. I didn't want to see anyone or interact, so I ducked into a nearby drevké, grateful at least for the fact that they were on nearly every floor of this stupid palace.

I collapsed onto a nearby bench and curled up as much as I could while still sitting, my body spasming from the sobs I was trying to hold back.

Your words may not have been the wisest spoken in a situation like this. Rhaegos's voice echoed in my head as anger and regret rose in reaction to her words.

"I know. I messed up. And I've probably screwed everything up like Kamira thinks. Maybe I'm not cut out for being High Queen." The thought that maybe the dragons had made a mistake with me crossed my mind, only to be swatted away by what I imagined was Rhaegos.

Things are not set in stone so much as you humans like to think. For better or for worse.

"What does that even mean, Rhaegos?" My voice rose in irritation. "I'm too tired to deal with vague bullshit."

The door to the drevké creaked and I shot back up, turning around as my defenses went up. Senja stood at the door, her hands raised in peace. Without saying a word, she closed it.

"At least no one will think I'm crazier than they already do for talking to myself."

Senja gave me a muted smile, but the rest of her expression was still serious. "Few people here would think you crazy for talking to your dragon kin out loud. I've yet to find a haldraga who hasn't done it." She waved her hand and the door started shimmering. "That said, I can ensure you have some privacy if you'd like."

I nodded, not wanting to deal with anyone, at least not any humans right now. Senja sat, legs crossed in front of the door. She closed her eyes and relaxed her arms on her lap as her hands morphed into claws and her skin shifted to scales. The thought popped into my head that those claws could be used to hurt or protect me at some point.

Senja knows what it's like to be human and what it's like to feel helpless and hurting. I doubt she'd use her claws against anyone who wasn't directly trying to hurt her. That said, they are a reminder that you are still dealing with dragons, little one.

Even the slight hint of chastisement made me want to curl up and die.

"I screwed up. No matter what I do, something goes wrong, and now Haldrek thinks I'm incompetent." That was what hurt the most right now. He thought I was a crappy High Queen and was probably regretting making me one, no matter how much he hedged his words.

You are dealing with crafty individuals. People who make the Isillas's illusions look like child's play. Do not punish yourself for their trickery. And do not assume Haldrek's thoughts. It will only hurt you more.

"And I don't deserve to be hurt?" The words popped out of my mouth before I could think. My mother and Robert were dead, yet the lessons they had taught me stuck in my mind like they'd been etched there. "I'm the village idiot. I don't deserve any of this."

Little one. Rhaegos's voice was firm, but there was a tenderness in it as well. I couldn't imagine why, though. I had messed up. Everyone hated me and I hadn't been able to control Henry or whoever was pretending to be him. *You don't deserve to be hurt. You never have. Not by yourself or by others. Both you and Haldrek are hurting. Your past and his past, as well as the youth you both carry, make it a struggle to understand one another. In time that will pass, but remember this: he's just as scared as you are right now.*

"He seems to be handling it better than I am," I choked out. Still, sympathy for him, love for him, bubbled up in my chest. I hated thinking he was scared and hurting. The last thing I wanted was for him to be in pain, especially if it was because of me. My anger from our fight receded a little. It was still there and I didn't agree with what he'd said, but I didn't want to hurt him, either. "I wish I could help him, but how can I? I'm incompetent. I *feel* incompetent, and he doesn't trust me anymore."

He trusts you. Even now. If what I sense from Teminth is true, he trusts you more than almost anyone in this place. But he is grappling with his new duties. He feels like he's floundering as well.

"He knows how to hide it better than me, though. Everyone loves him still."

He's had many years of training for this, so he does what he can to look strong for Lohikärra. As he said, even as a young child, people challenged him for his power. Teminth tutored him well, but Haldrek is still human. And young. His emotions will get the best of him sometimes.

"And then I come along and mess everything up." I sighed. That wasn't completely true. Even if it felt like it right now. "Have I ruined everything for him?"

No. The response was swift and firm, but still full of love. *Your actions have done little to hurt anyone in the grand scheme of things. There is still time to remedy what has been ruined. But now is not the time to waver. The other Henry still schemes. Go find him, so you can fully understand what is going on and aid Haldrek. Time is of the essence, but it is still on your side.*

I nodded to no one but myself and Rhaegos. Still, fear crept up inside me. Uncertainty at loose ends here in the palace. The other main person trying to bring about my downfall.

"What about Kamira? I know she'd love to jump into the mess of this and make things worse. She's already trying."

"I will tend to Kamira." Senja's voice made me turn around. "She will not interfere with you or Haldrek while you are on Rhaegos's errand." As she stood up, the magic on the door disappeared and she opened it. "But as Rhaegos has said, time is of the essence, so let no one and nothing hinder you."

Chapter Twenty-Three

That night, the bedroom felt colder than ever before. As soon as I left the drevké, I'd looked for Haldrek only to find that he'd already left for Bragidrattür. An early snowstorm, which had been threatening the city and surrounding areas, had blown in after his departure. It covered the city and palace in a decent layer of snow. Not enough to stop people from moving about, but enough to make everything white.

With Haldrek gone after our argument, there was little to keep me warm. Not even the small fireplace that usually kept the bedroom comfortable could keep out the chill.

By morning time, the fire had gone out and a heavy weight settled in my chest. All I wanted to do was hide and hope that things would get better.

Time to get up, Ina. Rhaegos's presence nudged me out of my stupor. I reluctantly pulled the blankets from my body. If today was going to be cold and miserable, might as well deal with it now.

I sat up and stared at my pendant. The thought of calling Haldrek was tempting. Apologizing before I headed out, just in case anything happened. I hoped nothing happened. But I knew I wasn't lucky enough for that.

"Haldrek Rodreksson." The number within my pendant—my skill level thus far—disappeared as the inky blackness within the clear stone rippled. It continued for a few moments and then stopped. My number returned.

I tried to ignore the weight in my chest as I stood. There were a hundred legitimate reasons for why Haldrek didn't answer. Maybe he was sleeping. Or he was giving out orders. Maybe they'd already met the imposter Henry in battle. I hoped it wasn't the last one. The image of Haldrek getting injured in battle seared through my head.

Haldrek is safe. But his heart is still hurting. Give him time, just as you need it, and all will be well.

I sighed. "Can you send a message to Teminth to keep Haldrek safe until I can apologize and make things right?"

Rhaegos huffed in the back of my mind and I couldn't tell if it was annoyance or amusement. Possibly both.

Remember, little one. I am far more than just a messenger. However, I will give Teminth your words. He will keep Haldrek safe.

I smiled a little as I began to put my armor on. "Thank you, Rhaegos. I'm grateful for that."

A sense of appreciation on her part flooded my mind and I felt better. Stronger and more confident.

When I was finally dressed and had eaten some food for the road, I left Haldrek's and my quarters. Walking down the hall, I caught sight of Kamira. As soon as she locked eyes with me, she stiffened up, shoving her nose in the air, and made a beeline for me. Her terrible injuries from only a few days ago had miraculously healed up and disappeared.

When she stopped in front of me, I ducked to the side, not wanting her to sour my mood further. She sidestepped into my path and poked her finger into my armor. If her attitude hadn't been so snotty, I would have laughed.

"Where do you think you're going?"

"I'm going to assist the dragons. They've requested my aid." I tried to duck around her again, but she slid in front of me once more.

"I doubt it. More likely that you're going to help the Blodnar spy." She smirked and attempted to look down her nose at me, despite only coming up to my chin. "Even if you were going to aid the dragons, there is *nothing* you could do to ever make up for the trouble you've caused Lohikärra and the High King."

I wanted to slap the bitch, but I knew I could actually hurt her in my armor this time, so I refrained. Instead, I took a long step forward, bumping her out of my way, and walked toward the nearest stairs.

"I look forward to the day when you are no longer Queen. When my cousin Haldrek's eyes are finally freed from your illusion magic and you are brought down low to the vulgar, half-breed piece of shit you are."

I spun around, my patience gone, and began to raise my hand to smack her again. Instead Rhaegos whispered in my head:

Remind Kamira that she must listen to her dragon more often before any of our kin would believe her worthy of the title of High Queen.

Fine. As much as I would have enjoyed hitting Kamira, I followed Rhaegos's lead. "Kamira, you should learn to watch your mouth. And perhaps listen more often to the dragon who decided to bind with you. You might think I'm vulgar and a piece of garbage, but none of the dragons believe you are worthy to be the High Queen with how you're acting right now."

She swung at me and I grabbed her wrist. "Don't try that. Regardless of what you think of me, I'm still a better fighter than you. If I wanted to, I could give your face an actual beating, one that would stay with you for the rest of your life."

Yanking her arm out of my grip, her expression changed from haughty and imperious to disgusted and rage-filled as she scrunched up her mouth and nose.

"You know nothing of the power *I* have. When I am High Queen, I will see you grovel before me." She spun around and hurried off, leaving me in the corridor with the handful of servants who'd watched the entire episode. I groaned to myself, hoping I hadn't messed up things even more.

You did well, little one. Kamira meddles with things beyond her understanding as she strives for power, and her dragon kin mourns for what the future may bring. Now go. Time is of the essence.

Without another word, I hurried off, hoping I'd complete my task and help Haldrek in time.

I rode for most of the day, though it surprised me that no one followed, at least that I could see. Part of me wondered if I should have brought a group of fighters with me. Although I didn't plan to get into any skirmishes, that probably would have been the better idea. I grimaced at my stupidity.

You are not alone. My kin watch over you as you complete my errand.

I glanced up at the sky to see a couple of dragons flying in the distance. Not so close that they were on top of me, but not so far that they were out of reach.

The sun had begun to sink behind the tallest, snow-crested mountains when I finally arrived on a ridge above a war camp. A Blodnar war camp. So Henry—or his imposter—had rallied those imprisoned in the city *and* more. Soldiers I could only assume had been harassing the countryside. Smoke wafted from various fires around the camps and movement along the edges told me it was heavily guarded.

From the distance I was at, it looked small—maybe around two hundred men—but I guessed they were intending to reinforce those already in Bragidrattür, a force whose numbers I didn't know.

"I wish I could take out this army myself."

Rhaegos chuckled in my mind. *Soon enough, little one. Soon enough. Tonight is for scouting and reporting.*

"Is that what my errand was? I'm sure Haldrek already knows about this group. He would already have scouts watching this camp. I'm sure of it. He knows about Henry's escape and the men he took with him. What information could I bring him that he doesn't already have?"

The other Henry is crafty in all his works. Haldrek knows the general area of this Henry's camp, but he still isn't aware of where exactly they are or their numbers. His scouts keep getting spotted, and there is illusion magic hiding the camp's true size.

"So how can I see the true size? Is what I'm seeing, the true size?"

It is. You see with my eyes right now.

That surprised me, and brought a flood of questions to my mind.

"Teminth can't tell Haldrek what he or the other dragons can sense?" I looked up at the quickly darkening sky and saw a couple of shadows glide through the clouds.

Dragons are not messengers, little one. As convenient as that may seem. Rhaegos's statement was a mere reminder, though I could sense some irritation behind it.

"Sorry. There are roughly two hundred men down there. How long do you think it will take them to arrive at Bragidrattür's thegn hall?"

A few days. But once they reach the thegn hall, it will be difficult for Haldrek's forces to defend against them and those already fighting. Bragidrattür doesn't have a large fighting force to begin with.

"So it'd be better if Haldrek intercepted this group before they got to Bragidrattür?"

Rhaegos said nothing, but a sense of approval flooded my mind.

I tried to see a little more of what was going on in the camp, even though the night was coming on quickly—one of the few things I hated about the winter months here. But as the sky darkened and the camp blended into one blurry circle, I sighed.

"Is Henry—or the person pretending to be Henry—down there?"

He is. The man who calls himself Henry leads this group with one purpose in mind.

"To destroy Lohikärra?"

To destroy Haldrek. When you refused to submit to his demands, he realized you were a more difficult foe. So now he goes after Haldrek.

A heavy weight sank from my chest to my gut. The imposter pretending to be Henry knew how important Haldrek was to me. How I refused to betray him. Now I wondered what he thought taking down Haldrek would bring. Given Drattüjert's opinion of me now, probably more chaos. I would be in line to be the next ruler of Lohikärra, but I doubted many would follow me. A thought popped into my head. The Henry I knew growing up would have never pulled a stunt like this.

"We need to let Haldrek know what's going on. Rhaegos?"

Hmm?

"The person leading this army, this isn't the real Henry, is it? Do you sense that too?"

I knew Henry's mother, but not the child himself. The person who you've been dealing with however... is not what he appears to be. When have you last used Freya's Menace?

"I've practiced with it, but I haven't fought with it since before we took back Drattü-jert."

When was the last time you used it to cut through illusions?

"Even longer. Not since Seirye."

Rhaegos stayed silent, but that was an answer in and of itself. The person I'd been dealing with *wasn't* Henry. Not the person I knew anyway.

"Rhaegos, how far is Haldrek's camp from here?"

Not far, little one. I will guide you in the darkness if you wish. I sensed a hint of approval in her tone, though I could have been imagining it.

"Do we have enough time to get there tonight?"

Only if you fly like the wind.

Chapter Twenty-Four

I t was pitch black by the time I reached Haldrek's war camp. The new moon and the cloud cover had done me few favors, but with Rhaegos's aid I'd made quick time. A sinking anxiety came over me as I came within sight of the camp, and I wondered if I'd be welcomed at all or if I'd have to sneak in.

Walk in and show no fear. Those here still see you as Haldrek's queen and ally.

I nodded to Rhaegos's voice and got off my horse as soon as I reached the night guard.

"Halt!" One of the guards walked toward me, his hand on his hilt. "State your reason for being here."

"I'm here to see the High King. I have information for him."

The man stopped, but said nothing as I walked into the light of the nearby covered torch. As soon as I did, he bowed to one knee.

"High Queen, my apologies. Your husband has us on high alert. The Blodnar are not far from here."

"I know. That's what I wish to speak to him about." I continued inside. One of the sentries within the camp took my horse's reins from me. Surveying the tents, I found the top of the tallest one and began walking in its general direction. If anything, Haldrek would be there preparing or talking with his men. After a few moments, I found myself facing it. Two guards stood in front of the tent flaps, confirming this was where I needed to be. I nodded to them and they let me through without a word.

As soon as I opened the tent flap, Haldrek grumbled at the makeshift table in front of him, not looking up.

"I told you I'd send a messenger when I was done figuring out our strategy."

"What if I told you I had new information for you?"

Haldrek's head snapped up and he stared at me as confusion, alarm, and then resignation washed over his face.

"Ina...What are you doing here? Why aren't you in Drattüjert?"

"I'm here because Rhaegos told me to come find you. And I wanted to apologize."

"You could have called on your pendant," he growled. Instead of hesitating, I walked over to the table and leaned toward him.

"That only works if you answer your pendant. It's not like they have voicemail."

He frowned, then shook his head. "A Fargo thing?"

"Yes. Either way, it's hard to apologize when the other person won't talk to you."

"What are you apologizing for?" He began to shuffle some of the scrolls and maps on his table, keeping his eyes focused on them.

"For yelling at you. Being mean. Telling you that you should fuck your cousin if she's going to be a better High Queen. That was a low blow. I..." I paused, not so much because I didn't feel sorry for my actions. I did. But I was afraid that if I told him my reasons for acting that way, he would think I was excusing them, not just explaining them.

"I what?" He looked up, and I saw a hint of tears in his eyes.

"I was hurting. And I know now you were hurting. Rhaegos told me as much. I didn't want to be mean, but... it's not like I learned how to have an argument without hurting the other person. I grew up with a lot of yelling and, I guess, violence. Now that I think about it." Tears flowed forth from my eyes. "I'm sorry I let Henry, or whoever is pretending to be Henry, run around Drattüjert. I thought there was a possibility for peace between the Blodnar and us if I entertained him long enough. I'm sorry you don't trust me. It's not that I'm trying to mess things up, I just... I'm sorry."

Bowing my head, I wondered if it had even been a good idea to come. I'd apologized, but who was I to think Haldrek would ever trust me, or forgive me again?

In an instant, I felt Haldrek's arms wrap around my body as his chainmail clinked against my armor. His breath was hot on my cheek as he squeezed me tight.

"I forgive you, Ina. You were trying to do the best for Lohikärra, even if Henry—or whoever—wasn't. I should apologize too. I was too sharp with you when I returned to the palace. And jumped to conclusions I shouldn't have. I took my frustration with everything out on you and I'm sorry for that."

I went to say something, but instead I started bawling into his armor. He held me tighter, until all of my tears were gone. His words were both strange and relieving at the same time. I couldn't remember if anyone had ever apologized to *me*.

"I love you, Ina. I always have. And I trust you, your intentions, more than anyone at Drattüjert." He pulled away a little to look me in the eyes. "Even with the whole Henry thing, I know you were trying to help, even if it turned out badly."

I nodded. "I definitely don't think the Henry I was dealing with in Drattüjert was the one I knew growing up. I asked Rhaegos and she asked me when was the last time I used Freya's Menace."

"You think the Blodnar spy is using magic to pretend to be Henry?"

"That would make sense. That would make a lot of sense for the way the Henry in Drattüjert was acting. And why everything felt off."

"Whoever was impersonating your friend is doing a good job, but not quite hitting all the marks."

I nodded again. "Whoever that person is, I'm betting they are Blodnar for real, trying to cause mayhem." I glanced down at the dirt floor. "I did a little bit of spying before I arrived here. You may already know this, but the Blodnar troops pulled from Drattüjert are on their way to Bragidrattür. I'm almost certain the person pretending to be Henry is leading them."

"How far away is their camp? Did you see how many soldiers were in it?"

"It took me almost an hour on horseback riding as fast as I could to get from there to here. I didn't get too close, but it's the entirety of the Blodnar forces that came to Drattüjert, plus more. Perhaps one to two sattars worth."

"So roughly the same size as my forces here." Haldrek groaned. "Thank you for letting me know. That was information I needed." He kissed me on the forehead and pulled away. "I need to talk to some of my men. I know we won't be able to attack the Blodnar head on and then help Bragidrattür, but if we can waylay them, that may give us the upper hand."

As he slipped out of the tent, the old familiar weight I'd been feeling for the last few months returned. I stared down at the maps and papers he'd been studying. The runes were still barely decipherable, but the maps were easy to read. Three groups looked ready to converge on the thegn hall of Bragidrattür, but at different rates. My mind began to go over the different possibilities. Things I should have done, could have done, what might have made this situation less difficult. Tears rolled down my face as I closed my eyes, mentally and emotionally exhausted.

It didn't seem like that much time had passed before I heard the tent flaps open again. Turning around, I saw Haldrek enter in a brighter mood.

"I think..." He hesitated as he saw my face. "You were planning on staying the night in camp, weren't you?"

I nodded. "Unless you want me to leave. Then—"

He stepped forward and pulled me into his embrace, my cheek pressing against the cold chainmail protecting his neck.

"I want you to stay. You don't know how much I missed you. How badly I wanted you by my side." He laughed. "I don't know if I'll be able to do long war campaigns anymore. At least not without you visiting." His mouth made its way down the side of my face, pulling my chainmail away from it with his fingers. He began nibbling on my ear. I gasped as a thrill went through me.

"I don't have to stay if you don't want me to." Leaning back against the table, I let him press his body against mine until I was straddling his waist. It was as awkward as it was enticing, given that we were both still in full armor.

He made his way down to my neck and made a low, rumbling noise of displeasure. His kisses stopped.

"I am so tired of making war. There is no end in sight and I need a break. I need *you* again." He began to pull at the sides of my armor.

"Where are you sleeping tonight? I don't know if I can't stop the fighting, but at least for tonight, we could make something else other than war." The table shifted and creaked under our combined weight.

He made the same low, rumbling noise, but it sounded happier this time. Grabbing the bottoms of my thighs, he hoisted me higher on his waist as I wrapped my arms around his neck. He walked through cloth flaps that divided the tent in half. The back side of the tent was much darker and I grunted as he laid me down on what I assumed was his makeshift bed.

His hands immediately felt around for the clasps that held my armor in place. "I used to know where all these straps were. And how to undo them."

I laughed as I helped him. Quickly, my armor and clothing were off except for my undershirt. I shivered as the chill from outside blew in under the edges of the tent. As he pulled his armor and clothing off, he muttered:

"You won't be cold by the time we're done."

"Oh? You have always been a furnace."

"I'm burning hot tonight with no desire to cool down."

I gasped as he slipped into the bed on top of me, his warm skin touching mine from head to toe. My undershirt was on the ground in a matter of moments. As he began kissing and licking my collarbone, I moaned.

Softly in the dark, I heard him whisper, "We may be fighting for our lives tomorrow, but tonight we make love like our lives depend on it."

I awoke to Haldrek still snuggled on top of me, his mouth next to my neck, the heat of his breath keeping me warm. I relished the moment. As soon as we were awake, he'd—we'd—have to fight imposter Henry's forces before they reached Bragidrattür's thegn hall. There was no way we could let them join with the Blodnar forces already on their way to besieging the estate.

As I took a deep breath and relaxed closer into Haldrek's embrace, the sound of tent flaps snapping open interrupted me.

"High King Haldrek! An urgent message! High King Haldrek?"

Haldrek's eyes snapped open in alarm. He looked at me for a moment in surprise, then got up.

"Give me a moment to rise and dress, messenger." He quickly donned his pants and an overcoat before slipping out into the main area.

Any chance of a relaxed awakening was gone now. I got up from the bed myself, all of my muscles stiff. Haldrek and I had made the most of last night.

Haldrek's voice was quiet from the front part of the tent. "Are you sure of what you saw?"

Silence and then a grumbled oath from Haldrek. "Thank you for telling me. Inform the gesiths to ready themselves."

The tent flaps ruffled loudly and Haldrek slipped back into the part where I continued to dress.

"The Blodnar spy has begun to move. We need to get going."

I nodded, a sudden prick of guilt in my heart. "I'm sorry."

As I finished tying up my own pants, Haldrek walked up next to me. "You have nothing to apologize for. Teminth had some sharp reminders for me about my own actions and inexperience. He's right. You did what you thought was best for Drattüjert. When things went badly, you did what you had to in order to fix them. Or at least try." He cupped my jaw in his hand and a thrill went through my whole body. *I would do anything for this man.* The thought popped into my head without warning and I heard Rhaegos's laughter in response.

Anything?

I ignored her as Haldrek leaned down for a soft, slow kiss. When he pulled back, he whispered, "I thought you were a dream as I was waking up. It's good to feel you next to me."

"You don't know how much I've missed you." I whispered. "After we defeat this Henry imposter, we need to return to Drattüjert and repeat last night. Over and over."

Haldrek laughed and kissed me on the lips again, leaving me hungry for more. "When I return to Drattüjert, we can repeat last night as many times as you want."

I paused. "You make it sound like you'll be returning to Drattüjert alone from this fight."

"Hopefully most of my warriors will return with me. But," he cupped the other side of my jaw with his right hand, stroking my cheek this time, "you need to return to Drattüjert.

After how many times we enjoyed each other last night, I would not be surprised if there was another aethling within you now."

My stomach twisted at the thought and I fought to keep the tears that had sprung up from flooding my eyes. Haldrek didn't mean to hurt me, but how could he know? We'd been trying for months. It would be impossible... maybe not impossible, but he couldn't be certain and if I wasn't pregnant again, I didn't want to be heartbroken once more.

"Ina, I'm sorry. I didn't mean—" He kissed the top of my forehead and pulled me into his embrace.

"I don't want to get my hopes up. If I'm in the battle, I can distract Henry's imposter. I want to take a swipe at him with Freya's Menace. Even if you're the one who ends him."

Haldrek's chest rumbled with laughter. "I'm afraid you being on the battlefield might distract me. I'd be trying to keep you safe."

"I'm a haldraga now. Rhaegos will keep me safe."

"Being a haldraga won't make you immortal, Ina."

"That's not what I said. But Rhaegos will keep me safe. If I return to Drattüjert, I'll be labelled a Blodnar-loving coward. Regardless of the outcome of the fight, I'm staying."

Haldrek stepped away. "I—"

The tent flaps slapped open, interrupting him. A young voice spoke from the other side of the tent divide. "My king, I was sent to aid you."

Haldrek grimaced as I continued to put on my armor. Without a word, he disappeared into the front part of the tent.

When I finished dressing, he was gone. A servant was packing up the maps and other items that had been left behind. He looked up at me in surprise. "High Queen Ina. I didn't know you were here. Otherwise I would have sent someone in to aid you as well."

I waved his words off. "Has the High King left already?"

He nodded. "Should he have waited?"

I shook my head, worry twisting in my gut. I'd wanted to settle things with Haldrek and now I wondered if I'd made the right decision. What was the right decision in this situation?

You were right. I will keep you safe. It is of utmost importance that you keep Haldrek safe.

Rhaegos's words surprised me. Not wasting another moment, I hurried out of the tent and found the corral where they'd placed my horse. It was already saddled and ready to go. The man standing next to it, bowed slightly as he saw me.

"My queen, your horse is ready. I saw the High King ride off not long ago. If you go quickly, you may catch up with him."

"Thank you." I let the man help me up and quickly made my way out of the camp, following the path of soldiers. Haldrek would be near the front, so that's where I needed to go.

As I reached the place where the warriors had begun to spread out, I kept my head high and on the lookout. Haldrek would be around here somewhere. Once I reached him, I could see how many men now fought beside the imposter Henry. I had a sinking feeling he might split up his forces if he thought Haldrek's warriors were easily defeated.

"Cease your action, Blodnar scum!" Haldrek's voice rang out with anger nearby. I steered my horse in that direction, coming up next to him, but not far enough to see Henry's imposter or his men.

Laughter boomed from beyond my view in an uncomfortably familiar voice. "Filled with rage that I can bed your wife in a night and then come and fight you in the morning? Where is your stamina, Lohikärran?"

I scowled in spite of myself and pushed my horse to line up with Haldrek's. Before he could say anything, I shouted, "You were not the man bedding me last night. I would never entertain a man with a tiny dick."

Laughter exploded behind us as the imposter's face went red. I glanced at Haldrek, who strained to keep a serious expression. But I could tell he was amused as well.

"Surrender, Blodnar, and your men may return to their homes without harassment."

"I am Henricus, a Prince of Norycium, and I will never surrender to a wild king." He raised his sword and the cracking thud of numerous arrows being released sounded behind him.

"Attack!" Haldrek shouted as he raised his shield above head and charged toward the imposter. I did the same, crouching under my shield as arrows hit it, most of which bounced off. I pulled my sword out and began cutting down Blodnar soldiers as they came at me.

I glanced up to see if I could find Haldrek or the imposter, though I knew the latter would likely be on the ground in the melee. I barely dodged a blade aimed at my neck, feeling the tip click against the chainmail and padding protecting my neck.

Before I could attack again, my horse dropped out from below me with a high-pitched scream. I rolled away and into a standing position, trying to avoid getting caught underneath the creature. As soon as I was up, Blodnar soldiers surged. I cut down a few, but tripped over a body and fell to my knees with a grunt of pain.

I blocked an incoming blow with my shield as someone pulled me up by my sword arm, plunging their blade into the soldier underneath.

"Stay standing and keep your balance!" Haldrek's voice boomed behind me, and my chest swelled with relief to have him by my side. I straightened up, pressing my back against his and cutting down Blodnar soldiers as they came my way.

After a few moments, the onslaught lessened and Haldrek's back pulled away from mine. I turned around to see him focus on a man in the distance.

"Henry." Haldrek charged him as I followed. I hadn't been lying this morning when I said I wanted to take a swipe at him myself.

A handful of Blodnar tried to take down Haldrek as he ran forward, but he ignored them, knocking them to the side with his blade and shield. The blue haze of spirits began to fill my vision and thicken as Haldrek and I got closer. Even with the imposter's armor shielding most of his face, I could sense an element of maniacal glee coming from him as he focused on Haldrek and then on me, something I'd never felt from Henry before. I stored that information without hesitation as more proof that this was not my friend.

The imposter dodged away from Haldrek at the last moment and lunged for me. I blocked the attack with my shield and launched my own attack. It hit the imposter square in his sword arm and he stumbled back.

"This is what you get, you faithless whore."

I braced myself for another attack. Instead the imposter spun around and stabbed Haldrek in the side. Time slowed as I watched the blade sink through Haldrek's armor, going deep into his side. I screamed as a look of terror and surprise crossed Haldrek's face. He stumbled back, his legs giving out beneath him. The imposter pulled his sword out and grinned at me. I lunged at him, missing his throat by a split second as he dodged away. He began running and I realized the remnants of the Blodnar army were falling back.

Turning to Haldrek, I knelt by his side and looked around, screaming for a healer. Several people ran over and I focused on Haldrek as they began to tend to him. Sweat beaded across his face and his skin was pale as I held his head.

"Focus on me, Haldrek. Listen to me. You're not allowed to leave. You're not allowed to go to the Realm of Ghosts. I love you. Stay with me." Tears blurred my vision as the healers took over. I could barely see anything as Haldrek's head went limp in my hands.

Chapter Twenty-Five

I stayed with the small group of warriors and healers who took Haldrek back to the camp. The entire time, I held his hand and begged Rhaegos and Teminth to keep him alive. Though his head had been limp in my lap on the battlefield, his grip on my hand stayed firm.

Please don't die on me, Haldrek. Not now. We'd had more than a few close calls together. Was this what our future would be? Was there any way to keep him safe? Or safer? My gut churned and I helped the healers as they lifted the light cot they'd put him on.

Rhaegos, please. Please don't let him die.

Though I felt her presence, she remained silent.

As we brought him into an empty tent and laid him on a table, one of the healers looked at me regretfully and pulled my hand from Haldrek's. I stood in the corner for a moment, numb and unable to move. Finally, one of the warriors took me outside the tent.

"I'm sorry, my queen. They need all the space they can get in there."

His voice sounded distant. I tried my hardest to focus on the words he spoke.

"Are they checking his pendant? Last time—" My voice sounded different too before it faltered.

The warrior shrugged. "I dunno. But maybe. Seems like a healer thing to do."

I nodded. The healers would know what to do. This was their job. Haldrek was their High King. They would do anything to keep him alive.

He won't survive if he stays in the camp. He needs Drattüjert's resources—and protection.

Rhaegos's comment confused me, and I frowned. But I didn't question it.

"We need to get him back to Drattüjert. How long will it take to get there?" I glanced up at the warrior whose eyes widened.

"Only way is by wagon. That'll take a day at least."

"Then we need to get a cart prepared. Now." I gestured for him to go and get the wagon and horses prepared and he hurried off.

A few hours later, after the remnants of our army returned to the camp, the head healer came out to where I was pacing. She bowed deeply.

"My queen, we have made sure the High King is comfortable and beginning to heal, but he needs more than we can give him in camp. I recommend we make preparations for Drattüjert."

"Agreed." I gestured to the wagon and horses behind me. "The dragons told me as much. Whenever you are ready, we need to leave."

The healer bowed once more and disappeared within the tent. Before I could blink, there was noise from inside and I stepped back as the cot holding Haldrek was brought out and hurried into the wagon. He groaned a few times, and as I got up on a horse and began riding alongside the wagon, his face looked as pale as before. It didn't look like the healers had done much except kept him from bleeding out. As much as I wished for a Hethurin healer, I was glad for what we had. If we could get Haldrek back to Drattüjert without him getting worse, I would call that a win.

And so I rode with the small group as quickly as we could without aggravating Haldrek's condition. During the quiet moments, I thought of what I would do that next time I saw the imposter and how I would defeat him. How I would get my vengeance for everything he'd done so far.

By the next afternoon, we had reached the walls of Drattüjert. Riding through the eastern gate felt more ominous than I'd expected. People watched us and hurried away. My mind told me it was because this was unusual. They had probably expected Haldrek to be on horseback and I wondered how many thought this wagon might be carrying a coffin instead. I glanced down at him. He was still pale, but his chest rose and fell slowly, telling me he was still alive.

"My queen!"

I looked up as we entered the main square and saw Egil the spymaster running for us. Getting off my horse, I stopped him.

"We need to get the High King inside. He was severely injured fighting the Blodnar—"

"My queen, you are in danger. There are people inside the palace who would see you dead. Rumors are spreading that you attempted to kill your husband in battle."

"There she is! Grab her!" Kamira's voice made me look up as she pointed a long finger at me. She stood at the main doors of the palace with a handful of guards behind her. They refused to move. "The rumors are true. She wants the throne for herself."

Haldrek's spymaster grabbed my shoulder, but I shook him off. "Kamira, shut your mouth! I would never hurt Haldrek. Anyone at the battle will tell you that." I ran up to when she was standing, a smug mocking look crossing her face.

"People you paid favors to, obviously."

Behind her, the healers took Haldrek into the palace and a crowd started to form around us.

"Move, or I will move you myself." I hissed from between clenched teeth. This was no time for stupid court politics.

"You really think people will believe you didn't hurt the High King if you hurt me?"

I pushed her aside and she stumbled dramatically onto the railing behind me as I entered the palace.

"She attacked me!"

I ignored her and followed the healers into a larger stairwell, where they slowly navigated the circular turns going up. Haldrek's eyes fluttered open for a brief moment and a tiny smile flitted across his face. Relief flooded me as we reached the floor with our quarters.

Just as the healers entered the door to the antechamber, one of them stopped me.

"I'm sorry, my queen, we will need space to help him."

I nodded, trying to keep my composure. "Is there anything I can do?"

The woman glanced inside. "If there is a long rectangular table, we could use it. Right now, he'll be on the floor."

I nodded, not knowing how they'd get a big enough table in, but I'd let the servants and healers deal with that.

Rushing back to the main hall, I gathered a few servants, sending them to find a table. As they left, I noticed a group walking slowly toward me, headed by Kamira, Lady Drifa, and the advisor Gizur. An ominous feeling fell over me as I noticed the guards with them reveal their weapons. Anger came to the forefront of my mind. Of all the times for court bullshit, this was not it. I gripped the hilt of my sword, not pulling it out, but waiting to see how they planned to proceed with every intention of defending myself. Servants scattered from the hallway as the group stopped a few yards from me.

"There is no need for bloodshed, Thegn of Svartån." Gizur cleared his throat. "It is clear what has been done and we would rather stop the violence than continue it."

"Bullshit. That's why the guards with you already have their weapons unsheathed. Your group is the one wanting violence, not me. I just want my husband to be safe."

"Why do you insist on calling him that?" Lady Drifa's unemotional tone made my blood boil. She picked at her fingernails, not even looking at me. When she finally finished and did look my way, she continued, "You never loved him in the first place. He was merely a means to an end."

I laughed at the absurdity. "What? You should speak for yourself. I actually love my husband."

She scowled and glanced away. Kamira snapped, "Then why did you kill him? Or have the Blodnar spy do your dirty work?"

"I would never hurt Haldrek. He's not dead yet. He'll survive this like he always does."

"Will he? Or is this the final straw so you can be in charge once and for all?" Gizur gestured for the guards and they ran at me.

I pulled my blade and cut down the closest man to me. Another one took his place and I got pushed back into the stairwell. As much as I had trained in the past few months, fighting in close quarters hadn't been something Haldrek had taught me much about.

Fall back. Kamira and her allies have no qualms with killing you. Haldrek is safe for now.

My chest tightened as I crossed swords with the guard in front of me. I disarmed him and glanced down the stairs. I wasn't on good footing and I needed that. Tumbling down the stairs wouldn't help me defend myself. One more swift attack put the guard on the defensive and I spun around, running down to a safer location.

I ended up on the same floor as the High Queen's Home and immediately heard shouts coming from nearby. Running down the hall toward that set of rooms, the cries and shouts got louder the closer I got.

As I turned around the corner, I found guards shuffling and roughhousing women and children out of the rooms before shackling them in heavy chains. Some of the smaller children slumped to the ground under the weight.

"What in the name of the dragons is going on?" My voice boomed louder than I expected and a few of the guards jumped as they spun around.

One of the younger priestesses of Tenelth pushed her way out from where a guard was blocking her and bowed to one knee in front of me.

"My queen, they're locking up the refugees! They're saying they're spies and murderers in disguise. Please, they won't listen to us." She stood back up as I marched forward.

One of the guards stepped forward as well, his arms crossed tightly against his chest armor. "The High King's advisors told us to take them to the dungeons. Can't be trusted no more."

"As the High Queen, I say you don't touch them! They are Lohikärrans, not Blodnar, and I will not have you hurting them this way." I glanced past him and saw the looks of terror on the women and children's faces. "Which advisor told you to do this? Gizur?"

"That's not information you need to know." He scowled at me and I stepped back enough to put my blade to his throat. He stiffened and stared down at Freya's Menace. I had no intention of killing him, at least now, but I needed to see the truth of this matter.

I expected to see some kind of illusion or disguise, but instead I saw his reflection in my blade, so I took another approach.

"I am the High Queen of Lohikärra. The Lady of Lohikärra. I swear by the dragons, you will not harm a hair on my people. Release them now."

Instead of being afraid, he laughed. "The advisors have told us of your betrayal. We will no longer listen to a Blodnar-loving whore."

I swung my blade back and hit him in the chest, knocking him into a few of his men. "The only Blodnar-loving whore was your mother. Now release them!"

"There you are! Seize her!"

I spun around to see Kamira with the guards Gizur had sent after me.

Fuck.

I hated fighting in close quarters, and there was no way I'd be able to fight all the guards around me without hurting the innocent bystanders.

"Hide!" I shouted as the guard behind me grabbed the chainmail at the base of my neck. I swung back, elbowing him in the throat. He dropped, much to my surprise, and I shot my free hand toward the guards with Kamira. If she got hit, all the better.

"Too-Salpama!" A lightning bolt streaked out from my hand, hitting one of the guards square in the chest and knocking him into the wall. Kamira stumbled back and stared at me in horror. The other guard stayed by her as if to protect her.

"You are a monster! First the High King, and then you protect these-these half-breed evil things." She gestured to the women and children behind me. I aimed my hand at her, trying to ignore the pain and tingling in my arm. I'd gotten better at controlling the lightning spell, but it still hurt when I fought with it.

"Did you order these guards to round up the refugees?" I shouted, ignoring her insults.

"What does it matter, they're all monsters and —"

"DID YOU ORDER THESE REFUGEES ROUNDED UP?" She flinched for a moment before returning to her haughty expression.

"Gizur did. But I supported him. Why take care of these people when they and you are responsible for every misfortune Lohikärra has dealt with? Why let them live when good men and women have died? Gizur was being merciful to let them rot in the dungeons. They should all die, have their souls sent to Lyrroth, and be punished for all of eternity for their crimes against Lohikärra."

I stared at her, realizing just how crazy she was. "They are innocent. They never killed anyone. They are the *good* of Lohikärra!"

"You never deserved to be Queen!" Kamira continued ranting, ignoring my words. "Look at everything you've done. Lohikarra has been destroyed because of you. The High

King is dead because of you! I just saw him. He is *gone*. And Lohikarra with it!" She glanced past me and gestured at someone behind me.

I swung around just in time to dodge a blow from the guard I'd knocked down. Without thinking, I punched him in the face with my fist and sent him staggering, blood pouring from his nose.

Unfortunately the other guards now had their weapons drawn and aimed at the refugees.

"Kill them! Kill them all!" Kamira began shrieking. "They are traitors to the High King and to Lohikärra!"

People started screaming and panicking as I dodged another blow from the guard. I cast another spell, fire this time and shoved him back with the flames. He stumbled to the ground as I shouted,

"Enough!"

Everyone paused and I swung to focus on Kamira. The fucking bitch. I would have my revenge on her eventually, but I couldn't do that now. Not when there were innocents who could die.

Fall back and I will keep your refugees safe. Even in the dungeons.

I hated that Rhaegos kept telling me to fall back. I couldn't keep falling back. That wouldn't work. I needed to fight and protect.

There is a time and place for all things, little one. This is not a defeat. Leave the palace for now and you will return triumphant.

I hesitated, not wanting to concede. I didn't trust Kamira or her cronies. But I trusted Rhaegos enough to take her word for it. "I will leave the palace if you promise to not hurt the refugees."

"I will make no promises to a traitor like yourself." She looked at the guards. "Execute them! Now!"

I pointed my blade at the guards and they stopped as it glowed red at them. Turning back to Kamira, I said, "Then make an oath by the dragons and to the dragons. Not to me. Make one to the dragons above."

"Why would the dragons care about these half-breeds?"

"Because Tenelth himself protected all who came unto him." The priestess spoke up behind me and I stepped back at the tone of her voice. It was commanding and sounded different—not human. I'd forgotten that she was there. Her hands glowed white, which I thought might be for healing but she didn't seem to be a mood for healing. In fact, she seemed in the mood for something else. An edge of violence colored her words. "The dragons give you one last opportunity, Kamira. Do as they ask and they will be merciful to you."

Rhaegos's laughter was soft but strong in the back of my mind and I was curious why. She knew something I didn't. Kamira's haughtiness disappeared and she scowled as she put her hands down.

"Fine." Focusing on me, she spoke with anger in every word. "I promise on the dragons that no harm shall come to these *refugees* if Ina leaves the palace. Now."

The priestess turned to me and I noticed that her eyes were covered in a whitish film. "Go now, Ina of Svartån, High Queen and Lady of Lohikärra. This oath is binding to both of you."

I didn't know what dragon was speaking to me, but I nodded and bowed. Glancing back at the refugees, I hoped Kamira would keep her promise. If she didn't, the dragons may punish her, but there would be many needless deaths.

With that thought, I left the palace.

Chapter Twenty-Six

I left the palace without harassment, but that was the least of my troubles. The sky grew dark and there was nowhere for me to go. I began making my way through the city as snow began to fall.

People whispered as I walked through the nearest market and I realized why. I was alone. I had no guards with me despite wearing my armor and symbols of the High Queen.

I also wondered how fast the rumors would spread from the palace. It had been only a few hours since Haldrek had arrived in a wagon, so people would know something serious had happened. And now I was walking aimlessly around the city?

Of course they would talk.

Rhaegos, what do I do now? I couldn't go back to the palace and I wasn't about to leave Drattüjert unless they forced me to.

Find a place to weather the storm. It's coming and you will need your strength when it hits.

I looked up at the sky. As gray and ominous as it looked, I had a feeling that wasn't the storm she was referring to. The sound of armored footsteps behind me caught my attention as I left the market, and I spun around to see palace guards following me. When one of the city guards came up to them, I saw them gesture toward me and say something.

Well, crap.

The city guard gestured for some men to join him and I began hurrying out of sight.

"Stop! You need to stop!" Something whistled on my right side and I ducked away from it, only to see a short blade sail past me. It clattered to the ground harmlessly, but screams from near me shattered the silence as people ran down nearby alleys.

The guards kept running, and in an attempt to stop them, I cast an ice spell on the ground. Ducking around the corner of a building, I heard them stumble and crash into each other. It was stupid and a short term solution, but it would give me time to find help.

If there was any help to be found.

I looked up to see people closing up their doors and hiding from me. Memories of Bolvo flashed through my mind and I tried not to get angrier than I already was. Too much of this whole situation was feeling like a repeat of Seirye. Illusion magic, Haldrek on the brink of death, people I thought I could trust rejecting me, people I wanted to protect being put into danger.

I swallowed down the hard knot of anger in my throat. I needed to think clearly, not give into my emotions. Back when I was fighting Seirye, I still felt like I had hope. Or maybe I'd been too stupid to know better.

Rhaegos, where can I go? No one here will help me.

She was silent as I walked down the streets, trying to stay away from the sound of guards or armor clanking. The palace guards weren't my friends anymore, and I'd seen them turn the city guards against me. As lantern light replaced the last bits of sunlight, I leaned up against what I thought was the northern edge of the city wall.

In the distance I could hear warriors and guards walking around along the top of the wall, but this part seemed fairly empty and quiet. I would take it for now.

"It would not be wise for a noble woman such as yourself to be out here alone."

The voice made me jump. A hand covered my mouth in the darkness and I bit it as I pulled out my side blade and spun around.

The person swore in Lohikärran and, even though I couldn't see them, I knew the voice was familiar.

"My queen, though I appreciate your quick reflexes, please don't ever bite me again. That hurt." Egil shook out his hand. Apparently he hadn't expected my reaction.

"Then don't grab my mouth," I hissed.

"Duly noted. I'm here to help you escape the city."

"Over my dead body. I'm not leaving Drattüjert in Kamira or anyone else's hands."

He snorted. "If you don't leave, it will be your dead body. Lady Kamira has sent out the palace and city guards to hunt you down and kill you for treason and attempted murder of the king."

"But she—" I stopped. She had never promised me anything. She'd only promised not to kill the women and children from the High Queen's Home. "Fuck."

"My sentiment's the same. Come, there is a short window of time before the guards at the north gate return. Go to the shrine of Tenelth above the city and stay there for the night. It is considered holy ground and no Lohikärran in their right mind would attack you there."

I hesitated. "How do I know that you aren't on Kamira's side? I didn't hurt Haldrek—that was the Blodnar bastard—but you weren't at the battle, were you?"

"I was not. But I have my sources. I know that Lady Kamira's schemes are more insidious than anything you would ever do. I hope you don't take offense to that."

"I don't. So you trust me? As High Queen?"

The spymaster sighed. "I trust that you would never harm the High King, nor try to destroy Lohikärra. Now we must go."

I started at the sound of clanking of armor near us and the spymaster grabbed my wrist as he began running.

"There they are! Grab them!"

I began running as fast as I could behind the spymaster, ducking and weaving through narrow streets and alleyways until we got to the northern gate. We slipped into the shadows of some nearby homes.

In front of us stood a handful of warriors, oblivious to our presence. The men who had been chasing us ran into the street and stopped, twisting around to find us.

"We are safe in the shadows." The spymaster's voice was next to my ear and I tried not to move as we watched the warriors cross in front of us and confront those at the gate. They began arguing and I sunk as close to the wall as possible.

After a few moments of watching the argument, Egil spoke again. "I'll cause a distraction and once the warriors disperse, you need to run as fast as you can. Understood?"

I nodded.

He began gesturing with his hands and muttering words I couldn't understand. All I knew was they made me feel uncomfortable. As panic welled up inside of me, I saw a mirror image of me peek out from the other side of the street and into the light. Without hesitation, the spymaster ran toward the illusion shouting, "My queen, wait!"

That got the warriors' attention. Soon the half dozen or so men started chasing the spymaster and his illusion into the darkness. I waited a few moments and as soon as I felt the coast was clear, I ran.

I fell to my knees as I reached the shrine. Tenelth's Shrine. The same place where a year ago Haldrek and I had sworn ourselves to Lohikärra and the dragons. That day had been unseasonably warm and lovely. Full of hope and optimism. Now everything was dark and cold.

There were male voices in the distance, but for some reason they didn't come up the path after me. Maybe Haldrek's spymaster had been right? Or maybe there was something blocking them. Did they know something I didn't? My heart sank further into my chest as I bowed my head before the altar. That had been my life ever since I'd arrived in this stupid city. I was a fish out of water. Even more than normal.

Now everyone hated me, thinking I'd betrayed and murdered Haldrek. All of the people I'd tried to protect were in danger because of me.

I'd tried so hard to be a good queen and Lady of Lohikärra. To be what the people here needed and wanted. And in the end, I had failed.

Damn it, Rhaegos. What am I supposed to do now? I've completely messed things up and everyone hates me.

No response, not even the sense of her in the back of my mind. My anger grew. So much for the dragons.

Footsteps crunched behind me and I stood up with a spin, hand on my sword's grip.

"Hold your weapon, Ina of Svartån." A commanding voice boomed from the man facing me. But there was no threat from him or the woman by his side.

Walking up between the benches in front of the shrine, Senja and Paavo raised their hands in greeting and I relaxed.

Neither seemed pissed enough to eat me right now, even if I really had ruined things.

"It's been a while since you've come to this shrine." Paavo stopped to glance up at the large and imposing stone statue of Tenelth before speaking again. "What brings you here this evening?"

"I need help." My voice cracked as I tried to hold back my tears. "I did everything I thought I was supposed to do and I failed." My throat tightened. "Haldrek is dying inside the palace as we speak."

Paavo nodded. "Teminth confirms that he is on the edge of two realms. If he is in the palace, gravely injured, why are you out here?"

"Because Kamira and the other advisors kicked me out." I glanced over at Senja, trying to contain my anger. She placed her hand on Paavo's arm.

"Kamira troubles her dragon kin as we speak. Ina tells the truth. She has been cast out."

"That doesn't bode well for Drattüjert." Paavo glanced to his left, over the city. I followed his gaze. It looked peaceful enough if you didn't know what was going on inside. "Though the Blodnar soldiers have been pushed back and their troops decimated, I can sense their commander close by."

Senja looked at him in surprise. "The one pretending to be Ina's friend?"

He nodded and I sighed, slumping to the ground, my head on my knees and my back to the shrine.

"Why do you give up now, little one? There is much to do." Paavo's words stung despite me not seeing his face.

"I'm *not* giving up." Not that the thought hadn't crossed my mind. If Haldrek was dead and everyone here hated me, what place did I have in Drattüjert? "I just don't know what to do. It's not like I have an army to take back the palace and kick out Kamira or the fake

Henry." If Paavo could sense the imposter nearby, that meant he was likely within the city. I would bet all my gold he was with Kamira. Anger and helplessness rose up inside of me. "How am I supposed to take back Drattüjert and the palace when I'm all alone? I have no allies."

"What did you do when the ice elves took Svangendom?"

I sat there numbly. "I snuck it, got my only known ally killed, then got sent to the dungeon. Seirye's pride and superstition is what got him killed. Then Haldrek came in to sweep up the last of the elves." My throat tightened up. "But I've pretty much killed him and I don't have any allies, hidden or otherwise."

Senja looked at Paavo and a slight grin crossed their faces. I scowled. How could they find anything amusing right now?

"Are you two going to help me storm the castle? If so, what do I do then? I'm going to have to fight at least the imposter and Kamira. If I fight her, the rest of the advisors and hersirs will get pissed off and I'll be in a worse situation than before."

"Was that not the same as Svangendom?" Paavo focused on me. "You are dealing with an enemy who uses illusion magic. This is not the first time you have done so."

"But everything feels bigger here, heavier. More dangerous. I don't know what I'd do if I lost Haldrek this time. Or if me barging in would hurt him more. What would happen if I failed? Would the imposter finish Haldrek off once and for all? I don't want to risk that." My voice cracked at the thought. It was one thing to risk my life, but it was another thing to risk other people's lives.

"If you had failed in Svangendom, Seirye would have killed your friends and allies too," Paavo countered as he walked toward me. Kneeling in front of me, he continued, "And he would have gone after Haldrek and his people."

I nodded. "That's true. So why does it feel so different now?"

Senja cleared her throat and we both looked up at her. "More responsibility lies with you when you are the High Queen. When it's your responsibility to keep all of Lohikärra safe, and those you thought you could trust want you to surrender, it can feel like all of Sethys is on your shoulders."

Paavo turned back to me. "But you aren't the first to face that challenge. Nor will you be the last." He held his hand out to me and pulled me up. "Now is not the time to surrender. Now is the time to hold strong and fight for those who can't."

I nodded. "How do I do it then? How do I get into the castle? And how do I defeat the imposter?"

Paavo nodded toward my sword. "Commune with Rhaegos and think on what you know about both your friend and the imposter. Then your future actions will be revealed to you." He stepped back and let Senja take his place. She gave me a tight hug and whispered,

"We will stay here with you until you leave the shrine. Then we shall aid you as we best can."

I nodded and she slipped away, taking refuge under Paavo's arm. The scene made me ache for the comfort of Haldrek's touch once more. Turning around, I took a seat on one of the empty benches, trying to clear my mind and settle my emotions. If nothing else, tonight I needed to focus my thoughts on how to best defeat Kamira and the imposter.

Chapter Twenty-Seven

The night passed slowly as I racked my brain for ideas on how to fight the imposter and Kamira. I doubted they would be far apart from one another, possibly scheming while Haldrek lay dying.

Who is the biggest threat?

Rhaegos's voice tickled, if that was the right word, and my body warmed up, as if a blanket were draped over me, holding off the night's chill and the surrounding snow. I was glad to feel her presence again.

Who was the biggest threat? If I took out Kamira first, there would be little to keep the imposter from going after Haldrek again. He'd already shown his ability to get past guards and servants alike. But if I offed him, would Kamira do something to make me look terrible again? Granted, if he was revealed to not be Henry, it would be hard for her to spin the narrative framing me as the bad guy.

Maybe that was it. The imposter would happily kill Haldrek if he got a chance. Kamira wouldn't. So if I could figure a way to defeat the imposter, I could...

My mind faltered. How could I defeat him? He had better magic skills than me by far and I'm sure he was fairly strong if he was using a body that looked like Henry's...

Appearances can be deceiving. You should know this by now, little one.

I squeezed my eyes shut tight and rubbed them as I tried to fight off the sleep. *Appearances* can be deceiving. The imposter wasn't Henry, but looked like him. He didn't act like him either. Would he fight like him too? Did Henry even know how to fight?

I laid down on the bench, exhaustion falling over me like a cold, hard blanket. Rhaegos's warmth encircled me.

As soon as my eyes closed, images of Henry danced in my mind, some of them familiar, some of them not. Memories of high school, of us playing the Lohikärra games—those were familiar and I sensed that it was Henry, the real Henry, who I was seeing. Then the images darkened. Henry looked like he'd been beaten up, and a young Blodnar man stood above him, clutching something around his neck and smirking triumphantly. That man felt familiar as well, but in a different way. He shifted into Henry's form and as he went to grab a large sword from the ground nearby, it slipped uselessly from his hand. Irritation flowed out from him and the image faded.

"Ina…" A hand jostled me awake. I opened my eyes to find the area around the shrine lighter. Daylight hadn't broken yet, but some time had passed.

"Shit. I fell asleep." I struggled to sit up and turned around to see Senja watching me. She relaxed and gave me a small smile.

"You needed rest. These past few days have been difficult. But it's time to rise. Do you know what you need to do?"

I shook my head. "Not exactly. But Rhaegos, or my dreams, or something… I saw Henry, the real Henry, and another man who shifted to look like him. The imposter. He doesn't have Henry's strength. He was smaller, less muscular. Not weak, but not…" I gestured with my hands as I tried to think of the word. "He wasn't built like Henry or Haldrek. Which is probably why he was less inclined to fight on the battle field." My mind went back to those moments when Haldrek and I were fighting the imposter. He wasn't using illusion so much as deception. The imposter was quick.

"So he may not have the strength your friend Henry has? Or had?"

I closed my eyes and shook my head again. "If I confront the imposter, he's going to use magic. Cunning. Tricks like Seirye. This isn't going to be a battle like when we took back the thegn hall of Heidrunefoss. Not so much brute force. It's going to be like fighting Seirye again." I groaned.

Senja placed her hand on my shoulder and put something warm on my lap. Opening my eyes, I found a small loaf of bread. I frowned and looked up at Senja.

"I may have sent Paavo into the city to acquire supplies. No one would question his being there or his intentions."

"Perks of being a dragon, I guess." Breaking open the bread, I felt the warmth emanate from it and inhaled deeply. It was a meat and vegetable bread—Svartån bread—and it both made me happy and want to cry.

Senja rubbed my back. "You will have to return to the palace today and you will need your strength. For yourself and for Haldrek."

"Did Paavo hear anything when he went into Drattüjert?"

"Haldrek is still alive, if that's what you're asking. Teminth is keeping him strong as the healers aid him. But the imposter knew exactly where to inflict the most damage."

I grimaced and began chewing the bread. The imposter was taking away nearly everything I loved. My friends, my family, my possible future. I didn't have an army or much at all, but if he thought he was taking me down, he'd be in for a surprise.

"Can you and Paavo get me into the palace without anyone seeing me?"

Senja smiled. "Of course. That will be a simple task." Footsteps crunched behind us.

"Are you making plans now, Ina of Svartån?"

I turned back to see Paavo join us. Instead of bread, he had a leather bag full of round objects. Pulling one out, he inspected what looked like a raw meatball before popping it in his mouth. I tried not to look too disgusted as my stomach churned. Meatballs weren't any worse than raw flesh after a battle, and I'd seen plenty of dragons eating that.

Instead, I focused on what I would do going forward. *The plan* was barely anything. First, I get into the palace through Paavo and Senja's help. Then I find the imposter Henry and kill him. And then what? What would I do after that? What would happen if I ran into Kamira? She'd attack if she saw me, though I wasn't afraid she'd hurt me. At this point, she'd done as much as she possibly could…unless she got to the imposter before me and joined him in an alliance. But then again, she might have already done that.

"Ina?" Paavo's voice pulled me from my thoughts.

"I get into the palace, find the imposter and kill him. If Kamira gets in my way, I beat her senseless. Or least do something to keep her from blocking me. If she calls the guards on me again…" I sighed and looked back at Paavo and Senja. Paavo walked away as if no longer interested.

"Wait—" I stood up as he got on one of the furthest benches from us. He walked backwards and then ran forwards, shifting into a dragon form by the time he was in the air. I gasped and Senja grinned.

"He scared me the first time he did that. I didn't know he was a dragon then."

I turned back to Senja in surprise. When this was all over, I was definitely getting her full story. She continued to stare at Paavo in the sky as he swooped around and down toward the city.

"He says the city guards are preparing for something. More Blodnar."

"More Blodnar?!"

Senja nodded. "They're waiting, quietly, outside the city gates. Which means…"

"The imposter is already inside. Likely in the palace."

"You are correct. Paavo also says he can sense some discontent from the city guards. They are anxious to fight the Blodnar, but a small group of the advisors has told them to refrain until further notice." Senja laughed. "The warriors grumble loudly."

"We need to get back to the palace." I glanced up to the east. The light over the horizon had increased. The sun wasn't quite out yet, but it would be by the time I reached the city gates. "Is there a way you can disguise me so I can get in?"

Senja shook her head, still smiling. "You don't need a disguise to get in. Do you have your plan, though?"

I sighed, placing the last bit my Svartån bread in my mouth, and nodded. "Yes."

"Then hop on my back and experience how dragons arrive at the palace in Drattüjert."

The flight on Senja's back was both terrifying and exhilarating. I clenched my whole body tight and buried my face in the fur or hair along the ridge of her spine. It made for an uncomfortable ride, but oddly enough, I didn't feel like I was going to fall off either. When we arrived on a balcony high above the rest of the palace, I stumbled off, right into Senja's tail. Trying to hold my stomach as much as I could, I leaned over the edge and vomited, not caring what it hit.

The sound of angry shouts made me recoil. Senja shifted and ran to the railing, hand over her mouth.

"Sorry! Rough landing!"

The anger below us settled into unhappy grumblings as the guards left their positions.

"That was easier than I thought," I whispered. Senja smiled and helped me up.

"This was your first time riding a dragon, right?"

I nodded, hoping my stomach would finally settle.

"It gets easier with time. When this is all said and done, I'll have to take you flying again."

"Okay." I couldn't say much more, as the mere idea of doing that again set my stomach on edge.

"Where do you think the imposter will be?"

"Anywhere," I grumbled. "If he's plotting, one of the meeting rooms, or if he's gloating, the throne room."

"Well, we need to get you in there soon. Paavo is distracting people in the front of the palace so—"

The door to the balcony creaked open as Senja and I froze. She stepped in front of me slightly as her hands shifted into claws.

"Senja, I thought that was you and Paavo I kept hearing last night." Taimi poked her head out the door and slipped onto the balcony with us. Salla followed her and shut the door.

"Taimi, Salla." Senja's tone was firm but respectful. I'd forgotten Haldrek's aunts had his same gift.

Taimi glanced around at me and bowed deeply. "Forgive an old woman, my High Queen. My own fears have gotten the better of me these past weeks. I should have been a better friend and ally."

My heart was torn between forgiveness and anger. They hadn't actively tried to hurt me, but neither Taimi nor Salla had come to my aid when Kamira had accused me of awful things, nor when she had forced me out of the palace.

"Why this change of heart now?"

Taimi looked up at me, at her sister, and then back at the ground as she knelt on the small patch of balcony that wasn't covered in snow. "We feared the man called Henry had swayed you away from Haldrek and Lohikärra. While neither of us trusted Kamira, she is easier to deal with than a foreigner. Especially a Blodnar foreigner."

"You didn't trust my loyalty to either my husband or the country I chose to be a part of?"

Taimi averted her eyes and Salla cleared her throat. "We were wrong, my queen. Unfortunately, we have seen many a thegn and other abthanry fall in love quickly, only to find out that their love was unrequited." Salla hesitated. "Though neither of us think you would try to betray Haldrek or Lohikärra, our fears were louder than our dragons."

"Even your dragons told you I was trustworthy and you didn't listen?" I glanced at Senja and she shrugged, as if this wasn't that uncommon.

Taimi stood back up. "We have erred. For that we are sorry." She twisted her attention between Salla and myself. "After Kamira cast you out, both of us realized our error. Now she has brought the Blodnar man back into the palace. We should have stood firmer with you and we should have trusted you. Even after your Blodnar friend came."

"He's not my friend. The man who arrived after Haldrek's departure is an imposter bent on chaos. He uses illusion magic to pretend to be my friend Henry, but the actual Henry would have never done any of the things the imposter has done."

"We believe you now." Salla focused her attention on me. "We've asked for your forgiveness, but at the same time both of us know we must show our loyalty to you and Haldrek as well. I'm assuming you have a plan. Is that why Senja brought you here?"

I nodded. "Get into the palace, find the imposter, kill the imposter. Possibly smack Kamira around if she gets in my way."

Taimi laughed, and then turned somber. "Sorry. I would not begrudge you if you smacked her around. Neither would many of those still in the palace. Come, we will get you inside safely and keep you from getting caught by Kamira or her allies."

I glanced at Senja and she nodded. "You are in good hands with Taimi and Salla. I'm going to see what Paavo is dealing with. He's gone quiet and that worries me. But I'll be near the palace still."

Stepping inside with Taimi and Salla, I heard a thud as Senja shifted and took off outside. I took a moment to adjust my senses to the much darker corridor ahead of us. A darkness that could either be to our benefit or not.

"Oh yes, Tesroan, Kamira is so silly isn't she? She walks around like she's the High Queen! Ordering people around like she's in charge and calling the real High Queen a traitor. Even though Kamira welcomed the Blodnar with more lavishness than Ina ever did. I think her dragon has all but given up on her." Sibila's voice echoed at the end of the corridor and made me more irritable. Not so much with Sibila, but with what it sounded like Kamira had done in my absence.

I had planned on going after the imposter first but now the idea of walking into Kamira on purpose and punching her out sounded fantastic. Standing up, I walked toward the end of the corridor, ignoring Taimi and Salla's hushed pleas to stop. I was done being nice.

As soon as I got to the next hallway, Sibila stopped in front of me and curtsied. Without a word, she pushed me back into the darker hallway, into an alcove I hadn't noticed before. I tried to push back, but she refused to move. The sound of clanking armor nearby stopped me.

Sibila continued to hum and fiddle with things around me as the clanking stopped.

"Who goes there?"

I froze, wonder what in the name of the dragons Blodnar soldiers were doing inside the palace. Was this Kamira's doing? The imposter?

"Oh dear child! We finally found you!" Taimi ran up to hug Sibila, who stopped and grinned at her. Salla hurried next to them, blocking any view of me.

"My sister and I were just looking for the girl. She's been cursed and sometimes gets lost in the passages here, you see?"

"Grandmother?" Sibila turned around to face Salla.

"Yes dear, it's Lady Salla. We've been looking for you all morning. Are you hungry?"

Sibila nodded and I heard some grumbling from the Blodnar soldiers before they starting walking away. Once the sound of them faded from earshot, I sighed.

"Thank you, Sibila." I whispered quietly, not thinking she'd respond.

"You're very welcome." She focused on me and I stared at her in surprise. "Tesroan tells me Kamira and the Blodnar mage are together right now, planning something. I think you would want to find them sooner rather than later. He weaves his magic much like my brother does and the little loyalty Kamira has to Haldrek and Lohikärra fades even now."

"Thank you." I cocked my head, then looked to Taimi and Salla to see if they were as surprised as I was by her sudden shift.

They weren't.

Instead Taimi released Sibila from her hug and asked, "Do you know where exactly Kamira and the Blodnar are?"

Sibila smiled and looked off distantly. "Follow me." She turned around and began dancing back down the hallway she had come from.

Chapter Twenty-Eight

We slowly followed Sibila as she danced and swayed down several sets of stairs to what I thought was the floor just above the throne room. This floor held many of the larger spaces for banquets and socializing, as well as the room where many of my meetings with advisors had been.

But outside of the main hall, it was relatively empty. I'd expected more people hurrying about.

Sibila danced and swayed into a small empty room near the staircase. The three of us followed her and as she sat on a bench near a small outer window, she said, "It'd be best to shut the door. They're coming."

Taimi quickly closed the door and leaned against it as she sat on the floor.

Speak with those who ally themselves with you. Their knowledge will be invaluable.

As much as I wanted to catch Kamira and the imposter, I knew better than to question Rhaegos's judgement. My only hesitation was how to go about getting said knowledge.

"Sibila? Can I ask you something?"

She turned to me and nodded.

I hesitated, trying not to say something horribly offensive. There was the question I wanted to ask, but there was really no polite way to ask it, so I took a different approach. "Why are you helping me? I mean...your brother is currently trying to destroy me and Haldrek, he's done horrible things to me and my loved ones, and your father basically sent a man to torment me from the time I was a little child. I know your mother sent you here for your protection, but do you care how things turn out?" As soon as I said everything, I wondered if I'd said too much.

Sibila glanced at her hands, then up at me, looking very serious. "I do care how things turn out here. If you are able to destroy my brother, that will be a dream come true for me. I've heard stories of your own upbringing. It wasn't pleasant, was it? Not just because of Hrothbere."

I shook my head, still stunned by her change in demeanor. "It wasn't. My mother was an awful person. Someone I'd be more than happy to forget for the rest of my life."

She nodded. "My father was the same way. Rorik is his eldest, but we are only half siblings. Rorik's mother died when he was either a baby or child, I don't know, but it was well before my existence. Still, our father saw him as his heir, his legacy. Rorik saw me as competition. Or a toy perhaps. Something to torment. Our father would look the other way, dismissing my mother as hysterical and jealous if she disciplined Rorik in any way." Sibila glanced up at Salla. "*Bestmora,* come sit with me. You look tired." Salla happily sat down next to Sibila.

I frowned. "Are you two... related?" If they were, I felt like there was an interesting story behind the family connection.

Salla shook her head. "Sibila's mother, Ingrid, is a distant cousin to my husband, Sigurd. When she and her sister, Nysa, were orphaned, they came to live at the thegn hall with us. When each of them got married and had children, I went to visit them. They were the daughters I never had. Their children are the closest thing I have to grandchildren. For better or for worse."

I nodded and Sibila continued. "My mother has always been very skilled at mage work and spells. For many years, she tried to ease the tension between me and Rorik. I learned that if I pretended to be ignorant of the world around me, Rorik and his friends would grow tired of tormenting me. I wasn't a threat and it wasn't fun anymore. It also gave my mother the excuse to hide me away."

"So she started a rumor that you'd been cursed in order to keep you protected?"

Sibila nodded. "It works, sometimes. When I finally became a haldraga, Tesroan promised me she'd keep me safe from those who would harm me by telling me when to keep up my ruse and when not to."

I nodded. "Is that why..." I hesitated as I tried to think of the best way to describe her behavior. "Is that why you've always acted the way you have? To protect yourself?"

Sibila nodded. "I have no love for my brother. Nor for my father. I wish I could, but I always saw anger and felt pain around them. The only people I've been able to trust are the dragons, my mother, and Lady Salla."

"Do you trust me now? If you've dropped your facade?"

She nodded. "Tesroan told me you were safe from the beginning, but I will admit I had to see for myself. While there are those who question your abilities with the Blodnar mage, I think you have handled him better than many in Lohikärra could."

I grew warm at the compliment. It felt good after weeks of being told how badly I'd messed things up. Though now I felt like I'd misjudged Sibila. Badly. Even if it hadn't been out loud. I could understand having to live under a facade to keep yourself safe. How long had I done that with my mother?

"Thank you. That means a lot." I glanced around the room and saw Taimi stand up. "Once we deal with Kamira and the imposter, I'll do what I can to make this place safe enough that you don't have to wear your facade if you don't want to." Turning back to Sibila, I watched as a grin lightened her face.

"I would enjoy that." She paused and then stood up, crossing her hands to the opposite shoulders and closing her eyes. "I promise on the dragons that I will aid you as I can. Lohikärra will suffer if Rorik is in charge, and I do not want to see that day happen."

"Thank you. I—" Loud voices interrupted me and I spun around as Taimi straightened up. She nodded to Salla and Sibila.

The voices got closer and angrier. They spoke a mix of Lohikärran and the tongue of the Blodnar. Palace guards and Blodnar soldiers most likely. If this was the first time they had come to blows, I would be surprised.

"We should go as soon as we can." Taimi waved her sister and Sibila over.

Sibila shook her head. "You two go. I will stay with the High Queen. Create a distraction and we will continue on to find Kamira and the Blodnar mage."

"Sibila..." Salla began to object, but stopped as Sibila walked up to me.

"I'll be fine, *bestmora*. I trust the High Queen now, and Tesroan has never steered me wrong yet."

More shouting came closer, as well as a thud against the door. I put my arm out protectively in front of Sibila.

"Come on, Salla, let's distract them before things become too chaotic." Taimi nodded to both of us as she grabbed her sister's hand.

Sibila and I slipped out of sight of the door as the two sisters opened it and disappeared into the chaos.

As soon as the hall quieted, Sibila went to the door.

"It's safe, my queen. Let's go."

Sure enough, the wide corridor in front of the eating hall was empty, and I wondered what Taimi and Salla had done. Sibila grabbed my hand and began leading me down another nearby corridor.

"Tesroan tells me that the imposter and Kamira are nearby. They are in an empty room on this floor."

"Your dragon is a very helpful friend."

"She is indeed. I—"

The sound of more armor, clinking like chainmail this time, interrupted Sibila. We froze right as a group of three Lohikärra warriors, palace guards, stopped and stared at us.

"Crap," I whispered. Their expressions turned from surprise to anger to amusement in a matter of seconds. Pushing Sibila behind me, I imagined these were some of Kamira's cronies. I pulled my blade out in defense, alongside the shield I'd grabbed in the last room, and set myself into a defensive position.

But instead of attacking, the men started laughing and the warrior closest to me, a tall, lean man with dark black hair, bowed deeply.

"It is a relief to see the true High Queen didn't abandon us."

I cocked my head, now thoroughly confused. Watching them for a moment, I realized their weapons were still sheathed and relaxed my stance.

"Who said I had abandoned you all?" I already had a thought, but I wanted to hear it from the men themselves.

"You know who, my queen." The way the other two warriors nodded and deferred to the dark-haired man, I got the impression he led them in some capacity. "Kamira announced last night that you had fled the palace once she had confronted you, and that now she was the new High Queen. A few questioned her, but she silenced them with help from the Blodnar spy."

"Seriously? How many people still support her?"

"Very few. But the Blodnar brought enough men to keep us from overthrowing her." The warrior's face darkened. "There are also guards loyal to her in front of the High King's quarters. They only let a few people in."

My heart dropped. "Has Kamira been in there?"

The dark-haired man nodded. "Last I heard, she'd forced all of the healers and servants out." He hesitated and then said, "Word is, she's hoping the High King is too far gone to recover from his injuries. Or that he's dead already."

I clenched my fists, thinking of what I'd do to Kamira when I found her.

Focus, Ina. Haldrek still lives.

Rhaegos was right. I pushed my thoughts of vengeance to the side. "And the imposter? Has he been in the High King's quarters?"

The warrior shook his head. "I do not know. The imposter seemed more interested in the throne room than in the High King's quarters. He seems to think the High King is already dead."

My stomach churned and I fought to push my anxiety away. "A curse on both of them. I will destroy Kamira and the imposter if it's the last thing I do."

The dark-haired warrior nodded and knelt to one knee. "I—and those with me—offer our loyalty to you, the true High Queen. We will fight with you to rid this place of those who don't belong."

"Thank you." This was unexpected, but I wasn't one to complain. "I accept your loyalty."

He stood back up. "I assume you have a plan, my queen? What would you have us do?"

"We need to eliminate Kamira and the imposter's support. Find those who do not follow them, those you trust, and let them know I am here, ready to protect the palace and the city."

The men nodded. "And then?"

"And then we get rid of those who support either Kamira or the imposter. Lock them in the dungeons, kill them, I do not care, but if they don't support Haldrek or myself, they are not to be running around the palace freely."

"What of Lady Kamira and the imposter?"

I glanced at Sibila, who nodded, and then back at the men. "We'll deal with them separately. Do any of you remember where you saw Kamira last?"

One of the warriors pointed up above us. "She was in her quarters, speaking with someone. Her guards, or rather the Blodnar soldiers now guarding her, wouldn't let anyone near the door, but she was shouting loud enough that the whole castle could hear."

I raised an eyebrow. "Angry shouting or otherwise?"

The dark-haired warrior grinned briefly in amusement. "It sounded like angry shouting. Unless Lady Kamira has a strange way of showing her enjoyment. Either way, I wouldn't want to be in that room with her with the mood she was in."

I nodded. "Thank you. We'll go see if we find her or the imposter." A thought crossed my mind. Perhaps the two of them were coming to blows already. That would make it easier for me to fight them. "Go find others to help, and may the dragons watch over us all."

The men bowed and disappeared down the hall they had come from. I looked around, trying to find the closest staircase.

"Follow me." Sibila took my arm and we hurried off into the corridor ahead of us.

Chapter Twenty-Nine

I t didn't take long for us to find Kamira and whomever she was talking to. Sibila had mapped out the palace in a way I had yet to grasp. It was almost as if she'd lived here her entire life and not somewhere else. As soon as we reached the floor above where we had been, Kamira's furious screech rattled around us.

"I know what I'm doing! How do you think you were able to get in here without so much as a fight?"

I couldn't hear the other person's voice, but given what Kamira had said, I only had one guess. I glanced around the corner and sure enough, there were a couple of Blodnar guards standing alert at the door.

"Now we just have to figure out how to get inside," I whispered.

"Distract the guards and distract the imposter." Sibila's voice was soft as if she was contemplating something. "Or let Kamira anger the imposter enough that he leaves, and then distract the guards."

"I feel like the second option will be the more successful one. But what do we do while we wait? Is there anything to get them more agitated at each other?"

Sibila had closed her eyes and started humming. I grimaced, knowing she was probably doing something useful, but still wondering what exactly that was.

"I am as good as Queen now. Don't underestimate me, Gaius!"

Gaius? I'd heard that name before. It was definitely a Blodnar name. Was that the imposter's name? I put my ear next to the wall, praying it wasn't too thick to hear Gaius's response.

"You are *not* as good as Queen now." Gaius's voice rose loud enough for me to hear it through the stone. "The High King is on his deathbed, but his Queen still lives, and you have told me yourself she will inherit the throne if he dies. Not your lover."

I gaped, glad that almost no one was in this small corridor. I glanced up as a servant passed us. She paused for a moment, then bowed her head and kept moving. I returned my attention to Kamira and Gaius's voices on the other side. The fact that Kamira had a lover was news to me. She had made it sound as if she'd wanted Haldrek as her lover.

Obviously that was a ploy. My heart twisted with regret at my angry words from only a few days before.

"Rorik isn't my lover. Not yet anyway. But I will be his Queen. One day."

"Not if that Svartån bitch still lives."

"It doesn't matter if she lives or dies. No one likes her outside of Svartån and Andrattür anyway."

"I highly doubt that. Though her allies are less than those of Rorik, she is still a threat. You will not be Queen until she is dead."

"That will be a simple task. She's not even a good fighter, and she's too gullible to be sneaky. I will be more than happy to stab a blade through her heart."

Both of them stopped talking, and as footsteps shuffled back and forth on the other side of the wall, I got the impression the imposter wasn't on board with Kamira's plan.

"It will be easier for you to ensure the High King's death than it will be me. You are correct—Ina is gullible. That's why I'll be the one to kill her. She may or may not still think I am her friend, Henry."

"Is that fool dead?" Kamira laughed and I wanted to choke the laughter right out of her. My heart hurt at the idea of Henry possibly being dead at Gaius or Rorik's hands.

"If he isn't, he will be soon. He pissed off Rorik, and you know how Rorik is when he's in one of his moods."

Kamira's laugh trilled with joy. "So the fool has probably been killed and risen again as Rorik's slave?"

"Yes. I wouldn't be surprised if he had."

There was a coughing fit from one of the guards and I turned my attention to the noise. Sibila was still humming with her eyes closed. I sighed and put my ear back to the wall.

"So what is your plan, Kamira? Or do I need to create one again?"

"I have a plan. I kill Haldrek, blame it on Ina because people already think she delivered him to you in that battle, kill her, and then get the other advisors and hersirs to follow me as I deliver Drattüjert to Rorik and become his Queen."

Silence. "Too many variables, but I suppose I can work with that." Something creaked in the room and I heard footsteps. Pulling away from the wall, I saw Sibila stand up and start prancing toward where the guards stood.

I reached out to grab her, but she dodged out of my reach and continued on her way, starting to sing now.

"Hey! Who—"

The door creaked open as Sibila passed by. The imposter's voice cut off the guards. "It's just the cursed girl. She's no threat; just let her dance. I'll deal with her later."

Sibila spun around and shook her head. "No, Tesroan, we must not breathe fire or poison on them. That would be very rude. I know they look like a tasty snack, but not today."

"See, she doesn't know what's going on. Come on."

The guards left with the imposter, a welcome surprise. Once they disappeared, Sibila danced back over to me and waved her hand around, humming some more. After a few moments, she stopped and knelt low, grinning wryly.

"No one can see you now. Kamira is alone in the chambers she chose for herself."

I didn't know so much about the invisible part, but I nodded. "Thank you, Sibila. Do you think you can keep anyone else from coming up here? I need to have a private chat with Kamira."

Sibila's wry smile turned into an amused smirk. "Of course I can, my queen." She turned around and started dancing again, singing softly as she did. For a moment, I admired her skill. But I hated why she had to act this way.

Slipping out of the hall, I snuck into Kamira's room. Her attention was on the vista outside her small window. She was oblivious to my presence.

As Sibila's singing grew louder outside, Kamira sighed in annoyance. "Will someone get that addle-minded brat away from me? I can't think!"

I kicked the door shut with my boot and stood up as she spun around.

"No, but I can get some answers out of you."

For a moment, Kamira looked surprised, then disgust and a certain level of smugness covered her face.

"I'm not even going to call the guards, because this works too."

"You really think you're going to succeed?" I pulled Freya's Menace out and pointed it at her.

"Yes, because even if you kill me, you've already killed Haldrek, and no one will accept you as Queen. Not even the dragons." She shifted her hand behind her and toward a pocket where I was certain she held a blade. I pointed my sword at that hand.

"Keep your hands where I can see them. I don't trust you."

"The feeling is mutual, half-breed. At least others trust me. I can't say that about you."

I wanted to laugh, but I knew better than to give her a reaction. "If that helps you sleep at night, keep on believing that."

She laughed. "You think people in this palace trust you? You think that once your beloved Haldrek is truly dead and my body goes missing that they won't look to you and want your blood?"

"I think they trust me more than they would ever trust you or Rorik, considering you let a Blodnar whom they *definitely* don't trust into the city and the palace. Also, you are far too loud."

She scowled at me. "Doesn't matter if the only people who heard me are Gaius's men and a couple of crazy women. And yes, I do know about Sibila's magic. It's not that hard to see if you've been dealing with illusion magic all your life." Her scowl disappeared and she cocked her head with a smug smirk. "Did you not know about that facade until just now?"

"I knew about it all along." Obviously it was a lie, but I doubted Kamira knew too much about Sibila's magic unless Rorik had told her. "I just know how to stay quiet, too."

Her smirk disappeared as she pulled a blade out of her other pocket and flung it at me. I dodged, blocking it with my sword so it skittered away under a nearby piece of furniture.

"Bitch." She waved her hand and I tried to block whatever spell she'd tossed my way with my shield. Instead, I got knocked back into the door, my breath disappearing from my lungs.

I tumbled to my feet with a gasp, and cast a lightning spell through my sword. "Too-Sal-pama!" She dodged it, rolling onto her already messy bed. The sheets twisted around her ankles and I took the chance to lunge at her. But she was quicker and cast another blast of air at me.

"Is that all you can do? Seriously?"

"No, but I'm not about to wreck this place. One day it will be mine. As it always should have been." She got the sheets untangled from her feet and ducked into an adjoining room. As I chased after her, she tossed a bucket of something foul smelling at me and I dodged out of the way, pushing the residue from me with my shield.

The smell was nasty as I jumped over what she'd just tossed and followed her into the next room. It was much darker in here and I had to stop, listening for her presence. Something creaked behind me and I swung, catching her with the edge of my shield as she toppled head first into the sludge on the floor.

"Ugh!" She grabbed whatever was on the floor and tossed it at me. I knocked it away as she scrambled up and wiped filth from her face and mouth.

"It suits you, given how much shit you've been talking about me over the past few months."

"At least I speak the truth."

"Do you? Because pretty much everything you've called me is what you've become. A monster, a traitor, selling out to the Blodnar. All of that was you. Hell, I bet you were even fucking that Gaius guy."

She stepped back toward the window with a smirk. "And if I was? He told me I was his most amazing lover. Something you wish you could be to Haldrek. Something you'll never hear from anyone."

"I don't care about who you have sex with. I care that you're slandering me. I care that you are destroying Lohikärra for your own pleasure and you don't give a shit about anyone but yourself."

"What are you going to do? Kill me? That isn't going to help you. People still hate you."

"I'm not going to kill you." I remembered her words about kicking me out of the palace and making an oath. "I'm going to make you swear an oath to the dragons."

She frowned at me, and then laughed. "You really think I'd swear an oath to you? Or promise you anything? You're the one who broke your oath by coming back into the palace. You should be watching your back for the dragons. They don't like oath breakers."

"You're right, but I don't think they'll consider it an oath broken when they were the ones who brought me to the palace in the first place."

Her eyes widened as fury colored them. I sheathed my sword and grabbed her by the hair, pulling her up from where she leaned against the window.

"Let's go."

I had no idea where I was taking her, but I needed to find that priestess of Tenelth again. Or at least one of them. There should still be a few still in the palace.

Forcing her back out of the room and into the main space, I saw Sibilia dancing happily in the center. An older priestess stood on the other side of her, looking anxious, as if she was trying to beckon Sibila back toward her. Sibila ignored her as she collapsed into a nearby chair, grinning.

"Just who I wanted to see." I smiled at the priestess, who looked at me and Kamira in surprise and disgust. The smell emanating from Kamira wasn't a pleasant one.

"My queen..." The old woman stared at me. "I thought you'd been cast out?"

"The dragons brought me back. You can thank Paavo and Senja. They weren't very pleased with what Kamira and her allies have been doing."

The priestess looked at Kamira and nodded. "Yes, Kamira has dishonored her dragon. Many, many times. I can hear it speak."

Kamira grumbled something under her breath I couldn't understand.

The priestess shook her head and focused on me. "What would you have me do, my queen?"

"Kamira—and I—wish to make an oath by the dragons."

The priestess hesitated. "Is this oath under duress?"

"It is! It isn't valid!"

I shook Kamira by the hair. "Would you rather me kill you and send you to Lyrroth for all the things you have done to betray Lohikärra and the High King?"

"Of course she wouldn't. She still wishes to join up with my brother and do more damage!" Sibila shouted from where she sat.

"I have no intention of joining up with Rorik! I would never defile Lohikärra."

"Then will you swear an oath to the dragons for that?"

Kamira was silent for a moment, and then nodded. "I swear by the dragons and to the dragons that I will never aid the necromancer Rorik of Etelaranikä." The old priestess's eyes glazed over with a white film as her hands filled with a white light.

"Promise you will leave the palace and Drattüjert forever on the pain of death."

Kamira hesitated and I dropped my shit-splattered shield before reaching for my side blade.

"I promise by the dragons and to the dragons that I will leave the palace and Drattüjert forever on the pain of death."

I released her and she stumbled to her knees, despite her feet still being on the ground.

The priestess turned to me. "And what do you promise, High Queen Ina, Lady of Lohikärra?"

"I promise to avenge my husband, the High King, defeat those who would see him dead, and protect Lohikärra for all of my days."

The priestess's hands stopped glowing and she exhaled. "Thus as it has been promised, so shall it be known by the dragons."

A warm sensation flooded my brain and I got the impression Rhaegos was pleased. Turning to Kamira, I said, "I'll be merciful, even though I have every right not to be. You have until nightfall to leave Drattüjert. Understood?"

She sneered at me. "And if I don't?"

The priestess cleared her throat. "You'll have to answer to the dragons. Something I wouldn't test if I were you."

Kamira paled and scrambled to her feet. Without another word, she ran off. Sibila stood up and began twirling again as she followed Kamira from a distance.

The priestess shook her head. "A sad thing, that child. But no matter, the dragons watch over her." She turned to me. "If you wish to take back Drattüjert from those who sully it and mock the dragons, hie yourself to the throne room. The Blodnar menace defiles your husband's seat as we speak."

"Thank you for letting me know." I grabbed my foul-smelling shield and slipped down the staircase to the throne room.

Chapter Thirty

I ran into the throne room, surprised by how easily I had defeated Kamira. It had almost been too easy, even with her verbal assaults. Despite the fact that she had attack me with her blade first, I felt like the fight had been more of a diversion. The more I thought about it, the more uncomfortable I felt about everything.

But Kamira would be gone soon enough, exiled from the city on pain of death. Let her go back to her grandfather, Raynord, or whomever else. For now, my focus was on finding her co-conspirator—the imposter.

"Ina..." A voice taunted me from the thrones and I spun around to see the imposter lounging in Haldrek's throne with a little hand wave in my direction.

"Stand and fight me, you coward." I pulled Freya's Menace from my sheath and readied myself for the inevitable.

"Didn't expect to see me back so soon?"

"I expected you. Doesn't mean I want you here." I stepped forward and he stood up.

"Is this how you treat friends? No wonder you never had many. Who could tolerate a violent, erratic girl like yourself?"

"Shut up. You were never my friend. The real Henry would never act this way."

The imposter pushed back his long brown hair and started walking around me. I turned to keep him front and center. "How long did it take you to figure that out? Did you even care? What I did to him?"

My throat tightened with anger. This was just as much a confession that the imposter had done something to Henry. He'd hurt not only my husband and my future, but my friend as well.

"I care. Probably more than you ever will. And I will take my vengeance on you for all you've done."

He laughed. "I doubt it. There have been plenty who swore vengeance on me. But look, I'm still here. What makes you think you are any more special than the others?"

"I am the High Queen of—"

His laugh interrupted me and my anger grew inside. "I have slain the High King of Lohikärra. If he is not dead yet, he will be soon. And he was a far mightier warrior than you can ever proclaim to be."

"But he has not had the experience with illusion magic as I have."

A flicker of doubt crossed the imposter's face, then he smirked. "How much experience has that been? I've heard of your feats with the Isillas up north. As talented as they think they might be, they are nothing compared to those who taught me." He waved his hand and his form shifted into that of Rorik. I steeled myself to keep from shuddering. "See, even you do not know my power."

"Illusion isn't just disguises. Anyone skilled in magic knows that." I lunged forward, knowing I needed to keep him on his toes. Otherwise he might actually start using more than just the tricks he'd shown me thus far.

He jumped back with a grin and suddenly split into three people who darted in various directions, essentially trying to get me to go after the wrong person and allow him to escape. Instead I stayed still and waited until he stopped moving.

"What are you waiting for, little queen?" The words echoed from each version. "If you think you are so smart, come and fight me."

I glanced around at the three nearly identical versions of Rorik. He hadn't shifted into another form, and I doubted he'd change into his true self unless I forced him to. Watching the three preen and wave their hands like idiots, I also kept an eye out for my sword to do anything in reaction to this magic. After a moment, the reflection in my blade shimmered as I passed it in front of one of the three imposters.

I smiled and lunged. Only for the person to disappear as my blade cut through it.

The imposter's laughter from behind me made my skin prickle with anger. I swung at him again as he sat in the High King's chair, barely missing him as he dodged out of sight and behind my throne.

"I expected you to be a better fighter than this for all the stories told of you. I wonder how many of them were your beloved actually defeating your foes for you?"

"None of them. I defeat my enemies on my own."

"Then prove it." He rolled out from behind my chair and disappeared into thin air this time.

"Shit." I spun around, knowing he couldn't have just evaporated. There had to be a shimmer of movement somewhere. As I thought about where he might be, the whiz of air past my cheek made me twist away and I swung in an arc, hoping to catch whatever had grazed me. For a split second, I saw someone's reflection in my blade before it hit an object and the imposter was rocked back into existence. He rolled back toward me and I jumped, my stomach churning as I felt heavier for a second. Spinning around, I narrowly missed a bladed star make its way past my left ear. A blond-haired young man, not much older than me, flashed into existence before shifting back into Henry's form.

Once again larger than me, the imposter started taking swings at my face. I twisted slightly with every swing, doing my best to keep enough distance between us and knocking each blow back with my shield. After a few seconds of this, I parried forward, stabbing through part of his illusion. He grunted and the illusion flashed away again, but he was still physically whole.

"Your illusions are just that. Illusions. You don't actually have the strength of bigger men."

"I don't need the strength of bigger men!" He shifted into Haldrek and swung at me a final time. I blocked the blow as it crashed into my shield and staggered me back.

Anger and indignation flushed throughout my entire body. "Don't you dare pretend to be my husband!" I swung again, this time with my shield, and knocked him to the ground. He collapsed, the breath knocked out of him, and released his illusion.

For a moment I felt pity. A sense of what he could have been flooded my senses and I felt grief for the person he never had the chance to be.

"You forget, little queen. Illusion magic can also change our feelings for people."

He rolled back onto his shoulders and pushed his feet into my chest. I went flying back, hitting the ground with a thud and cursing myself for giving him that opening. He jumped up as I pulled my shield into my chest and primed Freya's Menace for the attack. As soon as he stabbed down with his dagger, I met it with my shield and thrust my sword through his neck. His eyes widened with surprise as blood began to drip down my blade.

Pulling his body to the ground on my right side, I used my blade as a staff to push myself up.

"And I told you, I've dealt with illusion mages my entire life."

Horror filled his eyes as I pulled my blade out of his neck and his hands went to the wound. He flinched and his body tried to shift as a gasp came out. Then the unexpected happened. A black line spread out from the wound and around his neck. His eyes rolled up and his body shuddered, twisting the two apart.

I stepped back, forcing myself not to vomit as I stared at the now headless body.

"My queen!" A guard, one of the few who had supported me, came running into the throne room and stared at the body as well. He shook his head and focused on me. "The Blodnar are attacking."

My horror disappeared and I shrugged off the images in my head. "Then let's go fight them. The imposter is no longer a threat here."

I hurried behind the warrior, knowing that the imposter could still be a threat, despite my previous words. But his power would hopefully be gone, if I went by the fact that his death had separated his spirit from his body. I knew his ghost would likely try to cause trouble, but I had yet to see one cause more than annoyance.

As we reached the main doors, I saw chaos in the main square. Blodnar soldiers were fighting anyone and everyone. Where were Paavo and Senja? Were they in human form or dragon?

Do not worry for them. Rally the warriors of Drattüjert and show these invaders the might of a Lady of Lohikärra.

I didn't need Rhaegos to tell me twice.

Jumping up to the top of the railing, I balanced myself and shouted, "For Drattüjert!"

Was it stupid or cheesy? Probably. But it got people's attention, giving my warriors the needed edge. I jumped down, landing in front of a grizzled old Blodnar soldier, and slammed my shield into his face, knocking him to the ground and letting a couple of my warriors deal with him.

Running forward, I started cutting down any Blodnar soldier I could see. A few put up a fight, but each time several Drattüjert warriors would swoop in and overwhelm them. Within a few minutes, we had pushed the Blodnar to the eastern gate. I ran through it as they turned and fled. Those still outside the city hesitated, then raised their hands in surrender.

Several of the warriors ahead of me began to move toward those still in their makeshift camps. I realized that whatever the imposter had been doing, it had been less organized than he'd made it out to be.

"Stop!"

The Drattüjert warriors stopped and turned around, looking at me with surprise and anger.

"Don't fight them in their camps. We're not cowards who go after sleeping men."

A few of the Blodnar seemed to think this was a call to retreat, and ran forward. The Drattüjert warriors quickly cut them down. The rest of the Blodnar who had yet to fight slowly got up, still with their hands raised, as more warriors from the city joined me.

I focused my attention on the Blodnar, hoping by the dragons at least one of them would understand me.

Speak. They will know your word by the power of their gods and goddesses.

An interesting comment from Rhaegos, but I knew she at least was worshipped by them as a goddess. Perhaps the other dragons were as well.

"If you wish to die, stay here and fight against my people. If you wish to live, return to your lands and stay there. We have little love or mercy for fighters like you."

A few moments of tense silence passed, and then a few of the Blodnar nodded and backed away, taking up bedrolls and what I assumed were provision bags. I watched with my warriors as they slowly headed away from the city.

"They'll be back, my queen." One of the warriors next to me shook his head, staring at the ground. "You choose mercy over vengeance."

I was done with fighting for now. Chasing after these Blodnar would leave Drattüjert weak to our other enemies. "There has been too much blood. I know many who would have had the Blodnar give them mercy. *We* will give them mercy and they can learn what civilized people do then."

A warrior to my right scoffed. "You don't think they will cut down peasants on their way out of our lands?"

I grimaced. Of course they would. "Send a group of men to keep up with them, but not within eyesight. If they do anything to the innocents along their way...you understand what to do."

The man nodded and turned around as he began shouting orders.

I turned to see Senja and Paavo walking out of the gate towards me. Both of them seemed grim. Had I done the right thing?

"Hail Queen of Drattüjert and Lohikärra! Lady of Lohikärra!" Paavo's voice boomed across the area. He didn't sound pissed. For that I was relieved. But that meant their grim expressions had to do with some other bad news, right? Was Haldrek all right? Or had something happened while I'd been out here fighting?

I rushed over to them and a small smile crossed Senja's face.

"Calm, Ina. Haldrek is still in the Realm of the Living."

I exhaled. "What news do you have?"

"We have cast out the Blodnar out of the city. Would you have us make sure they don't cause any more trouble?"

I looked around. Some of the warriors watching us, including the man I'd told to follow the Blodnar at a distance. I knew they were eager to make sure they were out of Lohikärra once and for all.

"If you wish, but I've already ordered a few of Drattüjert's warriors to follow them and make sure they don't cause any more chaos."

Senja nodded. "Then you need to return to the palace. Some people have found the body of the imposter and there are rumors already."

"Seriously? It hasn't been fifteen minutes, has it?" I was exhausted. The physical exhaustion had begun to creep into my bones now that the adrenaline was fading away, reminding me of how little I'd slept last night. The mental and emotional exhaustion added more weight to my shoulders and legs as I tried to gather up the last dregs of my energy. I still had to cast the imposter's spirit into Lyrroth and that would be exhausting on the best of days.

She shook her head and put her hand around my shoulders, letting me lean into her. "Come. Now that the Blodnar are well and truly gone from the city, let us finish the business in the palace once and for all."

Chapter Thirty-One

I marched my way back to the throne room alongside Senja and Paavo, trying to ignore the fatigue threatening to engulf my body. The only thing keeping me upright was a renewed sense of rage and spite. Fury. The imposter had fooled me and taken away nearly everyone I loved. Henry, Haldrek, my future children, plus more. But he was dead now and I wasn't.

As soon as I stepped into the throne room, Senja and Paavo slipped away to some other quarter of the palace and I found a group of people surrounding the body, ignorant of my arrival. Haldrek's advisors, some of the hersirs, and a few servants. The few faces I could see expressed disgust, surprise and confusion at the now headless body, taking care to not step in the blood surrounding it.

"Do any of you still question *my* loyalty to Lohikärra and the High King?" My voice boomed throughout the room.

Several of the people jumped back in surprise and stared at me. A couple of Haldrek's advisors began murmuring, but grew silent as I stared at them.

"This man. The one you see beheaded on the floor. He pretended to be a dear childhood friend of mine. He promised peace while he engineered violence alongside Kamira. He is a liar, a con artist, and a villain above all. A person who took pleasure in others' suffering, both those of Lohikärra and of the Blodnar Empire. He planned his actions to keep Lohikärra weak, a wolf in sheep's clothing, and he fooled us all." I focused on each and every person as they looked away from me. "He fooled me, pretending he was an ally to Haldrek and I. He fooled many of you into believing your High Queen could not be trusted."

Pointing my blade at the man's body, I continued, "For that, he lost his life and his illusion to a blade that has protected Lohikärra for millennia. His spirit still wanders this palace, but just as I took care of him in the flesh, I'll handle his spirit, too."

One of the advisors lifted his head in an attempt to be haughty. It took me a moment to recognize that it was Gizur. Of course it was Gizur. "What of the future, High Queen? When the next illusion wielder comes begging refuge, will we be in this situation again?"

I hardened my expression. "No." I let snark color my next words. "At least I hope not. I know I've learned a few things, like whom I can trust in this palace. As for everyone else, I cannot speak." My tone softened as I surveyed the rest of the group. "But I hope—and believe—we'll be better prepared in the future."

The members of the group looked away from me. One by one, they began to leave the throne room, until it was only me, the beheaded body, and a fully intact spirit who kept its distance. The rage emanating from it filled the room and threatened to overwhelm me.

I looked directly at it. "It doesn't matter where you are. Here or anywhere else in Lohikärra. As soon as I do the rites over the body, you will leave the Realm of Ghosts."

The spirit rushed toward me as if to attack. I braced myself as it ran through me, leaving a wake of anger and vengeance behind it. I staggered and spun around, facing the ghost as it looked at its hands and then at me. The emotions resonating from it made me ill. Anger, disgust, fury at its failure. Each wave hit me with increasing intensity, aimed straight at my chest. In response, my dragon ring, given to me by Haldrek and blessed by Senja, Rhaegos, and Teminth, wobbled back and forth.

I glared at the belligerent ghost. "You aren't the first hostile spirit I've dealt with, and you won't be the last." The memory of the Isillas spy came back to mind and I felt the exhaustion again. Last time, I'd had Haldrek help me afterwards. Now I'd have to do it myself.

I hadn't done the rite for Lyrroth since I'd cast that ice elf there, but I'd heard the Priests of Tenelth repeat the rite enough times for many dead Blodnar soldiers and a few Lohikärran warriors who had fallen fighting alongside them. Closing my eyes, I focused on his spirit, watching the defiance ripple off and hit me like an avalanche.

Tenelth, Lohikarras første drage,

The spirit's blue form began to waver in my mind's eye, unlike anything I'd ever seen before, almost as if some kind of ghostly fire was consuming him. He was oblivious to it, whatever it was, but it scared me for a moment as I continued:

hastighet denne sjelen,

The imposter raised his fist, reminiscent of when he'd attacked me here only a few hours earlier. My fear shifted to anger, my rage returning. How dare he be angry? Indignant? After everything he'd done, it was evident he'd never had an ounce of honor in him. I spat out the next part of the rite:

vanære i liv og død,

He charged me and I braced myself for the onslaught of emotions he was about to batter me with. I bent over into a defensive position, feeling my dragon ring necklace spin and twist as the imposter's spirit ran into me and stop, the weight of his ghostly presence trying to smother me as I spoke the last words:

til Lyrroths ytre bunnfall.

He emitted a howl. The air was sucked out of my lungs as I got knocked back. As soon as I hit the floor, I gasped and opened my eyes. His blue essence twisted into a black vapor and fought against some kind of invisible bonds as I scrambled backwards. This was nothing like when the Isillas elf had been sent to Lyrroth. After a moment, the black vapor twisted tighter and tighter until it ceased to exist.

You sent him to Lyrroth, but the amount of dark magic he had worked in his short life came due. Not even Lyrroth will accept him.

"Where did he go then? Is he still in the Realm of Ghosts?" I collapsed to the ground as exhaustion hit me, stealing away every ounce of strength I had left.

No, he went to a place outside of the realms of death. A place of which we dragons even hesitate to speak. Which is why there is no death rite for that place. No one enters who does not truly belong.

I shuddered, not wanting to think about that place. There were more questions in my head, but they swirled around without much coherence as I closed my eyes.

As soon as I succumbed to the exhaustion, Rhaegos's presence wrapped around me like a blanket and I passed out.

My head throbbed as I opened my eyes. Bright sunlight streamed in from rooftop windows, blinding me as I regained consciousness. Someone was humming above me and footsteps on stone echoed in the distance. My body ached and my chest grew heavy with every breath, but I didn't know why.

"How are you feeling, little one?"

Bright lights, a feminine voice, and a nickname that only the dragons used. Was I in the Realm of Dragons for some reason?

"Rhaegos?" I whispered, my throat feeling drier than ever.

The voice laughed. "No, it's only me, Senja. I'll take the compliment though. How are you feeling?"

I twisted my neck so I could see her. Sure enough, it was Senja. "Sore, and sad. Where am I?"

"You are in the High King's throne room. You passed out after sending the man pretending to be your friend to Lyrroth. Rhaegos called out to me and Paavo. We came as soon as we heard her plea."

Plea? What had happened that would make Rhaegos plead for help? My memories began to piece themselves together and I remembered the imposter's spirit. "The ritual. Is that why I'm so exhausted?" I tried to sit up, but Senja kept me laying on her lap. The brief glimpse I had of the room made it look empty, but I vividly remembered the imposter's blood on the ground after we fought. Then when I had killed him—beheaded him...my body shuddered as that memory came back in full force. I still had no idea who the imposter was. Only that he had done so much damage. More than I could ever fix.

"Is it still here? The body?"

Senja shook her head. "No. Paavo and the others removed it. Some of the advisors thought you had died as well and wanted to move your body. I told them not to touch you."

"They would have been happy if I died too."

Senja shook her head. "You acted like a true Lady of Lohikärra today. Even your harshest critics will admit that."

I groaned in frustration, my head still throbbing. "What does that even mean? People keep saying it and I've looked for references to it, but nothing has been definite. There's no example of what a Lady of Lohikärra is."

"Because what a High Queen does to earn that title is different for each woman. The common thread is this: they are all willing to make heavy sacrifices in order to protect Lohikärra. Which is what you have been doing all along."

Tears flooded from my eyes as I thought of Haldrek and the refugees Kamira had locked up. Was that what Senja was talking about? If so, that wasn't the sacrifice I wanted to make. That wasn't fair to them.

"You didn't give up on Lohikärra, Ina. Not on your king or your people. As difficult as it may have been to do so, you fought someone you thought was your friend in order to protect your new homeland. Many, whether they be human, elf, dragon, or other sentient creature, could not do that. But you protected Lohikärra from the person you thought you knew. That willingness is what makes *you* a Lady of Lohikärra."

That made more sense. At least more sense than anything else I'd seen or heard.

"So were you a Lady of Lohikärra when you were human, Senja?" I stared up at her, trying to focus long enough to keep from passing out again.

She nodded. "Though it took me many more years than you before I gained that title. My actions in those days were part of why Paavo helped transform me into who I am today."

"A dragon?" I smiled, thinking about how crazy Senja's life must have been to have gone from being human to dragon.

She nodded once again. "How are you feeling now? Do you think you are able to sit up? Or do you need to rest some more?"

I tried to sit up, but even with Senja's help, my body was still worn out. The ritual had exhausted me. Not to mention the imposter had fought me both in this life and as a ghost. I felt bone tired. My head flopped forward as I struggled to sit upright.

"I'll carry you upstairs and you can rest with your beloved." She gently cradled me in her arms and stood up.

"I'm not heavy?" Given that I still had my armor on, I couldn't be that light.

She nodded to someone I couldn't see and began walking. "Part of being a dragon means being very strong. You are no heavier than any of my children ever were. Even as adults."

I closed my eyes as Senja carried me up several flights of stairs and into Haldrek's and my antechamber. My eyes welled up again with tears as we entered and I thought of Haldrek, still on the edge of death.

"Will Haldrek be all right?" I whispered, terrified at what the answer might be, but wanting the truth regardless.

"If he chooses to be, he will. Teminth is with him and his wounds, while serious, aren't grievous enough to kill him. But he will have that injury with him for the rest of his life. If he chooses to go to the Realm of Ghosts, there is nothing Teminth can do." She paused for a moment as she laid me down on the bed next to Haldrek. "But I don't think he's ready for the Realm of Ghosts. He loves you too much, and there is too much he desires to do still."

I nodded, taking his hand in mine. It was warm, but still limp. Opening my eyes, I watched as his chest rose and fell steadily.

Senja stepped away quietly. Before she reached the door, I looked up. Another thought came to my mind. Something I needed to deal with before I could rest.

"Senja?"

"Hmm?"

"The people from the High Queen's Home. Are they still in the dungeons?"

She nodded.

"Will you help them? They shouldn't be there. They should be somewhere safe and warm."

"Of course." A smile crossed her face. "You rest and I'll make sure they are taken care of."

I relaxed back on the bed, falling into an uneasy sleep, my hand in Haldrek's.

Chapter Thirty-Two

The next morning, I awoke with a start. The room was still dark as I heard Haldrek groan in pain.

"Haldrek?"

He groaned again, but I couldn't tell if it was in response to my voice or not.

"My queen?" A sleepy voice spoke from behind me. The curtains opened, revealing soft, wintry light outside of the bed. How long had I been asleep? "Are you wanting breakfast?"

"Um, sure. What time is it?"

The young servant woman glanced to her right. "Still morning. The sun rose maybe an hour ago. We were under orders from the dragons to let you and the High King rest. But if you are hungry, I can fetch you some food."

I nodded. My stomach rumbled, but I was still waking up. "Have you all been checking on Haldrek while we've been asleep?"

"The healers have. So far, they say he is no better and no worse." The maidservant paused. "Let me get you your breakfast and if you wish to get up, I can dress you."

I nodded. "Thank you."

She slipped away, leaving the curtains slightly cracked. Haldrek's chest rose and fell some more as he continued to rest. I squeezed his hand gently as I got up, hoping for a response or some kind of gesture. Some piece of hope. Instead his hand remained still as I sat there.

After breakfast and getting dressed, I made my way down through the throne room and to where the closest entrance to the dungeons were. The weight of everything from yesterday still felt heavy on my shoulders, but as the High Queen—and a Lady of Lohikärra—I didn't have much time to rest. Instead I focused on the door in front of me. It was small and obscure, and I wouldn't have known what existed behind it had Haldrek not shown me months ago. I grabbed the door handle and pulled.

"My queen?" A guard's voice spoke behind me. I paused, and turned to find the man looking at me in confusion. "Is there something you need down in that area?" He looked around and while I guessed my personal guards were around somewhere, the rest of the hallway was empty.

"I'm going to release the women and children who were sent down to the dungeons by Kamira. They pose no threat to Drattüjert and they shouldn't be down there."

He bobbed his head. "I believe those people were brought out yesterday. There was quite a scene between the guards stationed beyond that door and the dragon woman who confronted them. I remember a large group leaving soon after."

My chest grew lighter as I smiled. "Thank you. Do you know if they were taken back to the High Queen's Home?"

He nodded. "I believe so. Would you like me to escort you there?"

I shook my head. "Thank you. I'll be fine." Hurrying off before he could say anything else, I relied on my memory to get me to the rooms that had been set aside.

As I neared them, the subdued chatter of women and children met my ears before I saw anyone. They sounded happy. As happy as one could be after their ordeals. Turning the corner and entering the room, I stopped as everyone's attention turned to me. The chatter faded away and one of the older Priestesses of Tenelth walked up to me, concern etched on her face.

"Is there news, my queen?"

It took me a moment, but I realized they were expecting something else. I shook my head. "The High King still lives and I heard that Senja rescued you all from the dungeons. I—I'm sorry for what Kamira did to everyone. I wish I could have protected you better."

The priestess's expression relaxed and she waved her hand in the air, as if to dismiss my words. "You have done all you could, my queen. There is no animosity among this group toward you." She hesitated, "Feelings of mistrust have arisen in regards to other members of court who still reside here, but it is our fervent wish that those may be remedied in the future."

I nodded, trying to think of something eloquent and noble to say. "I agree."

The priestess bowed and hurried off as the chatter returned. I clasped my hands and let them hang down in front of me as I walked through the more public areas, making sure there wasn't anything amiss or that I couldn't help with. As I passed one room, I saw movement and stopped.

An older woman darted out of the room and bowed fully toward me. "My queen, I wish to thank you for all you've done for my family. You have our eternal gratitude, and I am glad to see you as High Queen again instead of that wretched child, *Lady Kamira.*"

I smiled, trying not to be too amused. The woman was vaguely familiar as I tried to search my still fuzzy memory for her.

"Though my family and kin are from Etelaranikä, you and the High King have our eternal allegiance, as will the aethling you carry. You, he, and your descendants will have the allegiance of many from Etelaranikä for generations to come." She bowed deeply, falling to her hands and knees as her body trembled.

My amusement at her words disappeared and I glanced briefly at myself. The way my hands fell, of course, made my stomach stick out a little. I grimaced and pulled my hands apart, wiping them on the sides of my dress. After the last few months, I didn't need any more rumors or gossip going around.

"Thank you for your allegiance, and that of your family." I hesitated, trying to force the lump from my throat. "Unfortunately, I'm not pregnant right now. One day soon. But not yet."

The woman shook her head, rising unsteadily. Another woman from the room hurried to the old lady's side. I nodded for her to help her friend. She whispered, "Mother, let's go back in the room. The High Queen is busy."

The old woman batted her away. "I know what the dragons have told me. You do not remember me, my queen. That is understandable. I do not expect you to. But I only speak to the visions the dragons have gifted me. I have seen you and the High King in my visions. Dressed as you are now and large with child. When I asked the meaning of this, I was told you and the High King were expecting an aethling."

"When was this vision?" Though I hesitated to call it such, I was still willing to humor the old lady for the time being. At least while I was in public. "Do you know why the dragons have gifted you with visions?"

The woman scoffed. "Of course I do. I am Runa of Halsar. My father was a member of the abthanry, and so am I, gifted with the ability to bind with dragons. My mother's kin have always been chosen to walk as Vollr. My twin sister is one of them now, though they age as the dragons, so she is not the eldest. But between the two lineages, I may see the future if the dragons grant it."

I nodded and glanced at the younger woman aiding Runa. "Is this true?"

The younger woman nodded. "My grandfather was a minor abthanry, the illegitimate grandson of the Thegn of Etelaranikä many years back. While my mother has her dragon with her, she is the last of our family to have the right. My mother also speaks true, that her sister was chosen to be a Vollr. I have seen this with my own eyes."

The lump in my throat grew tighter and Rhaegos stirred within my head, as though confirming what these women had said. Yet the thought terrified me. I couldn't handle thinking I was pregnant and then finding out I wasn't. Not now.

Plastering on a smile, I focused on Runa again. "Thank you for your words then. I... I hope they are true." That was the truth and the most I could say. Without another word, I hurried away, hoping I'd reach Haldrek's and my quarters before I broke down crying.

Over the next few days, I could barely sleep despite my exhaustion. Haldrek still rested and while I was awake, I could see his chest rise and fall with every breath. A sure sign that he was still alive, but only just. There was still no reaction when I touched his hands, and with every passing day, I was terrified I would eventually wake up and find his spirit standing over me, wanting to be sent to Mirroth. Despite Rhaegos's comfort and assurances, I still didn't know if Haldrek blamed me for getting injured in the battle and part of me was afraid I'd wake up in the Realm of Ghosts to him chewing me out for doing something stupid when we'd been fighting the imposter.

But while I was awake, I could make sure he was still alive. I could still have hope.

"My queen?" I turned to the voice, startled out of my thoughts. The servant gestured to the almost empty plate of food next to me. I nodded and he gestured to the potion bottle on the side table next to me. It was half-full with a purple liquid. "Would you like me to take that as well?"

I shook my head. "It's for the High King when he has recovered."

The servant looked confused, but nodded and slipped back out of the room.

I turned back to the purple potion bottle and silently wished once again for Haldrek's swift recovery. Rhaegos's presence warmed my core. Tears bubbled up from my eyes. I trusted her. More so now, but seeing Haldrek still in such a weakened state broke my heart. I wanted him to be well. I needed him to recover.

Brushing my tears away, I held his hand, still warm but limp. "You're not allowed to go to the Realm of Ghosts, Haldrek. Not now, not for a long time. We still need to fight Rorik. Defeat him. You know he'll mess with you there. You're stronger than him in this realm." I tried to be objective. There was so much Haldrek needed to do in Lohikärra. He was the Restorer. Lohikärra was far from being restored. And I couldn't do my job without him. How do you reform a place without first restoring it? The two went hand in hand. One couldn't happen without the other, at least not here in Lohikärra.

"I need you, Haldrek. I love you. There's never been a question in my mind. Not with anyone, and especially not with that person pretending to be Henry." I paused, my voice choking on the lump in my throat. Whoever that bastard was, I was going to find out who sent him and how he was connected to Henry. There was so much I needed to do, I wanted to do. But all that would have to wait.

"The Blodnar have been ousted from Lohikärra once and for all. The imposter's forces were the last dregs scooped up and mashed together. Those we didn't kill are gone now, even from Bragidrattür. Now we focus on fighting Rorik. His forces are still pushing through Etelaranikä and they threaten Bragidrattür, but your cousin seems less worried about them than the Blodnar." I squeezed Haldrek's hand and waited for a response. Nothing still.

"The city's defenses are nearly back to normal. For all the grief the imposter gave us, the troops he rounded up actually did a good job of repairing the walls. Those overseeing them have double checked the work to make sure it's solid."

Haldrek's chest paused for a moment and I froze, waiting, watching, willing it to rise again. It finally did so and I exhaled in relief.

Rhaegos, please do what you and Teminth can to heal Haldrek. Please help him get better soon.

There were no words, only a heavy weight of chastisement. Like Rhaegos didn't need me ordering her around. Not that I blamed her. If Senja was right, the dragons were doing all they could to help Haldrek. I sighed and returned my attention to him, a flicker of frustration growing inside me.

"Haldrek, you better wake up. I can't do this alone. Kamira may be long gone, but there are still others here I don't trust. I need you to work with them. If you die, I become the full on ruler of Lohikärra. Alone. I don't want that! I want you. I want to rule *with* you. I'm still a—" I paused, trying to thinking of a better word than the one stuck in my throat. After a moment, I continued. "I'm still new to all of this. You've been ruling here in Lohikärra for nearly your entire life. I haven't." Still no response.

There was still one last thing I hadn't shared with him. Something I was too afraid to openly speak myself. Something I wanted to share with him when he was awake. The one bit of potential joy I wanted to hold onto. I glanced at the purple potion bottle before turning back to him.

"Haldrek. You need to get better. *I* need you. I need to tell you that you were right that one morning. Before we fought the Blodnar imposter." I laughed through the tears that were now falling down my face. "Remember? You said we'd enjoyed each other's company so much the previous night that you were sure I had an aethling inside of me?" I paused, trying to push the lump out of my throat so that I didn't choke out the words. "You. Were. Right. And damn it all if I'm going to have to raise your kid by myself *while* ruling Lohikärra." I laughed at the absurdity of my words, but my laughter turned to sobs.

Of course of all the times Haldrek and I had enjoyed each other's company, now would be the time I got pregnant, right when he was on the edge of death. I was excited for the child, but terrified at the same time. Terrified of ending up like my mother, of *becoming* my mother, of another miscarriage, even though I wore Haldrek's dragon ring, the one Senja had infused with a powerful protective ward to keep me safe from any dark magic while I wore it.

"Haldrek, you are not allowed to die right now. I need you to help me raise this child. Our child." I squeezed his hand once more, then sunk my head down between my hands and knees. Grief and hopelessness washed over me so fully that I couldn't even feel Rhaegos anymore. As I embraced those emotions, there was a pressure on my hand. Light, but firm. Like someone holding onto me.

"Haldrek?" My head popped up, vision blurred from my tears. Another squeeze to my hand, firmer this time. My heart raced as I squeezed back, gripping his hand. Rhaegos's presence pushed back through the heavy emotions, adding her joy to mine. Haldrek's hand squeezed mine harder before one of his fingers stroked the inside of my wrist. I watched his face as a slight smile made his mouth curve.

He lifted one eyelid enough for me to see his eye focus on me. His smile widened.

"*Mine drawing.*"

The Lohikärran Chronicles

<u>**Visions of Lohikärra (Prequel)**</u>
A mysterious young woman, an elven invasion, and the tokens of the High King
Haldrek Rodreksson has known his entire life where his future lies and what is expected
of him. But on the eve of battle, soothsayers show him three visions of a different future:
a mysterious young woman, a new invasion, and theft of the High King's tokens. Visions
which make him question his future and that of his homeland, Lohikärra.

When the capital of Lohikärra falls, Haldrek's world is thrown into disarray and he must
scramble to keep the young woman from his visions safe.

Injured, weaponless, and with little support, will Haldrek be able to save the woman and
change the visions he was given? Or will he, his homeland, and his loved ones fall to their
enemies?

<u>**Heir of Svartån**</u>
Lohikärra was just a game. Until it wasn't.

Ina Svanunge lives in North Dakota, avoiding attention and counting the days until she's
free of her abusive mother. But when she and best friend, Mattie, sit down to play the
newest release from their favorite video game series, they find themselves in the game's
world, Lohikärra. Only it's not the game - Lohikärra is real.

Once there, Ina finds out her long-absent father was a powerful thegn - and she's his
rightful heir. Unfortunately, she isn't the only one claiming his title, and the others are

more than willing to kill her for it. On a journey across Svartån, Ina must fight for her birthright or risk rejection from the world she has long wished to be part of.

Will Ina be able to claim her rightful title with help from Mattie and their handsome new friend, Haldrek? Or will she end up dying in a foreign, unforgiving land?

Thegn of Svartån
She will be Thegn of Svartån. If Svartån still exists.

Ina Svanunge is the rightful thegn-heir of Svartån, but she must fight to lead and protect her new homeland's people, even as she's still learning how to do both. Can she learn to lead and bring her people together before they are brutally conquered?

An invasion from the Isillas elves - Svartån's most ancient enemy - looms imminent and Ina's first priority is to prepare her new homeland's defenses. Which would be easier if not for the deep hatred held by many of her subjects against their half-elven neighbors. With the Isillas at their doorstep, Svartån is fractured and in need of a leader to unite it once and for all. Racing to improve not only her fighting and leadership skills, she finds herself out of time when the Isillas attack and endanger not only Svartån, but those closest to her.

Weakened and alone, will Ina be able to protect Svartån from the Isillas? Or will she both lose her hard fought title and risk the destruction of Svartån?

Queen of Drattüjert
Old enemies. New challenges. Ina is thegn, but can she be queen?

It's been almost two months since Ina Svanunge officially became the Thegn of Svartån. With the Isillas conflict behind her, she must now aid her fellow thegns against an even bigger threat: the Blodnar Empire from the south.

Lohikärra will never be whole without its heart: the capital city of Drattüjert still under Bloodnar control. Ina and her fellow thegns have a plan to take it back, but there are traitors amongst their ranks bent on obtaining their own power and glory. The last thing Ina's beloved country needs is the emergence of a necromancer bent on destroying both Lohikärra and its dragons entirely.

When traitorous calamity strikes, Ina and Haldrek are forced into a race against time to save their loved ones, Lohikarra, and even Ina's hometown Fargo. But the cost could be Ina's life.

Lady of Lohikärra
With great power comes great responsibility. And greater enemies.

Fully embracing Lohikärra as her new home, Ina has taken her place alongside Haldrek as High King and Queen. But Lohikärra is a broken country on the verge of civil war. Respected by some, despised by others, Ina must rebuild the capital city of Drattüjert while Haldrek rebuilds Lohikärra.

When Henry, an old friend from Fargo, arrives in Drattüjert offering a solution to all her problems, it'll either be her saving grace or too good to be true.

Will Ina figure out which before it's too late? Or will fractured loyalties cause her to lose everything she holds dear?

Heart of Lohikärra
Coming June 2023!

About the Author

L. L. Nelson is a full-time librarian, history buff, and author of numerous stories and poems. In short, she is a word nerd with a passion for poetry, fantasy, historical fiction, and just a little bit of romance. She's been creating worlds and figuring out the 'what ifs' in her stories since she was old enough to read the words 'Egg Roll King' on a local Chinese restaurant sign in 1992.

In college, she took all the creative writing classes she could to feed her need to write. This gave her enough credits to graduate with a minor in English and the ability to second guess her work like a true writer. It also introduced her to a variety of genres and their tropes that she now uses in her stories and poetry.

As a librarian, L. L. Nelson has honed her research skills to a science. (A library science.) This has given her mad talent when it comes to finding obscure facts to use in her stories and poetry. (Like the fact that the Vikings used rap battles as a form of combat.)

When not dealing with her scripturient nature, L. L. Nelson is a mom, inventive cook, wannabe linguist, and dreams of being not only a 'word traveler' but a world traveler. Fortunately, she lives in Southern California with her husband and kids, so she can go to Disneyland once a year and pretend that she's actually traveling around the world, even when she isn't.

Love it?

Leave a Review!

Did you enjoy *Lady of Lohikärra*? If so, I would be delighted if you left a review. (If you already have, thank you so much!) As a new author, book reviews are golden. You can leave reviews wherever you purchased the book, Goodreads, or other places as well. Book recommendations on social media (Youtube, Instagram, Twitter, TikTok, etc) is also awesome.

Follow me!

Website: https://www.llnelsonauthor.com/
Newsletter: https://www.llnelsonauthor.com/newsletter/
Facebook: https://www.facebook.com/llnelsonauthor
Instagram: https://www.instagram.com/llnelsonauthor
TikTok: https://www.tiktok.com/@llnelsonauthor

Acknowledgments

My utter gratitude goes out to a whole host of people, without whom this book would have taken a lot longer to write. Among them are the *many* friends I've made at the various 20Booksto50k conferences I've gone to since 2021 (especially Meryl Yourish and Cady Hammer), my editor for this book—Karie Crawford, my fellow mom writers, and of course, my family. Your support and help have been priceless.

www.ingramcontent.com/pod-product-compliance
Lightning Source LLC
Chambersburg PA
CBHW032158190726
48289CB00007BA/2278